FLEECE THE CAT

ALSO BY LOUISE CLARK

The Nine Lives Cozy Mystery Series

The Cat Came Back

The Cat's Paw

Cat Got Your Tongue

Let Sleeping Cats Lie

Cat Among The Fishes

Cat in the Limelight

Fleece the Cat

If the Cat's Away

Forward in Time Series

Make Time For Love

Discover Time For Love

Hearts of Rebellion Series

Pretender's Game

Lover's Knot

Dangerous Desires

FLEECE THE CAT

THE 9 LIVES COZY MYSTERY, BOOK SEVEN

LOUISE CLARK

Without limiting the rights under copyright(s) reserved below, no part of this publication may be reproduced, stored in or introduced into a retrieval system, or transmitted, in any form, or by any means (electronic, mechanical, photocopying, recording, or otherwise) without the prior permission of the publisher and the copyright owner.

This is a work of fiction. Names, characters, places, and incidents either are the product of the author's imagination or are used fictitiously, and any resemblance to actual persons, living or dead, business establishments, events or locales is entirely coincidental.

The scanning, uploading, and distributing of this book via the internet or via any other means without the permission of the publisher and copyright owner is illegal and punishable by law. Please purchase only authorized copies, and do not participate in or encourage piracy of copyrighted materials. Your support of the author's rights is appreciated.

Copyright © 2022 by Louise Clark. All rights reserved.

Book and cover design by eBook Prep
www.ebookprep.com

May 2022
Paperback ISBN: 978-1-64457-240-5
Hardcover ISBN: 978-1-64457-241-2

ePublishing Works!
644 Shrewsbury Commons Ave
Ste 249
Shrewsbury PA 17361
United States of America
www.epublishingworks.com
Phone: 866-846-5123

CHAPTER 1

"Mrs. Jamieson to see you, Mrs. Jamieson."

Christy Jamieson, currently the de facto head of the Jamieson family and the CEO of the Jamieson Trust, looked up, frowning. Bonnie King, blond, always beautifully groomed and the receptionist for the Trust, was standing in the doorway to the conference room where Christy was going over agenda items for the first quarter of the year with Isabelle Pascoe, the Trust's office manager. Bonnie's blue eyes were wide, and she was biting her lower lip.

Christy struggled to figure out what the worried expression and the strange introduction meant. She was still trying to deal with Isabelle's last agenda item that they had fifteen—fifteen!—requests for interviews with Christy. She could understand one or two, but fifteen? It boggled her mind.

"I'm sorry, Bonnie, you said Mrs. Jamieson. You meant Miss Jamieson, of course." Except that Miss Jamieson, Ellen Jamieson, had just left for a holiday in Tahiti with Trevor McCullagh the Third and was not expected back until the middle of February. Since it was only the second week in January, Christy had no idea why her aunt by marriage would be back in Canada again so soon.

But Bonnie was shaking her tousled blond head. "No, Mrs. Jamieson, I did mean—"

"She meant me." The person who interrupted Bonnie had clearly followed her from the reception area to the conference room. She was a young woman, close to Christy in age, although perhaps a few years older. Her hair was dark, spilling over her shoulders in waving curls skillfully created with hair mousse and a flat iron. Brown eyes with a gleam of wicked amusement dominated a narrow face. High cheekbones accentuated her eyes, and a rather wide mouth softened her beak of a nose. Put together, the face was striking rather than pretty.

Raising dark brows, Christy watched as the woman sashayed into the conference room, her slim hips undulating seductively, her balance on stiletto heels perfect. She was wearing a leather jacket that wouldn't do much to keep out the cold on this damp winter's day over a thin black wool turtleneck sweater. Tight black trousers made the most of long legs and those slender hips.

Whoever this woman was, she made Christy feel dowdy. Christy's dark hair was short and layered, a practical cut, not a sexy one, and she was wearing an understated powder blue skirt suit designed to create an image of an efficient businesswoman. Annoyed at the invasion, and not about to call this woman Mrs. Jamieson, Christy said, "I don't think you've been invited in, Ms....?"

The woman's mouth quirked up into a smile full of confidence. An irritating, deliberately provocative smile in Christy's opinion.

Looking around the conference room, the woman's gaze lingered on the gleaming teak table, the soothing blue walls, and the windows that overlooked English Bay. "Very nice," she said, as she sat down in a leather-covered chair opposite Isabelle Pascoe and at an angle to Christy, who sat at the head of the table. She raised carefully plucked and shaped brows. "Your decorating, I presume?"

So far neither of them had called the other by the Jamieson name and Christy had no intention of being the first to do so. She straightened and clasped her hands in front of her on the table. "You were not asked to sit."

The woman's smile broadened. "I wasn't, was I? Yet here I am."

And she clearly wasn't planning on leaving any time soon. Christy's mouth tightened. She looked over the woman's shoulder to Bonnie King who still hovered in the doorway. "Call security, Bonnie. This lady needs some encouragement to help her decide to leave."

Bonnie nodded and disappeared.

The woman laughed. "Don't you want to know why I'm here?"

"Not particularly," said Isabelle Pascoe, speaking for the first time. Isabelle was a middle-aged woman with olive skin and long dark hair she wore parted in the middle and tied in a knot at the back of her head. Like Christy, she was dressed soberly, in her case in a brown suit and gold blouse. Her dark eyes were disapproving as she said, "You've come here for some sort of fraudulent purpose, that much is obvious. The details are irrelevant."

The woman shook her head slowly, her mouth pursed in a disappointed way, her eyes amused. When she turned to Christy, her smile was smug. "What is that old saying? The devil's in the details?" As Christy frowned, she nodded. "Yes, it's the details, Christy dear, you're going to want to know. I think you should hear what I have to say. Evicting me from the property is not in your best interests."

"Nonsense," Isabelle said, and stood up.

Whoever this woman who called herself Mrs. Jamieson was, she was not here to help Christy in any way, of that Christy was certain. "I doubt that's true, but in the very unlikely situation that it is, I suggest you contact McCullagh, McCullagh, and Walker, the legal firm that represents the Jamieson Trust."

The woman sat back in her chair and moved long, slender fingers on the table in a lazy way. Her nails were blood red and pointed. "I guess you need a bit more incentive before you decide to enter into a conversation." She shrugged one shoulder dismissively. "Fair enough." The smug smile widened. "What if I told you that Frank Jamieson was a bigamist?"

Isabelle Pascoe sucked in her breath and flopped back down into her chair.

Christy's heart skipped a beat, then began to pound erratically. She held herself together and said in a level voice, "I wouldn't believe you."

The woman shook her head and drew a small breath. "I thought you might not." She straightened, then reached into the purse she'd placed on her lap.

As Christy watched those red-tipped fingers sink into the bag, she had a sudden vision of a bird of prey, talons extended to snatch its victim in a quick, indefensible strike. A chill swept over her. She firmed her jaw and waited.

The woman withdrew a small booklet. Carefully placing it on the table, she slid it across the smooth surface where it came to rest in front of Christy. "Frank Jamieson was not only my husband, but we have an eleven-year-old son together."

The booklet was a miniature photo album from the days when people carried around print pictures, displaying them in the cellophane sleeves that made up the pages of the booklet, rather than including them in a digital photo gallery on their phone. Christy didn't open the slim volume. Instead, she used her finger to flick it back to the woman. "I don't know who you are, or what you expect to accomplish with these slanders against my late husband, but—"

The woman raised her perfect brows and smiled in a superior way. "Have I not made myself clear? I am Mrs. Frank Jamieson and my son is the Jamieson heir."

"I doubt that," Christy said. She kept her features expressionless and her voice even. Everything this woman did was designed to shock and dismay her audience, possibly with the goal of having Christy or Isabelle make an impulsive statement that could later be used to support the woman's claims. So far, she hadn't succeeded, and Christy was determined to ensure she didn't.

The woman shook her head, that annoying, superior smile implying she thought Christy was a gullible fool worthy of pity and little else. It was an expression meant to goad a reaction, but Christy met it with silence.

The false Mrs. Jamieson sighed. "Anyone looking at the pictures of my son will realize he is Frank's as well. He resembles his father at the same age." She raised her eyebrows. "I suppose, since you had to vacate the Jamieson mansion, you didn't keep all the family photos."

Christy laughed. "Family photos are the sort of thing we did keep." Some of them had ended up in Ellen's English Bay condo and as far as Christy knew were still there. Others were in storage at her Burnaby townhouse where she now lived with her daughter, Noelle. A few had even made it to the Trust's office and were in a cupboard in the supply room.

For a moment, the woman's confident expression slipped, and she looked uneasy, then she smiled again and said, "Fabulous. They'll prove my point then."

Isabelle, having recovered somewhat, cleared her throat. "It would be much more efficient if you supplied your marriage license and the child's birth certificate to McCullagh, McCullagh and Walker. The lawyer you should talk to is Mallory Tait."

"Mallory Tait!" The woman's eyebrows shot up and Christy thought she saw something akin to triumph gleaming in her eyes.

"Do you know Mallory?" Christy asked, curious. What kind of relationship would evoke that flicker of satisfaction?

The woman had herself well in hand and her self-satisfied smile gave nothing away. "Oh, yes. Mallory and I go back a long way." She laughed. "I'm delighted, actually. I'm quite sure Mallory will find my credentials perfectly in order."

That sounded ominous, but then this woman specialized in theatrics aimed at undermining confidence. So Christy ignored the concern gnawing at her gut and said, "Good. Then we're done here."

"I suppose we are." The woman pushed back her seat. "You'll be hearing from me." She stood up.

Christy didn't rise. "I sincerely hope not."

The woman laughed and shook her head. "So unsociable."

Bonnie King appeared in the doorway. "Security's here." She stepped into the conference room and was followed by a dark-haired man. He appeared to be in his early thirties. His uniform consisted of a crisp black shirt and pressed trousers, and he was carrying a two-way radio on his belt. His shoulders were broad, his belly tight, his hips slim. A scruff of a beard and mustache highlighted a sensual mouth. Black lashed dark eyes scanned the room looking for the person he was here to escort out.

The false Mrs. Jamieson's face lit up. "Oh, my. Aren't you delicious."

The man's eyes widened, then he said gruffly, "Is this the woman?"

Bonnie nodded. "Yes."

"If you'll come with me, ma'am," he said, gesturing toward the doorway.

"I would be absolutely delighted to," she replied. She glided toward the door, her hips swaying seductively with every step, a smile on her lips and promise in her eyes. When she reached him, she linked her arm with his and gazed up into his beautiful eyes. "You must tell me your name. I want to know absolutely everything about you."

The security guard cast an appalled glance at Bonnie, who was staring at their visitor in amazement.

Isabelle looked at Christy and said, "I'll go along and see her out."

"Good idea," Christy muttered.

The woman ignored them both and gave the guard's arm a little tug. "Do come along. We have so much to discuss." As they moved into the doorway, she looked over her shoulder. "Goodbye, for now, darling. We'll meet again soon." She and the guard made a grand departure into the hallway. Bonnie scuttled after them and Isabelle, after a fuming look at Christy, followed.

"Not in my lifetime," Christy said, glaring at the doorway as the lilting sounds of the woman's voice faded as she moved through the Trust's suite.

CHAPTER 2

Fuming, Christy flipped to a new page in the notebook she'd been using to jot down ideas during her meeting with Isabelle Pascoe. Whoever the woman who called herself Mrs. Frank Jamieson really was, she was a problem. Hopefully, Christy thought, she would turn out to be more nuisance than threat.

Hopefully.

Christy grimaced and tapped the notebook with the end of her pen. The woman struck her as the kind who would do anything to achieve her goal. She had the potential to drag the Jamieson name into the spotlight, and not in a positive way. Christy's pen hovered over the page. What she needed was a plan. She nodded in a determined way. That plan would have to start with Frank.

A year and a half ago, Frank Jamieson, Christy's husband, and the heir to the Jamieson Ice Cream fortune, disappeared. Along with him went Stormy, the family cat, and most of the Jamieson fortune. Rumor placed him in Mexico with a girlfriend, living the high life on embezzled millions. His disappearance, the embezzlement, and the police search that followed were a media sensation. It went on for what seemed like an eternity to Christy but was closer to a month. Eventually other scandals eclipsed it and Christy was left to pick up the pieces of her life and make radical changes that would change both her and her daughter Noelle's future.

The Jamieson Trust, created by Frank's father before his tragic death when Frank was a pre-teen, was depleted except for a few minor investments that provided Christy with a small income to support herself and Noelle. Worse, the Jamieson mansion, an enormous property in the exclusive Shaughnessy district in Vancouver, had been sold. The proceeds disappeared, along with the rest of the Jamieson fortune. Christy and Noelle were forced to move, which was why they were now living in a townhouse in Burnaby. And it was there, to that modest home, that Stormy the family cat finally returned to them.

By the time Stormy reappeared, Christy had begun to wonder if Frank truly was in Mexico or if he'd returned to Vancouver. Or, more grimly, if he never left Canada and was dead. It wasn't long after the cat's return that Christy began to hear a voice in her head that sounded remarkably like Frank. For a time, she wondered about her sanity, until her neighbor, Roy Armstrong, revealed he could hear the voice as well. Together, they discovered that Frank's essence had taken up residence in the cat after he had indeed been murdered.

When Christy tracked down Frank's killers, she assumed he'd leave the cat and move on to whatever came after death, but he didn't. Instead, he remained in the cat and became a fixture in Christy's small household.

Proving Frank had been murdered had also revealed who had stolen the funds in the Jamieson Trust, and, eventually, all but a small portion of the money was restored to the Trust.

The return of the Jamieson fortune had occurred only a few months before, around the time Karen Beaumont was murdered at a gala Christy was attending. Christy suspected that the publicity around Beaumont's death and the attention it brought to the Jamieson name was why the unnamed woman had come to the office today. She thought she was safe bringing forward the claim of a relationship with Frank when he was a young man. After all, he wasn't alive to deny her story. To prove she wasn't what she said she was, the Trust would have to expend money and time disproving her claim. She probably assumed it would be easier to just pay her off.

What she didn't know was that all Christy had to do to find out what lay behind her story was ask Frank what he remembered about his life around the time the woman described. And that was exactly what she was going to do when she returned to Burnaby that afternoon. Oh, yeah, she and Frank were going to have a conversation, you could bet on that.

Christy lifted the pen from the page, pausing to review the hurried notes she'd scratched into the book. She tapped her chin with the end as she thought about the woman and the child she claimed was Frank's. She had said the boy was eleven, which meant the relationship had begun twelve or thirteen years ago. That was close to the time Christy met Frank. It had been his fourth year at university and her freshman year. Had Frank really known this woman and had a physical relationship with her such a short time before he met Christy?

Christy's mouth flattened into a hard line. She wouldn't have believed it then, back when she was a freshman and Frank a senior at the university where her parents were professors. She didn't want to believe it now either, but her years with Frank had taught her that not everything was as it seemed on the surface. She had to at least consider that the woman's story was true—for now, anyway.

What if Frank really had married this woman? Her son would be the Jamieson heir and Noelle would no longer be his legitimate daughter. Would that mean she would no longer be an heir to the Jamieson fortune?

On the other hand, it was possible the woman lied about being married to Frank but told the truth about Frank being her son's father. If that were the case, the boy would be the illegitimate child. Would he still be a Jamieson heir?

Of course, if the woman had lied about her marriage, she could also have lied about having a relationship with Frank, meaning Frank wasn't the child's father at all.

Christy made a low sound of frustration and decided those questions could wait until she had a chance to talk to Frank later today. In the meantime, she'd do what she could here in the office. She made a note to check the provisions of the Jamieson Trust to see what the criteria were that defined who could be an heir and so eligible for the benefits of the Trust. She followed that with another to call Mallory Tait, the Trust's lawyer, to let her know what had happened and to find out what the process going forward would be.

She stared out the bank of windows that made up one wall of the conference room, but she didn't see the spectacular view of Vancouver's harbor and the North Shore Mountains beyond. Grimacing, she acknowledged that the woman's allegations would have to be checked out. The search could be done by a private investigator, but because of her connection to Frank she would have access to information that had no paper or electronic trail, which might prove difficult to pass along to an outsider. That meant she'd have to do at least some of the digging herself.

The trouble was, most of the people she trusted to help her out were away and so not available. Frank's aunt, Ellen Jamieson, was in Tahiti with Trevor McCullagh for a romantic holiday. Quinn Armstrong, the man she was falling in love with, was in Toronto. A respected journalist, he was working on a documentary based on his book about the search he and Christy had made to discover Frank's fate. Like Ellen and Trevor, he wasn't expected to return to Vancouver until the end of the month, if not later. Sledge McCullagh, Trevor's son and part of the rock band SledgeHammer, was in Los Angles working on a reality television show. That left Roy Armstrong, Quinn's father, and a well-known Canadian novelist, as her sole ally.

And of course, Frank in Stormy the Cat.

Roy and Frank liked to work together, with sometimes startling results. They would have to be enough.

She paused in her scribbling, this time rubbing the tip of the pen on her cheek as she thought. There was one more ally she could access—Detective Billie Patterson of the Vancouver police department. Patterson was the detective who'd been assigned to Frank's case after he'd disappeared, when there were fears he'd been kidnapped and held for ransom. It had been Patterson who began Christy's investigative career. When she received information that Frank had returned from Mexico and was back in Vancouver, she passed it along to Christy. Frank's embezzlement was low on her department's priority list, but Patterson knew Christy wanted to find her husband. The two could work together, benefiting both.

Since that time, Christy had worked on five other cases with Patterson and the woman had become a friend. She wasn't sure, though, that Patterson could become involved in a case like this one, so she wrote down the detective's name with a big question mark beside it.

Isabelle Pascoe walked back into the conference room. "What a dreadful woman," she said, sounding worried and annoyed at the same time.

Christy put her pen onto the fold of the notebook and sat back in her chair. "Did you get anything more out of her?"

Isabelle shook her head. She pursed her lips in an expression of distaste. "No. She was too interested in seducing that poor security guard." She sat down in her chair. "Honestly, I thought she was going to gobble him up as if Bonnie and I weren't there watching the whole disaster unfold in front of us."

"Did you get her name?"

Isabelle shook her head. "Not that I didn't try. She said she wanted to keep it a surprise for Mallory Tait. What's that all about?"

Nothing good, Christy thought. She said, "I have no idea. Call Mallory and give her a heads up so she'll be prepared. Tell her I'll phone her this afternoon after I've collected Noelle from school." And talked to Frank, and hopefully figured exactly who this woman was.

Isabelle made a note. "I'll contact her as soon as we're finished here."

Christy nodded. "Isabelle, what are the provisions in the Trust for situations like this?"

Frowning, Isabelle said, "You mean, that Frank Jamieson had a wife other than you?"

Christy shook her head. "No, for a child Frank might have had outside our marriage."

"Ahh. Yes, of course." Isabelle was nodding thoughtfully now. "You think the woman was lying about being Frank's wife, but not that Frank was her child's father."

"Frank never mentioned any other children, but it's possible the woman didn't tell him about her baby." Christy shrugged. "Though why she would do that, rather than seek some kind of support for the boy, I don't know."

"I don't believe the woman was married to Mr. Jamieson, or that he's the father of her child," Isabelle said briskly. "But to answer your question about the terms of the Trust, Frank Jamieson and his children are the beneficiaries. I don't believe it specifies that the children must be the product of a legal marriage."

Christy considered that. She already knew the annual stipend she received was as the parent of the Jamieson heir, rather than Frank Jamieson's widow. Financially, then, it was largely irrelevant to her whether the unknown woman had ever been married to Frank. "So, proving or disproving that this boy is Frank's son is vital. All right, you let Mallory know what's coming her way. I'm going to dig through the photos in the storage room and see if I can find any of Frank when he was eleven years old. We may need to compare them to the woman's photos."

"Or," Isabelle said, "to the boy himself."

CHAPTER 3

Christy was unable to find a picture of Frank as a young teen amongst the photos in the storeroom. The albums focused on his parents and their dear friends who became the original trustees for the Jamieson Trust. She wasn't interested in those images, but she thought Noelle might enjoy seeing some snapshots of her grandparents and Aunt Ellen as a young woman, so she set those aside and boxed the rest.

Carrying the selection of photos she'd saved, she headed home to have a serious conversation with Frank. The weather was indulging in its usual January dither. The temperature was down around freezing with a nasty wind off the ocean that added to the chill, but instead of snowing it was trying to rain. The result was precipitation somewhere between wet snow and ice that made Christy's drive home an exhausting commute on slippery roads with too many drivers who hadn't bothered to replace the summer tires with winter ones on their vehicles.

Frustrated by the traffic, brooding over the woman who called herself Mrs. Frank Jamieson, and the possibility that Frank really was the father of her son, Christy parked in her driveway. A quick glance at the dashboard clock told her she had about an hour before picking up Noelle from school, so she sat for a moment gathering her thoughts.

Once again, Frank was the center of a great, big problem she was going to have to deal with. The resolution would begin with a conversation he wasn't likely to want to have, which meant it would probably become a confrontation, rather than a simple exchange of information. Frank did confrontations well. She didn't.

She drew in a deep breath and told herself to chill. It was unfortunate that the woman—the slinky, beautiful, horrible woman!—had been so sure of herself and her position, but the worst thing Christy could do was condemn Frank without hearing his side of the story. Still, the woman must have known Frank in some way. The problem was how.

Almost as if her thoughts had conjured him up, she heard his voice in her head. *Hey, babe. You're home early.*

As Frank greeted her, Stormy, the Jamieson family cat, jumped onto the hood of the still-cooling engine and pressed his nose to the windshield.

Brought back to the here and now, Christy jumped guiltily. Her distracted gaze sharpened, then refocused on the unexpected sight of the cat's face pressed against the glass. She screamed. The cat bounced backward, then he arched his back, spiked his fur, fluffed his tail, and did a straight-legged hop away from the windshield, before leaping from the vehicle and bolting.

Christy sighed as she climbed out of the van. Frank was always grumpy when someone frightened Stormy. He was protective of the cat and didn't like him to be upset, so he wouldn't be happy about her reaction. She exited the carport, heading for the short concrete walk that led to her townhouse. There she found Roy Armstrong ambling down the sidewalk between their units.

"What's up?" he asked. The cat twined around his ankles, peeking between them, and glaring at Christy. "Frank says you nearly gave Stormy a heart attack."

Both cat and man appeared oblivious to the cold, misty drizzle that had made her commute so stressful. Christy resisted the urge to sigh again as she looked down at the cat, who stared back, refusing to look away. "Frank's overreacting. Stormy jumped onto the hood when I parked and shoved his nose against the windshield. I wasn't expecting to see a flattened cat face staring at me through the glass, so I screamed." She tightened her lips and frowned at the cat. "If anything, I'm the one who should be complaining of an unexpected shock."

Roy raised his brows, amusement in his eyes. He was a robust man in his early sixties who had never had much use for social conformity. He wore his greying hair long and tied at his nape and preferred casual button front shirts and jeans to more formal wear. He looked down at the cat, who was now sitting on his foot, staring up at Christy in a baleful way. "See? I told you Christy wasn't mad at Stormy."

You didn't have to scream.

"It was an involuntary reaction."

The poor guy was just trying to be friendly.

"I know!" Christy drew a deep, steadying breath. "I wasn't expecting to see him on the hood of the car. I was surprised, that's all."

This was greeted by a moment's silence. Then, *he accepts your apology.*

Christy rolled her eyes. "Thanks. I think."

Roy laughed.

So why are you home so early?

Brought back to the situation on hand, Christy said, "I need to talk to you."

About what? The cat left Roy's foot and strutted over to Christy, where he rubbed against her leg, marking her as his territory.

Christy narrowed her eyes. "Your son."

The cat froze in place and looked up, green eyes wide.

"Oh my," Roy said. His eyes were bright with curiosity.

What are you talking about?

"I don't want to discuss this on the sidewalk. Let's go inside. Roy, would you like to join us?" Since Roy was now one of the trustees who managed the Jamieson Trust, including him in the discussion made good sense. As well, they might also be able to extract more information out of Frank with both of them asking questions.

Roy's expression said hell yes! He replied politely, "If you don't think it's too personal."

Christy shook her head. "I think the Jamieson Trust has become the target of a shrewd woman, but I want to hear Frank's side of the story before I take action."

His brows rose. "Sounds ominous."

"It may be." Christy turned up the walk toward the house. The wood siding was painted a warm mocha, the trim a bright white. The porch, with its five stairs, which Christy liked to sit on in the summer, was a beige designed to accent the mocha siding. As Christy mounted the steps, the cat tore up them as well, ensuring he reached the top before her. Prancing to the door, he looked up in a challenging way. Reading the demand, Christy deliberately spent more time than she needed rummaging through her purse for her keys. Unlocking the door, she pushed it wide. The cat bolted inside. Christy waited for Roy to join her on the porch, then ushered him into the vestibule.

After ridding themselves of their outdoor clothes, they headed up a flight of stairs. The townhouse was a good size, but tall and narrow. A living-dining room combination led into a spacious kitchen with a breakfast nook beside a wide bay window. Christy offered Roy a coffee and made one for herself. They sat at the kitchen table, the coffee mugs in front of them, the cat crouched in the middle of the rectangular, maple wood table.

"This morning a woman walked into the Trust's office claiming she was Mrs. Frank Jamieson," Christy said. She watched the cat for a reaction, although how she expected to interpret the actions of an animal known for its inscrutability she didn't know. Still, it seemed the right thing to do.

The cat stared back. *You're Mrs. Frank Jamieson.*

"She claims her marriage to you predates mine." There was an edge of accusation in her voice. Christy reminded herself she was giving Frank the benefit of the doubt and letting him tell his story his way.

The cat rose from its defensive crouch and stretched, arching his back in a languid way before he settled into his alert, neat and tidy sitting position, back straight, and tail wrapped around his paws.

Don't be jealous, Chris. The only woman I ever married was you. There words were straightforward, the tone was amused.

The frustration and annoyance that had been eating at Christy all day flared into anger. "I'm not jealous! Frank, this is serious. A woman came to the Trust claiming she was married to you and that you have an eleven-year-old son together. I need to find out who this woman really is, and why she thinks she can pass off herself and her child as your family. If I don't, Noelle's future and the future of the Trust are in jeopardy. Is her claim true or not?"

Not!

Roy listened to this exchange with raised brows. "Did she give you any other details, like her given name? Or the kid's name?"

Christy sucked in a deep breath and counted to ten as she shook her head. "She refused to supply any details. She said she'd give them to Mallory Tait."

Roy shook his head. "Sketchy."

A con artist. There was a sneer in the voice, which Christy couldn't fault. The Jamieson wealth had always attracted people who wanted to relieve them of it and now that the family's fortune had been returned, Christy suspected this woman's claim was merely the first of many that would follow.

"Probably. But, Frank, I need to know if there's anything in your past that's going to jump out at me. Is it possible you had sex with this woman, even if it was just a one-night stand, that resulted in a pregnancy?"

The kid is eleven, you said?

Christy nodded.

There was silence. She assumed Frank was thinking back, figuring exactly when the relationship might have taken place.

It must have been the summer before my fourth year at university.

She nodded again. "That would be my guess."

I came home to Vancouver that summer. Unlike many Vancouver teens who attended one of the local colleges or universities, Frank had enrolled at his parents' alma mater in Ontario. He'd returned to Vancouver at the end of each year, though, spending time with a peer group of wealthy, entitled young adults who had no need of summer jobs to pay for their tuition and a lot of time to get into trouble.

I hung out with Aaron DeBolt and his crowd. There was a pause, almost a mental shrug. *Aaron always had girls buzzing around him.*

Aaron DeBolt was not one of Christy's favorite people. She couldn't stop her voice from hardening. "Names, Frank. I need a name."

The cat blinked at her. *There's Brianne, but she's gone.*

Murdered by the same people who had murdered Frank. "Anyone else you can think of?"

There's Pam Muir. But—

"But what?"

She came on to me, but I thought she was more interested in other guys.

"What did Pam Muir look like?" Christy asked grimly. The woman she'd met this morning certainly had no hesitation in showing her interest in the security guard. With luck, she and this Pam Muir might be one and the same person.

There was silence again while Frank thought. The cat scrunched down in a crouch on the table. *Dark hair. Thin face. Big nose. Nice lips.*

Christy drew a deep breath. "That sounds like the woman I met today. Frank, I need to know everything you remember about Pam Muir."

Not much. I told you; she was just there, part of Aaron's crowd. We hung out, but I never slept with her.

"Okay. So there's no way the child is yours?"

None.

Christy stared at the cat, who compressed himself into an even smaller size and wouldn't meet her eyes. She shifted her gaze to Roy. "I need to find out all I can about this Pam Muir."

"I'll get my computer. I'm not as good at research as Quinn is, but I can do a deep dive into social media. I bet we can discover a lot about this chick." Roy cast a considering look at the cat. His expression told Christy he thought there was more the cat wasn't telling them.

Christy thought there was, too, but Roy's willingness to delve into the research released tension she hadn't thought she was holding in. "Thanks, Roy. I'll take you up on that."

CHAPTER 4

Christy left Roy to do his computer research while she dug out the family photos from the storage cupboard in the basement. There were several cartons, carefully labeled by someone with dates and contents. Three boxes, packed full, chronicled Frank's baby and pre-teen years, but after his parents' death, the record dwindled. Only one container was needed for the years when he was eleven to twenty-two. Then he met Christy and the boxes again expanded.

One box, Christy thought with a mental sigh. It didn't seem right that such a formative time in his life would hardly be documented. She pulled out the lone box and hauled it upstairs to the kitchen.

She was greeted by Roy, deep into his project and full of enthusiasm. "I've been searching through social media for Pamela or Pam Muir. It's not an uncommon name and I found several people who might be here in the Vancouver area. I narrowed it down to two possibilities. Both have dark hair and sons. One has a landline and telephone listing that puts her address in Surrey. The other is either unlisted or doesn't have a landline."

Christy thought about the phony Mrs. Jamieson and said, "The unlisted one is probably our Pam Muir. The woman I met this morning was slinky and smooth and modern. I can see her not bothering with an old-fashioned telephone hook-up." She plunked the box of photos on the table and circled round it to look over Roy's shoulder at his laptop screen. "What does she look like?"

Roy brought up a page. The profile picture consisted of a dog lolling on its back with its feet sticking up in the air and its tongue hanging out of the side of its mouth.

"Not very helpful," Christy said.

They contemplated the picture for a few moments. Roy said, "The dog looks happy. That's a positive."

Christy sighed. "I suppose."

"According to her page, the dog's name is Buster. That's the kind of name a kid would give his dog."

"I guess." Christy thought back to the night Stormy had arrived in their lives. He'd been a feral kitten, brought to an animal sanctuary Christy supported. When they'd called, asking if the Jamiesons could provide a home, Frank had answered the phone and immediately said yes. They went together as a family to pick up the tiny scrap of life and Noelle, seven years old at the time, had fallen in love. She wanted to call the kitten Madeline in honor of one of her favorite storybook characters, even though the little creature was a male. Eventually, they'd compromised on Stormy, because the day he'd come to them was windy, cold, and wet, much as this day was.

"Any pictures of the woman herself?" Christy asked.

Roy nodded. "Some with her and her kid." He pulled up photos showing a dark-haired, overweight woman and a scrawny pre-teen boy on what looked to be Ambleside Beach in West Vancouver.

Disappointed, Christy said, "That's not her." She leaned closer to the screen and squinted at the image. "Even if she's lost a ton of weight since that picture was taken, the nose and eyes are wrong." She straightened. "Pity. I figured the unlisted number was a perfect match.

What about the other Pam who lives in Surrey?" She didn't have a high expectation for this one either. Surrey was the suburbs and the woman who had invaded the Trust's office this morning wasn't a suburban mom type.

Roy opened a tab he'd set up earlier and said, "What do you think? Is this her?"

As soon as the profile picture came up, Christy knew they'd found her. "A bit younger than today, and she's wearing less make-up, but yeah, that's her." She pulled up a chair and made herself comfortable beside Roy. "What do you have on her?"

Roy angled the computer so the cat could view the screen too. "Family photos—an older couple who appear to be her parents, her son at various stages of his life, his first name—which is Carson—but not his surname. The TV shows and movies she likes, her favorite album. That's about it."

"So not much."

Roy moved the laptop back toward him. "It's a beginning. Now I know this is the right Pamela Muir, I can access some of the databases Quinn uses for his research and pull out more details."

The kid has my coloring, but he doesn't look like me—or anyone else in my family.

Roy pulled up a picture of the boy, a close-up that was clear and well focused. He turned the laptop to give the cat a better view. "You're sure?"

Yes.

Christy stared at the picture. "I have to agree with Frank. I can't see anything of the Jamiesons in that child. Hopefully, when I dig through our photo collection, I'll find one of Frank about the same age we can use for comparison. Before I do that, though, I'd better phone Mallory Tait and fill her in on what we've discovered."

Roy shot Christy a quizzical look. "How are you going to explain finding out the woman's name?"

"I hadn't thought of that." She groaned. "I don't know."

Tell her the truth.

Christy made a derisive sound as she cast the cat a sarcastic look. "Yeah, like that's going to be helpful. Mallory would think I was nuts."

Roy chuckled. "She is very uptight."

Mallory Tait was in her early thirties. She had a mane of natural blond hair that she wore pulled back in a severe knot, chiseled cheekbones in a classically beautiful face, a killer figure that was only accentuated by the tailored skirt suits she wore, and long legs that seemed longer with fashionable sky-high heels. Despite her looks, she was all business. Christy figured that if she couldn't sort a problem with her undoubted legal smarts, she'd have no hesitation using her physical charms to ambush the opposition.

Christy picked up the landline handset and carried it out to the living room. She wouldn't admit this to Roy—or anyone!—but Mallory Tait intimidated her. The woman might work for the Trust, and so for Christy, and she undoubtedly knew her stuff, but she was a highly polished career woman and Christy... Well, Christy was first and foremost a mom and she was still amazed she'd become the representative of the Jamieson family. She was soft corners where Mallory was hard edges, and in a confrontation, hard edges could easily lacerate soft corners.

She sat down on the couch and stared at the phone while she gave herself a pep talk and decided how she was going to explain the discovery of the mystery woman's name. Then she drew a deep breath and dialed. She was put through to Mallory Tait almost immediately.

"Mrs. Jamieson, I'm glad you phoned," Mallory said, her voice brisk, her tone all business. "Isabelle Pascoe warned me about the situation, but the woman hasn't contacted me yet. I expect to hear from her soon, though. If she was brazen enough to storm the Trust's office, she wants her payday. She'll be in touch."

"I fear you're right about that," Christy said. "I don't believe she was married to Frank, though, or that her child is Frank's son. I've been looking through family papers and there's no record of a previous marriage or a birth."

"That doesn't mean either isn't true, but it does weaken her case," Mallory said.

She sounded impatient. Christy could imagine her tapping a pen on a pad of lined paper, anxious to get the legal competition underway.

The no-nonsense tone continued as Mallory said, "When she contacts me, I will be asking for the child to be DNA tested, as well as the usual marriage license and child's birth certificate."

That surprised Christy. "But how can that be done? Frank has been gone for almost two years. I don't think I still have anything with his DNA on it."

"We have your daughter and Miss Ellen Jamieson, his aunt," Mallory said. She sounded smug, like she'd just scored a slam-dunk. "Comparing their DNA with the child's will tell us if there's a family connection at the very least. If the boy is not Frank's child, and the woman hopes it will be easy to fleece the Jamieson Trust because Frank Jamieson is deceased, requesting a DNA sample is the kind of thing that will have her pulling away fast."

Mallory sounded eager now, as if she was excited about crossing legal swords with the scam artist. Christy could almost see the gleam of a toothy smile through the phone lines. "Okay. What do I do if she comes back to the office?"

"Do not connect," Mallory said. "Admit to nothing, promise nothing. If she comes to the office, she's looking for something."

"Like what?"

"An admission, a promise, a casual agreement she can distort and use against you. Don't talk to her at all!"

Easier said than done. "I didn't want to talk to her this morning, but she just barged in and sat down. She wouldn't leave until we gave her your name."

"If she comes back and won't go away, tell her you'll speak to her, but that you'll be recording the interview. That should make her stop and consider. In fact, it might make her leave immediately." That thought seemed to please Mallory.

"Why?" Christy asked.

"Because you'll have a record of the conversation," Mallory said, the hint of a sigh in her tone, as if she couldn't quite believe Christy could be so naive. "She'll be unable to twist your words or make outrageous claims. Always talk to her with a witness present and record the conversations."

"Sounds paranoid," Christy said, trying to imagine the scene.

"Better to be paranoid than taken in by a hustler," Mallory retorted.

Christy heard paper rattling in the background. Notes, she guessed, from this conversation and the earlier one with Isabelle Pascoe. That speculation was confirmed moments later.

"When Isabelle phoned this morning, she said the woman refused to give you any name other than Mrs. Frank Jamieson. She told me you planned to look through family records. Did you have any success? Do you have any idea of who she might be?"

This was the opening she needed. Christy said, "There's a possibility she might be a young woman named Pamela, or Pam, Muir. Frank met her through Aaron DeBolt in the summer between his third and fourth year of university."

There was silence on the other end of the phone line. Guiltily, Christy imagined Mallory wondering how Christy had discovered so many specific details.

Instead, Mallory said urgently, "Pam Muir? Are you sure?"

"I'm not sure at all," Christy said. "But there's a Pam Muir who lives in Surrey and whose profile picture on her main social media site looks an awful lot like the woman who dropped in this morning."

"Pam Muir. So that's what she's up to these days," Mallory said, so softly Christy wasn't sure she'd heard correctly.

"Do you know her?"

"Oh, yeah." Mallory cleared her throat. When she spoke, her tone wasn't as confident as it had been moments before. "Okay, Mrs. Jamieson, thanks for the tip. I'll be ready for her when she comes in."

Christy frowned at the sudden change. There was something going on here, but she wasn't sure what. "When she refused to give her name to Isabelle, we decided it was because she wanted to blindside you. Is there something between you two?"

"You're probably right about that," Mallory replied. Her voice tight, she added, "And, yes, we go back a long way, though we were never friends." She paused and when she spoke again, her delivery was once more brisk and full of authority. "Now that I know who the woman really is, I'm quite sure this is a hustle. Remember, don't make any promises, or give her information she can use against you. I'll be in touch when she's contacted me."

With that, she rang off before Christy could even say good-bye. She disconnected, wondering more than ever how Pam Muir would fit into their lives.

CHAPTER 5

Three days later, Christy opened an email from Mallory Tait with a calendar attachment inviting her to a meeting with Tait and Pam Muir for the following Wednesday, almost a week later.

She frowned when she noticed Mallory had chosen the Jamieson Trust as the venue for the meeting and wondered why. Wouldn't it be more official to have it in the conference room at McCullagh, McCullagh, and Walker? Then she shrugged. Mallory must have her reasons.

After adding the date to her schedule, she sent an email to Isabelle and Bonnie to let them know about the meeting and asked Bonnie to organize refreshments. She added a request that Isabelle arrange to have a recorder in the room so the discussion could be taped.

Then she started to worry.

The email from Mallory was remarkably terse. There was no information on how the initial interview with Pam Muir had gone, what documents the woman had produced, whether Mallory had asked for a DNA test, nothing but the uninformative calendar invitation. After an unproductive half hour imagining all kinds of scenarios, from the best case where Pam supplied obviously forged marriage and birth certificates, to the worst case where the documents were real and she was married to Frank, Christy realized she'd drive herself crazy if she kept speculating about the woman and her scam from now to next week. Resolutely, she told herself to focus and get on with today.

That worked until Monday of the following week, when the software app that alerted her whenever the Jamieson name was mentioned on the Internet, sent her a notice that an article had appeared in one of the Vancouver dailies.

She'd set up the alert last fall after the press labeled her a suspect in a murder that occurred at a gala she'd been attending. That had led to all kinds of unwanted side effects, notably renewed interest from Joan Shively, the child services worker who'd been assigned to assess Christy's parenting skills when an anonymous tip branded her a bad mother.

The tip had been a diversion meant to stop Christy's hunt to find Frank and later his killer, but even though Christy proved it was malicious in origin, Shively couldn't be persuaded to drop the case. She'd long since decided Christy was too self-indulgent to properly parent an impressionable child and was working hard to prove it. After a year with no proof, Shively had to back off, but the press surrounding the murder at the gala had brought her roaring back into Christy's life. Proving she wasn't the killer had forced Shively to take a step back once more. But Christy knew any bad press would bring Shively into their lives once more. She didn't want to be blindsided that way again.

Now she stared at the notice, her mind racing, anticipating every kind of disaster. Her body, though, was frozen, unable to act. She stared at the screen for what seemed like an eternity, but which was probably about a minute and a half. Panicky thoughts told her that any article was a bad thing and would lead to nothing but trouble, mainly in the form of Joan Shively. Calmer ones suggested the article probably had something to do with the Jamieson Foundation, a non-profit organization Christy had set up to coordinate the Jamieson

Trust's charitable activities. If so, it was harmless, if not actually a good thing.

She took a deep breath and moved her cursor to the alert. Speculating over the content wasn't helping. She clicked and the article came up.

Her panicked thoughts were right.

ICE CREAM KING'S HEIR BIGAMIST, the headline screamed. Christy's heart skipped a beat then began to thump at racing speed. She gasped for air, while her brain screamed, *No, no, no, no!*

A scan of the article quickly proved Pamela Muir had somehow been involved, either writing part of it, or supplying most of the content. The story was basically the one she'd told Christy, only in the news report she was identified by name. The article included a picture of her, much younger than she appeared today, standing beside a smiling Frank. The photo was grainy, as if it had been taken from quite far away, but the man was definitely Frank.

Christy leaned closer to the screen, peering at the image. A portion of Frank's left side was gone, and Pam was at the edge of the picture on the right. Was it possible the image had been cropped so other people standing beside Frank were eliminated to make it look as if he and Pam were alone together?

She searched the photo for shadows or stray bits of people that had been missed in the cropping but couldn't find any. Disappointed, she sat back.

What was Pam Muir doing? Their meeting wasn't scheduled until Wednesday, two days from now. Was she trying to pressure Christy with this article so that by the time they met she'd acquiesce to anything just to get the Internet trolls off her back?

Isabelle walked into her office, the expression on her face puzzled. "Bonnie says the phone lines have exploded with reporters asking for interviews. Do you know what's going on?"

Christy turned the computer screen so Isabelle could see it.

The office manager sucked in a quick breath. "Oh my heavens." She leaned closer to read the article. "Pamela Muir! I should have known it. What's that woman thinking?"

"At a guess?" Christy said. "I'd say she doesn't have the proof she needs to verify she was married to Frank or that he's the father of her son. She's trying to get public opinion on her side so we'll buy her off to get rid of her."

Isabelle shook her head. "I'm afraid you could be right. What a horrible thing to do. I'll tell Bonnie to say the Trust has no comment. Unless..." She peered at Christy. "Do you want to make a statement?"

Christy shook her head. "I'll leave that decision up to Mallory Tait. I'll call her now."

Isabelle nodded and went off. Christy picked up the phone and dialed.

Mallory had already seen the article and it was clear from her tone of voice she was furious. "When I saw Pam last week, she provided a poor, badly reproduced photocopy of the marriage certificate. The print was so light, it was hard to make out the information on the page. It was obviously a fake and I told her so. She said she'd bring the original when she came to our meeting on Wednesday, but I don't believe her, because I don't believe there is an original. Same thing with the birth certificate. Frank Jamieson's name was on the document as the father, but she only brought a copy. Even then it looked as if the father's name had been added later. I bet the original said 'father unknown'."

Since Christy had Frank's word he wasn't the father, this didn't surprise her. "What do we do?"

"We put out a press release saying the Trust is investigating the allegations and has no further comments at this time," Mallory said. There was an undercurrent of outrage beneath her usually brisk, business-like tone as she added, "And on Wednesday, Pamela Muir better bring clear, original documents that prove her allegations. And they better be real and not faked up. If she doesn't, I'm going to set the cops on her for attempted fraud and I'll sue her in civil court for defamation of character with damages that will ensure she's in debt until her dying day!"

That sounded harsh, but Mallory's furious rant pretty much said what Christy was feeling at this moment, so she didn't protest. "I'll see you Wednesday morning, then."

Mallory said, "Yup," and hung up. Christy disconnected more slowly and hoped Mallory's press release would smooth over the negative publicity.

It didn't. Social media went mad, with most of the support being for Pam Muir, who became something of a heroine for outing the promiscuous Frank Jamieson. Frank was slammed as a rich bad boy whose life had been nothing but wasted entitlement and opportunities lost. Christy faired a bit better—she was simply portrayed as the rather dim party girl who'd been taken in by the reprehensible Frank.

Pam Muir spent Monday writing posts and thanking her supporters, then she gave up as the volume of comments increased, only popping into her social media sites occasionally to do bulk thank yous or to reply to a particularly juicy comment. Christy figured the woman thought she had what she needed to convince the Trust to provide for her and make her son an heir, no questions asked. Which wasn't what was going to happen, Christy told herself on Tuesday afternoon as she left the office to pick up Noelle after class. Pam Muir was in for a fight.

At the school, she wasn't surprised when she was asked to go down to the principal's office, and once there was told Joan Shively had made a school visit that morning. Christy sighed and explained the circumstances. The principal reassured her that Shively hadn't been allowed into Noelle's classroom, which relieved Christy.

That evening, Quinn called from Toronto. He'd seen the article and was keeping tabs on the social media storm, and he wanted to know if she needed him to return to Vancouver. Christy hoped desperately that the meeting the next day would provide resolution and put an end to Muir's claim, so she said no, and they spent the rest of the call talking about each other.

The meeting the next morning was scheduled for ten o'clock. Christy dressed carefully in a teal blue suit with a white silk shell beneath and was in the office by eight forty-five. Mallory, striking in a power red skirt suit and butter soft red suede boots with four-inch heels, arrived fifteen minutes early, at nine forty-five. As they waited, she briefed Christy on how they'd handle the meeting. At ten, they were ready, but Muir hadn't arrived. Mallory took the opportunity to advise Christy on how to deal with the Shively situation.

By ten fifteen, Mallory was tapping her foot with annoyance. At ten thirty, she went out the reception area to quiz Bonnie and to make sure the door was unlocked and the office accessible.

By eleven, she was calling Muir rude names under her breath. At eleven thirty, she said, "I'll give her another half an hour. Then I have to go."

"Of course," Christy said. In fact, she was surprised Mallory hadn't called a halt already. "What do you think is keeping her?"

Mallory hardened her jaw and narrowed her eyes. "This is deliberate. She wants a buy-out and she's trying to disconcert us. You can bet she's going to get an ear full when she phones to reschedule."

At noon, Mallory snapped her file folder closed and stood up. "Okay, that's it. I'm going back to the office. Mrs. Jamieson, I suggest you leave as well. I don't want you talking to her without me." She stuffed the folder into her briefcase. "And tell your staff not to allow Muir into the office."

Since Pam Muir had walked into the conference room without permission once already, Christy stood as well and smiled at Mallory. "I'll go one better. I'll give Isabelle and Bonnie the rest of the day off and close the office completely."

Mallory blinked, then she smiled, showing her teeth in an expression that was remarkably predatory. "Good idea. I like the way you think, Mrs. Jamieson." Picking up her briefcase and tucking her purse under her arm, she headed for the door. "I'll call you after Muir makes contact again."

"Sounds good," Christy said. As she watched Mallory walk away, she wasn't sure if she was relieved or concerned.

Maybe both.

∼

That afternoon Christy curled up in one corner of her couch with her cell phone. Roy had just left after she filled him in on Pam Muir's mysterious absence that morning. Frank and Stormy were downstairs watching Noelle and Mary Petrofsky play. Christy had a few minutes to herself, and she planned to enjoy it with a FaceTime call to Quinn in Toronto. She thought he looked tired, or maybe frazzled, when he appeared on the screen, but then he smiled at her. His face lit with pleasure, and she was reassured.

"Hey, beautiful. How did this morning go?"

She wrinkled her nose. "The stupid woman didn't show."

He frowned. "Really? What kind of excuse did she give?"

"None. Mallory thinks she doesn't have the documentation she needs to prove paternity, and that her initial visit was a kind of test to see how hard we'd push back. We pushed and she caved."

His expression turned thoughtful. "Maybe." He shrugged. "Mallory Tait is the expert, I suppose. She should know what she's doing."

"Apparently, she also knows Pam Muir. She doesn't have a lot of respect for her, though, which could be coloring her thinking." Christy sighed. "I'm worried about what Pam might do, though. Maybe she's decided she's going to soften us up with more news articles about the wicked Jamiesons. The one that came out on Monday was bad enough." And if there were more, they'd only add fuel to Joan Shively's quest to prove Christy an unfit mother.

Quinn smiled at her with both lips and eyes, in a way that spoke of tenderness and concern. Christy's stomach did a little flip and she wished he was here beside her and not thousands of kilometers and three time zones away.

"The principal has your back this time. Noelle will be okay."

"Yeah." She touched the screen, tracing the shape of his cheek, and his smile deepened. "How's your day going?"

He blew out a breath and shook his head. "Slow. We're still wrestling over whether the show will be a straight documentary or a docu-drama, with performers playing you and Frank and acting out key scenes. My agent wants to sell movie rights to the book, so she's digging in her heels and demanding it be a straight documentary with narration and interviews." He grimaced. "I should come home and let her and the producer fight it out, but I seem to have been cast in the roll of mediator. I sit in on all the meetings and listen to them bicker until they reach an impasse, then I have to figure out a way around it." He shook his head. "Frustrating."

Christy laughed. "Sounds like they're keeping you on your toes."

But he shook his head again. "I'm bored to tears. I came here to write a script for a documentary. These format details should have been completed before I arrived. And, to be fair to my agent, they were. The agreement she drafted was for a straight documentary, with me as the host. It would be planned and written in Toronto but filmed in Vancouver. All this stuff about dramatization and using actors was all sprung on us when I got here. Now we can't do anything until the format is finalized."

Christy scrunched her mouth into a pout. "So you're not coming home anytime soon."

He shook his head. "Sadly, no."

She sighed. "I miss you."

"I miss you too," he said softly.

They spoke for a few minutes longer, but while it was only three-thirty for Christy in Vancouver, it was three hours later in Toronto and Quinn had to leave to go to a dinner being put on by one of the network brass. After they said good-bye, Christy sighed and wandered into the kitchen to empty the dishwasher she'd run earlier that day.

By Friday, two days later, Pam Muir still hadn't been in contact, and Christy's worries were growing. She checked the news feeds regularly, searching for articles that included the Jamieson name. All she found were normal, everyday problems. The province was worried about climate change, crime was up as witnessed by the first murder of the new year, which had occurred a mere eighteen days in, and the city was over budget, so taxes were going up. There was nothing about Frank Jamieson being a bigamist or the possibility of a new Jamieson heir. That was good, but Christy didn't quite trust the silence. She spent her lunch hour paging through the morning newspaper, then she called Mallory Tait.

"McCullagh, McCullagh, and Walker. Mallory Tait speaking."

Christy visualized Mallory reviewing a document and scrawling notes onto a yellow legal pad at the same time as she absently said her name into the phone. Best to get straight to business. "Hi. It's Christy Jamieson. Have you heard from Pam Muir yet?"

There was hesitation. Christy imagined Mallory sitting up straighter and shifting her telephone from one hand to the other as she focused on Christy's question.

This time when she spoke, her tone was crisp. Christy had her full attention. "No, and I don't expect her to make contact, Mrs. Jamieson. I don't believe she has the documentation she needs, so there's no point for her to continue her insinuations. She won't be back."

"You sound certain." Christy wished she was as confident.

"I am." There was another moment of silence, then Mallory said, "Pamela Muir isn't a woman with deep emotions. When she sees an opportunity, she seizes the moment. If she can score a win, she's all in."

Mallory's voice was so cold, it was brittle. Christy shivered. "If she can't?"

"She cuts and runs."

Now there was a sneer in Mallory's voice and Christy imagined her shrugging dismissively.

"Trust me, Mrs. Jamieson. That's exactly what she's done on this scam."

Trust me. Well, Christy did. Sort of. She rubbed her forehead. The specter of losing her daughter because of malicious bad press haunted her. It would take more than Mallory's reassurances for her to believe Pam Muir had gone away for good. "Shively has been to the school."

"We're moving forward with the case to dismiss the allegations against you," Mallory said. "I don't believe Joan Shively and Child Services will be a problem for you much longer."

Christy resisted the urge to say Mallory believed a lot of things that Christy was uncertain about. Instead, she said, "Please call me immediately when you hear from Pam Muir."

"Of course. Have a good weekend, Mrs. Jamieson."

Christy murmured a reply and hung up the phone. With Quinn in Toronto and Pam Muir lurking just out of sight, a good weekend was something Christy was quite sure she was not going to have.

CHAPTER 6

The weekend was better than Christy expected, because she got in another FaceTime conversation with Quinn. On Saturday, Noelle's pal Mary Petrofsky came for dinner and remained for a sleepover.

She let the two girls stay up later than usual and the three of them sat on the living room couch and watched the latest Disney epic. They shared two bowls of popcorn, one seasoned with white cheddar flavoring and lots of butter, the other plain. They all thoroughly enjoyed the movie.

On Monday, Christy went back to her compulsive checking of the news feeds but could find no stories that included Jamieson references. That left her edgy and worried. When she went to pick Noelle up from school, she expected to find that Shively had visited, and was fully prepared to defend herself, but the day had been quiet, and she returned home with Noelle feeling oddly deflated.

Tuesday followed the same pattern as Monday, except that Christy talked to Quinn and for a little while she focused on the problems he was having in Toronto instead of her own.

On Wednesday, Christy entered the Jamieson Trust offices very much aware that it was a full week since Pam Muir was supposed to have provided the documentation proving her son was also Frank's son. After a quick scan of the news feeds, where she found nothing, Christy walked briskly out of her office and over to Isabelle Pascoe's.

Isabelle's head was bowed as she focused on a paper document on her desk. As usual, she'd tied her long hair into a knot at her nape and the dark brown strands gleamed in a shaft of weak sunlight. She looked up as Christy entered and smiled.

"It's been a week and we've heard nothing," Christy said, not bothering to clarify. She felt as if doom was pressing down on her shoulders, and she needed to do something—anything—to avert the impending disaster.

Isabelle nodded. She didn't have to ask what Christy was referring to. Pam Muir and the threat she posed was on both their minds. "Perhaps Ms. Tait is correct—the woman doesn't have the proof she needs and has decided to give up on her absurd claim."

Christy sat on the chair in front of Isabelle's desk. "You were with me the day she came here. Did she strike you as the kind of woman who would give up because she ran into a roadblock?"

Isabelle's smile faded. "Not having documentation is a sizeable roadblock."

Christy made a faint, impatient sound in her throat and waved her hand.

Isabelle laughed. "But, yes, I agree with you. I don't think she'd let a little thing like legal proof stand in her way if she wanted something."

"Then why hasn't she contacted us?" Christy heard the desperation in her voice and wished it wasn't there, but worry was eating away at her. She didn't have control of this situation, Pam Muir did, and all she could do was wait until the woman made her next move. That didn't sit well with her. "Or has she decided to soften us up some more by arranging for another article smearing Frank's name?"

Isabelle shrugged. "Maybe she's trying to get past the roadblocks, but she hasn't quite made it yet."

Christy tilted her head and shot Isabelle a sideways frown. "Meaning?"

Isabelle sighed, as if thinking about Pam Muir and her shenanigans tired her out. "She hasn't found a forger able to create birth and marriage certificates that look real and the reporter she used to write the Jamieson article didn't get good enough results from the first article, so won't do a second."

"Maybe," Christy said. But she brightened a little.

"Or," Isabelle said, and this time she laughed. "Maybe Ms. Muir was so taken by our poor security guard she fell into bed with him that afternoon and hasn't come up for air since."

Christy's eyes widened, then she laughed too. "What an interesting idea." She shook her head. "I don't think I want to go any further with that one, though."

"Me either," Isabelle said, wrinkling her nose.

The conversation shifted to other matters, but the absence of Pam Muir remained on Christy's mind like a throbbing abscess that wasn't going to go away until the poison was drained from it. As the morning progressed, there were a half a dozen moments when her hand hovered over the telephone as she considered phoning Mallory Tait to see if she'd heard anything. Each time she told herself that Mallory would phone if she had news and so she waited.

At eleven-thirty, an email from Mallory dropped into her box. The subject line read Discussion re JS and when Christy opened it, she was surprised to find it contained nothing more than a calendar invitation for lunch at noon that day, just a half an hour away. She stared at it, frowning. JS must mean Joan Shively, but what about Pam Muir?

Puzzled by the brevity, which hardly seemed necessary, Christy pondered the invitation. Added to the mystery, Mallory had suggested a popular family style restaurant that would probably be busy and along with it, noisy—not the kind of place Christy envisioned for a planning session on a delicate subject. Wondering what was up, she sent an acceptance reply, then told Isabelle she was having lunch with Mallory. As Isabelle nodded, Christy added that she'd head home after the meeting. She wasn't sure how long it would last, and she had to be back in Burnaby by two-thirty.

Mallory had already secured a booth when Christy arrived. Dressed in one of her perfectly cut, always pressed, suits, with her hair sleekly tied in a knot at her nape, she oozed high-end, high-power vibes that didn't fit with the location. Focused on her phone, a frown between her brows, she seemed oblivious to the other patrons of the busy restaurant, but when Christy sat opposite her, she put her phone away before Christy or the hostess spoke.

As the hostess dropped a menu on the table, she said "Let's order before we talk."

That sounded fine to Christy. It didn't take long to review the menu and pick an item. When the waitress was gone and they were alone with cups of endless coffee Christy said, "Have you heard something about the suit?"

Mallory was stirring cream into her cup. As Christy spoke, she looked up. Her expression was baffled. "Suit? What suit?"

"The one against Child Services." As Mallory continued to look confused, Christy raised her brows. "Your email said you wanted to talk about Joan Shively."

"Oh! We can talk about her, of course, but no, that wasn't the real reason I suggested this meeting."

"But—"

Mallory held up her hand, palm out. Her face was expressionless, but Christy thought she detected worry in her eyes.

Mallory drew a deep breath, then let it out slowly. "The cops visited me this morning. Pam Muir is dead."

Christy stared. "Dead? How?"

"Murdered. Her body was found in the parking lot of the Jamieson Ice Cream Building." Jamieson Ice Cream, the company that created the Jamieson fortune, had long since diverted its dairy to the suburbs. The head office, and the offices of the Jamieson Trust, remained in a sleek building in downtown Vancouver.

It was Christy's turn to suck in a deep breath before she spoke. "She was on her way to our meeting."

Mallory nodded. "That's my guess. Apparently, there was no ID on her body when she was found, so the police thought it was a mugging gone wrong. There are several large companies with offices in that building, and their initial expectation was that the victim would be an employee of one or the other. Then a missing persons report was filed for Pam Muir. The cop who visited me had just come from interviewing Muir's parents, who knew about our meeting last week."

Christy searched Mallory's face, trying to figure out what was behind Mallory's closed expression. She supposed that hiding thoughts and feelings was a useful talent for a lawyer, but right now she wished the woman wasn't quite so good at it. "You're telling me I can expect a visit from the police sometime or other."

Mallory nodded. "Sooner rather than later, I'd think. Tell them as little as possible."

Apart from Christy having a positive relationship with the police, and one specific detective, she didn't believe in cover-ups. "I'll answer the questions as asked."

Mallory nodded. "Exactly. Nothing more, nothing less."

Annoyed at that advice, Christy tilted her chin up a fraction and looked down her nose. "I'll offer insights if I find them."

Alarm flared in Mallory's eyes, and she frowned. "Mrs. Jamieson…"

This time it was Christy who put her hand up. "I have nothing to hide and my working relationship with the police is a good one. If I can help them solve Pam Muir's murder, I will."

"Mrs. Jamieson..."

Christy shook her head. "I'm not going to actively go out and look for clues if I don't have to, but Pam Muir was coming to my office to meet with me." She tapped her chest with her forefinger as she spoke. "No parking garage is completely secure, so her death could have been an unfortunate act of violence, but..."

"You doubt it," Mallory said.

"Don't you?"

With a sigh, Mallory nodded. "Okay, Mrs. Jamieson. I get your point. I don't like it, but I understand."

"Thank you," Christy said. She paused to drink her coffee while she cooled down and gathered her thoughts. "If the press gets hold of this and links the Jamieson name to Pam's death, Joan Shively will be all over it." She put the mug back onto the tabletop. "I'd like to see this murder solved quickly."

"I understand," Mallory said. "If the Shively woman becomes obnoxious, let me know and I'll do what I can to get her to back off."

"That will only encourage her," Christy said, feeling gloomy. Joan Shively was nothing if not dogged in her approach to Christy's case.

The waitress appeared with their lunches, a spinach salad with a skewer of grilled chicken for Mallory, and a chicken salad sandwich with fries for Christy. When the food was served and the waitress was gone, Christy dipped a fry in ketchup, then nibbled the tip as she studied Mallory. "I'm curious. Why did you say you wanted to meet to talk about Shively when it was Pam Muir's murder you intended to warn me about?"

Mallory stripped her chicken from the wooden skewer. "I thought it was more discreet."

"Discreet?" Christy took a bite of her sandwich and chewed while she contemplated Mallory. Either the woman took online security to extreme levels, or there was something more going on here.

"I didn't want to implicate the Trust by committing anything to paper. Getting a search warrant to examine computers and network servers isn't all that difficult and the cops are pretty sophisticated these days. Even if you delete an email, their techs can still find the lingering shadow file. And if you wipe your computer clean, the service provider may well have back up files."

Christy couldn't see how an email that said 'I was just visited by the police who told me Pam Muir was dead' could possibly implicate the Jamieson Trust any more than they were already implicated. She wasn't a high-priced lawyer, charged with protecting her client, though, so she munched her sandwich and nodded acceptance.

"Now," Mallory said briskly. "The cops won't make an appointment, they'll drop in, and they will try to shake you up with their questions, to get you to admit more than you want to. If you feel at any time that you don't like the way the interrogation is going, tell them you want a lawyer present before you'll answer any more questions."

"Okay," Christy said. It was good advice. She doubted she'd have to use it, but it was good advice. She looked down at her plate and chose another fry to dip into the ketchup. "You said the police knew about the meeting. Did they know about Pam's attempt to extort money from the Trust?"

"Apparently not. Her parents thought she was meeting me at my office. They weren't aware we were gathering at the Trust. I guess that's why they didn't come forward earlier. They didn't connect their daughter's disappearance with the first murder of the year." She shrugged. "The cop, whose name was Jones, wanted to know when I'd last seen Pam and where I was on Wednesday morning."

Christy ate another fry as she studied Mallory. "You met with her on the Friday before her death, didn't you? When she came to your office to talk about the paternity suit."

Mallory pushed her fork into the salad, spearing chicken and spinach leaves. Her face was expressionless. "We did meet, it's true, and I admitted as much to Jones. I also told him Pam had come to my office to discuss a case. He tried to bully the details from me, the obnoxious little toad, but I refused to answer. The information is confidential. It made for a short interview."

Christy, who had a healthy respect for Vancouver's police detectives, said gently, "It won't take Jones long to figure out what the meeting was about, and he'll wonder why you were so cagey."

"Let him." There was a spark of defiance in Mallory's eyes. "I will not implicate a client in order to ease the way for the police."

Christy nodded and went back to her sandwich. Mallory Tait could take care of herself. Right now, she was more worried about how being implicated in another murder would affect her status with Joan Shively and Child Services.

CHAPTER 7

Christy was right—it didn't take long for the police to pay a visit to the Jamieson Trust. Mallory was correct as well, though. When the cops came to interview the staff, the visit was unannounced. They arrived shortly before nine o'clock on the morning following Christy's lunch with Mallory. Since she didn't have any meetings scheduled that day, Christy hadn't rushed after she dropped Noelle at school at eight-thirty, and she arrived at the Trust's downtown office at nine-thirty.

"Morning, Bonnie," she said, as she walked through the door. The thick pile of the pale beige carpet swallowed up the sound of her footsteps and the door itself closed silently behind her. The morning was cold, the air heavy with impending precipitation, so she was wearing a thick wool coat she only had to use for a month or two each winter. As it buttoned from neck to mid-thigh, she was busy releasing the fastenings as she spoke, looking down and not paying attention to what was around her. She was about to shrug off the coat when she realized Bonnie hadn't replied to her greeting. She looked up, frowning.

Bonnie sat ramrod straight at her desk. Her complexion was pale, her eyes wide. When she saw Christy's gaze focused on her, she whispered, "Mrs. Jamieson."

Christy's frown deepened. There was fear in Bonnie's barely spoken words and the poor girl looked devastated. "Bonnie, what's wrong?" She took a step toward the desk, her coat forgotten, every protective instinct on high alert. "Tell me."

Bonnie swallowed. Her voice wavered, then strengthened as she spoke. "The police are here. A man and a woman. They were waiting when I arrived to open the office. I said they couldn't come in until you or Isabelle arrived, but they insisted. Well, the man did. The woman was more polite, but she went along with him."

A man and a woman. Christy supposed the man was the detective who interviewed Mallory Tait yesterday. She hoped the woman was Patterson. "Did the detectives give you names?"

Bonnie nodded. "The woman is Detective Patterson. I knew her because she's been to the office before."

Christy nodded.

"The man said he was Detective—"

"I told you to alert me when she arrived." The man's voice was deep, his tone harsh, and his words silenced Bonnie like a slap across the face. She whitened and looked even more frightened than she had before.

Christy turned slowly to face the owner of the voice. Pulling on her Jamieson persona and remembering the way Ellen had faced down a squad of heavily armed police the day they came to Burnaby to arrest Tamara Ahern, she tilted her head in an imperious way and shot the cop a cold look. "She has a name and it's Mrs. Jamieson. Remember that and use it when addressing me or referring to me with my staff. I gather you are the policeman Bonnie was speaking about. I assume you also have a name?"

"It's Jones, Mrs. Jamieson." The statement was made in Patterson's usual unruffled tone, but there was the hint of disapproval beneath the cool calm. Evidently, she'd followed Jones into the reception area. Now, she came further into the room to stand beside him. Isabelle Pascoe hovered behind, in the opening to the hallway.

Christy looked from Jones to Patterson and saw the disapproval echoed in her eyes. Relief surged through her. She trusted Patterson and knew her sole objective was to discover who had done the crime. She was open to new theories and evaluated the facts she unearthed in an impartial way, rather than trying to make them fit a preconceived suspect.

"Detective Patterson," Christy said. She nodded briefly, hanging on to her Jamieson persona even though it was Patterson she was talking to. There might be amusement in Patterson's eyes, but her expression was guarded. She wasn't working this case on her own, but with a colleague who wasn't just obnoxious, but who seemed to be a bully. Christy figured Jones would probably enjoy going after Patterson if he had a chance as much as he seemed happy to make the unfortunate Bonnie cringe.

Her quick assessment was confirmed when Jones said, a sneer in his voice and a curl to his lips, "I've heard you two are pals."

Christy studied him. He was a tall, lanky man with a baby face, flawless skin, a thatch of black hair, and a sad attempt at a stubble beard. She suspected he got a lot of ribbing and had developed the obnoxious manner to compensate for his unintimidating appearance.

What sort of cues would this man respond to? If she let him intimidate her, as Bonnie apparently had, he'd walk all over her. She needed to assert control and keep it, but she also had to do it in a way that would be unexpected and would confuse him.

She smiled, and as she watched his eyes narrow she knew she was on the right path. He wasn't sure why she would smile at him when he'd been deliberately antagonistic. She decided this was going to be fun. "Detective Jones," she said in the most patronizing tone she could command. "I have friends. I have acquaintances. I have associates. I do not have 'pals' of any kind."

He blinked and drew his head back, then frowned as if he couldn't quite figure out her meaning. Good, she had him off balance. She continued on using the same tone. "I assume you are here for some purpose and that you will share that purpose with me momentarily. I suggest you and Detective Patterson make yourselves comfortable in the conference room."

To her satisfaction, she saw that Patterson was fighting a smile and that fury had twisted her colleague's pretty features. Apparently, the good Detective Jones didn't like to be dismissed by someone who might, or might not, be a suspect. Hiding her own rather gleeful smile, she turned toward the reception desk. "Bonnie, please supply these police persons with refreshments."

Bonnie, eyes still wide and complexion pale, nodded quickly. "Of course, Mrs. Jamieson. I offered earlier, but they said they wouldn't take anything."

Christy waved her hand in an airy, dismissive way. "I'm sure they will appreciate a beverage now. We have fresh cinnamon buns in the kitchen, do we not?"

Bonnie nodded.

Christy turned back to Jones, avoiding Patterson's gaze. She smiled in a superior way that contrived to show she had absolutely no respect for him at all, and said, "The police do enjoy sweet pastries, do they not? Please accept the hospitality of the Jamieson Trust. I will be with you in due time."

Jones opened his mouth. Whether he had planned to demand her attention now, or to protest he didn't need any refreshments, Christy never knew because at the end of her speech she simply sauntered past him as if he didn't exist.

Isabelle followed her into her office. She shut the door behind her and leaned against it, as if she was afraid Jones would invade Christy's sanctuary if she didn't. "You were marvelous!"

Christy stripped off her coat and threw it on one of the chairs in the small conversation area in one corner of her office. She turned to face her office manager. Her tone was brisk. "Fill me in, Isabelle. What's been happening?"

"They were interviewing Bonnie when I arrived. There, in the reception area. Jones was leading. Detective Patterson was standing to one side, watching, and listening. Bonnie was terrified. I could see it on her face. I intervened, demanding to know why they were here and what they wanted. Detective Patterson was the one who told me."

"They're here because of Pam Muir, aren't they?"

Isabelle nodded.

Christy sat down at her desk. "Well, that was quick. Mallory Tait figured they'd be here soon, but said she refused to provide them with any details about Pam's claims against the Trust."

Isabelle left her post at the door and came to sit down in one of the visitors' chairs in front of Christy's desk. She leaned forward. "Mallory might not have told them, but they do know Muir's allegation that your husband was her child's father." She sat back, looking thoughtful. "I'm not sure if they know she was also asserting they were married."

"We have to assume they do. After all, it was all over social media not so long ago." Christy thought for a moment. "I take it they've interviewed both you and Bonnie?"

She nodded. "They were questioning me when you came in. I made them go into the conference room to do it, but Jones insisted the conference room door remain open so they'd know when you arrived. As soon as he heard your voice, he jumped up and rushed out. Detective Patterson looked annoyed, but she followed him to the reception area."

Christy drummed her fingers on the desk. "So, he's gunning for me. He probably likes me as his main suspect. Okay, I think I know how to handle this." She looked at the door. "We've been sitting here for a good five minutes. I'd better go in there and keep my advantage, or Jones will be storming my office."

Isabelle nodded. "Is there anything you want me to do?"

"Yeah. Calm Bonnie down. Make sure she's okay."

Isabelle nodded again and slipped out of the office. Christy waited a moment longer, carefully smoothing her skirt and making sure her hair and make-up were perfect. Then she walked purposefully down the carpeted hallway to the conference room.

There she found the table laid with a platter of cinnamon buns, jugs of milk and cream, a sugar bowl, a coffee urn, and a dozen spoons. The china was the finest porcelain, the coffee urn and spoons sterling silver. Mugs of coffee were placed in front of Jones and Patterson, while a third was at the empty chair at the head of the table. Her empty chair. Christy smiled. Bonnie had done well.

Patterson had a plate in front of her and she was pulling apart a cinnamon bun as Christy entered the room. She stopped and wiped her fingers with a starched linen napkin. "Mrs. Jamieson. Thank you for meeting with us."

Jones sent his colleague a fuming look before he turned to Christy. "Took you long enough."

"It's my pleasure, Detective Patterson," Christy said. She paused to pick up the platter of sweet rolls. "My, you are impatient, Detective Jones. Do have a cinnamon bun." She thrust the platter under his nose and was pleased when he lifted his hand to take one.

Jones was made of stern stuff, though. He grimaced, then dropped his hand. "We're not here to socialize."

"No, of course not." She chose a cinnamon bun before she put the platter down. After placing it on her plate, she sank gracefully into her chair at the head of the table. "Now, detectives, please tell me what you are here for."

"Murder," Jones said, leaning forward in his chair, both hands resting flat on the edge of the table. Patterson continued to eat her cinnamon bun and watch silently.

"Dear me," Christy said, raising her brows. "I assume you're talking about the unfortunate death that was mentioned on the news the other night?"

"Don't be coy," Jones said. His voice was loud, his tone aggressive. "You know all about it."

Christy raised her brows. "I know my lawyer, Mallory Tait, told me you came to see her yesterday and you wanted information on her relationship with a woman called Pam Muir. I also know Ms. Muir's body was found in the parking lot of this building. That," she added, looking down her nose at him, "was courtesy of the independent media who stated that Vancouver's first murder of the year took place my parking lot."

Jones jabbed a finger at her. "You knew Pam Muir."

"Yes, I did," Christy said candidly. "As I am sure both Isabelle and Bonnie told you."

"She came here wanting to bust into your fancy trust. Afraid of losing your millions to some upstart, Ms. Jamieson?"

Patterson made an impatient sound that had Jones glaring at her. Christy brought the focus back on herself. "I assume you are referencing Ms. Muir's claim that my late husband was the father of her son?"

Jones glared at her. Patterson said quietly, "We are. Can you tell us about it?"

Christy let her Jamieson princess persona slip as she turned to Patterson with a smile. A real, very warm smile. "Of course. First, though, would you mind telling me what you know about her allegations?"

Patterson studied her for a moment, then she nodded. "Why not?"

"Police business!" Jones shouted, aggrieved.

After one long, cold look that silenced him, Patterson said, "Ms. Muir's parents knew Frank Jamieson was the boy's father. For years, they told us. Apparently, Ms. Muir recently decided to make the Trust aware of the boy's existence."

"Interesting." Christy stored the information away for later consideration. "Well, Detective, there isn't much I can tell you about Pam Muir. She showed up here a couple of weeks ago claiming Frank was her son's father. That was the first I'd ever heard of my husband having an illegitimate son."

"You didn't believe her."

"Honestly? No."

"Why?" Jones demanded. "Frank Jamieson had a bad reputation. There's no reason to believe the kid isn't his."

Christy locked eyes with Patterson for a moment. When she turned to reply to Jones, her expression was haughty. "There is every reason to believe, Detective Jones. If Ms. Muir had said her son was five years old, or younger, I might have accepted her claim. However, her son is older than my daughter. My relationship with my husband deteriorated over the years, but in the beginning we were very close. If the child was his, I would have known." She paused, studying him coldly. When he opened his mouth to blurt out yet another annoying question, she added emphatically, "Then there is the absurdity of a woman who knows the father of her child is wealthy beyond her wildest dreams and does nothing about it." She made a small dismissive sound. "Please! If Frank was the boy's father, Pam Muir would have been feasting on the Jamieson Trust from the day of his birth."

Jones looked as if he'd like to dispute that, but Patterson intervened. "So you didn't accept her claim when she first approached you?"

"Of course not! I told her she needed to speak to the Trust's lawyer, Mallory Tait. She was reluctant to leave without a promise, which I wasn't prepared to give her. We had to get security to usher her out. Fortunately, when she met the guard, she was quite happy to go."

"What?" said Jones. He was frowning again, apparently baffled by the comment.

Patterson raised her brows. The cynical quirk of her lips told Christy she had a good idea of why a woman would enjoy being escorted from the building by a man.

Christy smiled at her, but turned to Jones and said coolly, "The guard works out, Detective. His body was buff, and he had the eyes of an angel. Yes, I'm quite sure she enjoyed spending time with him."

She had the satisfaction of watching Jones redden. He humphed and deliberately tapped his pen on his notebook. "What was his name? We'll need to speak to him."

Christy gave him the name of the guard and the company he worked for.

Patterson said, "Ms. Muir had contact information for Ms. Tait in her phone, but when we spoke to Ms. Tait she cited lawyer-client privilege and refused to divulge anything beyond that she had met with Ms. Muir. Can you provide us with any details about the meeting?"

"I don't know exactly what was said, of course, but I know Mallory planned to tell Pam she would have to supply legal documents proving her assertions. We were to meet here last Wednesday at ten o'clock when she was to present them to us. We would then move forward depending on what those documents showed."

"So you were prepared to accept her son as the Jamieson heir, if she had the proof?" Jones sounded skeptical, almost contemptuous.

This was a question Christy had wrestled with before she confronted Frank all those days ago. What would she do if this boy was indeed Noelle's half brother? Could she welcome him into their lives? Could she not?

She wasn't going to give Jones the satisfaction of knowing of her struggle, though. "The key word in that question, Detective, is 'if'. She didn't have the proof because it wasn't true. However, if by some fluke the boy was a Jamieson, he would be entitled to an equal share of the Trust with my daughter."

Jones' eyes gleamed. "Cuts into her inheritance, doesn't it?"

Christy sighed. Audibly, impatiently. "Detective Jones, the Jamieson Trust is well endowed with funds, enough to support my daughter and myself, as well as a dozen other people. There is nothing in my daughter's life that would change because another person is receiving an allowance from the Trust."

"Your receptionist told us Ms. Muir didn't come to the meeting," Patterson said.

Christy turned. There was a faint smile on the detective's mouth, probably because she knew Christy was doing everything in her power to make sure Noelle lived as an ordinary little girl, not the pampered daughter of wealth.

Christy nodded in agreement. "That's right."

"Did she contact you ahead of time? Tell you she was running late? That she had another meeting?" Patterson asked.

"No. We heard nothing from her. We waited until noon, but she never showed. At that time, Mallory said she was leaving, and if Ms. Muir did arrive, we weren't to talk to her without Mallory present. I decided to close the office and send Bonnie and Isabelle home early, just in case."

"You were afraid of her," Jones said, a sneer in his voice.

Christy turned to him with a superior smile. "I was afraid I would have to summon that poor security guard again and sacrifice him to her in order to get her to leave."

Patterson made a sound perilously close to a snort of laughter as Jones reddened once more.

I've got your number, Christy thought with rather malicious glee. She raised her brows. "Is there anything else you would like to ask me, Detective Jones?"

He squared his shoulders. "Where were you between nine and noon that Wednesday?"

"I was here, along with Bonnie and Isabelle," Christy said, somewhat impatiently. "Mallory Tait arrived about nine forty-five. As I said before, we were all together until noon, when Ms. Tait left. Then I closed the office and Bonnie and Isabelle and I went down to the parking lot together. I don't know what they did after we parted ways at my car."

Looking as if he'd just struck gold, Jones smiled in a malicious way. "You said you were in at nine?"

Christy nodded, wondering what had made him look so pleased with himself.

He twisted his features into a scowl that was meant to be intimidating but didn't quite cut it and leaned forward. His eyes bored into Christy's. "You claim you were in at nine, yet today you didn't arrive until almost nine-thirty. How do you explain that, eh?"

Christy blinked, totally unprepared for the attack. Being disbelieved because her morning arrival times differed from day-to-day was the last thing she'd expected. She drew a deep breath, gave her head a mental shake, then skewered him with a look. "My explanation is simple, Detective. I had a meeting scheduled that morning. If you had been so polite as to book an appointment today for nine a.m., I would have been here before nine, waiting for you, ready to greet you. However, you did not, and I didn't know you would be waiting." Her tone was frosty, liberally laced with derision and she was pleased when Jones reddened even as he glowered at her. Adding steel to her voice, she said, "On that Wednesday morning, I made sure I was in the office by eight forty-five because Pam Muir was my guest—and because I didn't trust her. I didn't want to subject Bonnie and Isabelle to whatever pressure she might try to bring to bear. I also wanted to be sure I was prepared for whatever games she might play." She looked from Jones to Patterson. "Now, is there anything else I can tell you?"

"No, I think we're done here," Patterson said.

"For now," Jones snapped.

The idiot man was rescuing his ego, Christy thought, probably telling himself he'd been in charge throughout the whole interview. She pushed back her chair and stood. "Good. I'll see you out."

CHAPTER 8

They didn't speak as they traversed the hallway from the conference room to the reception area. Jones strode toward the door, ignoring Bonnie. Patterson followed, but she nodded to Bonnie and smiled faintly. Bonnie smiled back in a hesitant way. Christy shook her head and glared at Jones' retreating back.

As Jones put his hand on the doorknob, Patterson said, "I'd like to take a look at the murder site."

He turned away from the door to frown at her. "We passed it as we came up here. The body's gone and the site's been cleared. There's nothing to see."

Patterson gave him a level look. "You pointed in a general direction as we walked from our parking spot to the elevator. I'd like to stand where the murder was committed and get a sense of what the victim and her killer saw. I want to study the location."

Jones shrugged, his massive ego evidently untouched by the hint of reprimand in Patterson's comments. "Sure. Whatever."

Patterson narrowed her eyes. Christy wondered how she could

separate Patterson from Jones for a private conversation without Jones taking umbrage.

At that moment, his phone rang. He pulled it out of his pocket and turned away, hunching one shoulder, and showing them his back. There was a minute of silence, then he said, "Yeah. Sure. Right. Yeah, I'm coming in."

Christy raised her brows and smiled faintly at Patterson, who watched Jones with expressionless features.

He punched the disconnect button and turned back to Patterson. There was excitement in his eyes and voice. "That was the station. There's been a break in a case I've been working on for weeks. It could be what we need to make an arrest. I have to follow up on the tip."

"I can make my own way back," Patterson said.

Jones nodded. He wrenched the door open, then disappeared without a word. Patterson watched him go in equal silence. The door slowly closed. At the final, quiet click of the latch, she turned to Christy. "Do you have a moment? I'd like to speak to you privately."

Relieved she wouldn't have to cook up some excuse to convince Patterson to stay, Christy said, "Of course. Would you like another cup of coffee?" She smiled faintly. "Another cinnamon bun?" Patterson had consumed hers while Jones bullied his way through the interview.

Patterson shook her head, but she smiled as well. "I'm tempted. Those buns were delicious."

"They're from a little bakery a couple of blocks away. I'll give you the name before you go," Christy said, leading the way back down the hallway. They entered her office. She gathered up her coat, which she'd left on one of the comfortable chairs in the conversation area and hung it up on the hook behind her door. "I'm glad you offered to stay, Detective. I have a couple of things I'd like to ask you."

"I thought you might." Patterson sat in the chair Christy indicated, but she didn't relax. She sent Christy one of those wordless looks filled with meaning. "Jones hasn't been plain clothes for long and he's anxious to make a name for himself."

Christy sat down opposite her. She nodded silently, not sure where Patterson was going with this information, but willing to listen.

Patterson's jaw hardened, her gaze was level. "When the body was found, it looked like a simple crime, a woman in the wrong place at the wrong time. Jones was assigned the case."

Christy nodded again. If Pam's death had been the result of a mugging, the straightforward case would be a good opportunity for the inexperienced Jones to learn how to evaluate and assess clues.

"Initially, the victim's identity was unknown, but the location of her death did cause concern among the brass." When Christy raised her brows, Patterson smiled humorlessly. "The Jamieson name has influence in this town and Pam was killed in the parking garage of your building, Mrs. Jamieson."

"Jamieson Ice Cream and the Jamieson Trust are not the only tenants of this building, Detective," Christy said with some heat.

Patterson's rather grim smile warmed into something close to amusement. "You do have a way of getting yourself involved in capital crimes, Mrs. Jamieson."

Christy pursed her lips, feeling annoyed. Patterson had a point.

"When Jones linked the victim to the missing persons report, he went from interviewing the parents to questioning Mallory Tait before he reported in. And that was the point when my superiors decided Pam Muir's murder was much bigger than a purse snatching that turned violent. I was assigned to work on the case with Jones."

"Does he resent your appointment?" Christy asked, thinking of Jones' hostility.

"I'm senior, so I out rank him." Patterson shrugged, as if Jones' hard feelings were both unsurprising and inevitable. She leaned forward. "The thing is, Mrs. Jamieson, Pam Muir was in your parking garage, on her way to a meeting with you, on the day she was killed.

Jones knows that and he's hot to make a name for himself. He figures that if he can tie you, or someone associated with you, to the killing, the media will be all over it. The case will be big news and he'll be the cop who solved it."

Christy shuddered. Shively was already intrigued by the reports of murky goings-on in the Jamieson family. If she was implicated as a suspect in yet another murder, Shively would put her under more scrutiny than ever. Christy's worst nightmare was that Shively would decide she had a reason to remove Noelle from Christy's care. The threat of that terrified her, especially when she didn't have control of the circumstances causing it.

Christy realized Patterson must have understood her inadvertent dismay when the detective said, "I saw the article that claimed your husband was a bigamist. Are you getting flack from that Shively woman because of it?"

Christy grimaced as she nodded. "We're trying to get the file against me at Children's Services closed, but that's still in the works. As soon as the article was published, Shively went to Noelle's school. I'm concerned that connecting the Jamieson name with the murder of the woman who accused Frank of being a bigamist will cause a firestorm in the press and make it impossible for us to win our case with Child Services."

Patterson nodded. "I get that. At the moment, the press isn't particularly interested in the murder. It was our first of the year, so that got attention, but we didn't attach Ms. Muir's name to the file until later. As far as the press is concerned, the murder was a mugging gone wrong." She smiled faintly. "As I prefer to work out of the spotlight, I don't plan to make any announcements."

"Thank you," Christy said. "I appreciate that."

"But," Patterson said, "bear in mind I can't control the press. If someone else leaks her name and ties her murder to her claim against the Jamieson Trust, this could become a huge story."

"Jones, you mean," Christy said.

Patterson didn't respond.

Christy sighed. "I'll keep my fingers crossed that doesn't happen, then."

Patterson nodded. "As far as I'm concerned, Mrs. Jamieson, neither you nor your staff are prime suspects. However, since we don't have the exact time of death, and because of her involvement with the Trust I do have to keep you on the list."

Christy nodded. She hesitated, then said, "I know Pam was in the parking garage because she was coming here for a meeting that would arouse a lot of strong emotions, but is it possible it really was a mugging gone wrong?"

"It's true her purse was gone, so it could have been. Anything is possible, Mrs. Jamieson, but to me this murder looks personal."

Christy noted that Patterson didn't provide any details about the death, beyond what had already been released to the media. She allowed herself another small sigh. "Well, it was a thought. A hope, really."

Nodding, Patterson stood. "Thank you for your cooperation today, Mrs. Jamieson. I'll be in touch."

This time, when Christy escorted Patterson to the reception area, the detective did leave the office. As Christy watched the door close behind her, she wondered how long it would take before the news broke that Vancouver's first murder victim of the year was the woman who claimed to be Frank Jamieson's real wife.

∽

That worried feeling continued as Christy left the office and walked through the parking lot to her van. The underground garage was illuminated by well-spaced florescent lights, but the rough, gray concrete absorbed light and inevitably there were shadows. As the heels of her knee-high leather boots tapped on the concrete floor she wondered, not for the first time, where Pam Muir had been parked on that fateful day.

Had she just climbed out of her car when she was assaulted? Was she unaware someone was lying in wait for her? Or was she attacked on her way across the lot to the brightly lit glass encased cubicle that housed the elevator? Were her heels tapping on the concrete floor as she walked, even as Christy's were now? Did she know her killer and pause to speak to him? Or her, Christy reminded herself. She didn't know how Pam had died, only that she'd been assaulted. A woman could also be the killer.

She shivered and was glad when she saw her van and was able to unlock the door with her key fob as she neared. She took a quick look inside just to be sure no one was lurking there, then flung open the door and climbed into the driver's seat. After locking the door, she paused and drew a deep breath. Only then did she start the engine.

Pam Muir's murder was getting to her.

She acknowledged that as she navigated downtown traffic on her way back to Burnaby. It wasn't just worry about her own safety as she made the daily walk through the parking garage, it was the edginess that came from waiting for Shively to find out about the Jamieson involvement in the first murder of the year. She believed Patterson when she said she wouldn't blab to the press about it, but Patterson was right when she said she couldn't control the media. It would only take one person leaking a juicy tip for it to blow up in Christy's face.

She needed to get ahead of the story, but how?

That excellent question kept her mind busy mulling over possibilities for the rest of her trip home, but when she parked in her carport, she didn't have an action plan. She didn't even have any ideas that could be the beginning of a plan.

The gray sky had darkened into rain clouds, and it was cold enough that the precipitation was coming down in the form of sleet.

She went into the house and changed from her business suit into jeans and a sweater. For the walk over to the school, she donned a down jacket and sturdy, flat-soled footwear. No sense in ruining fine leather boots with three-inch heels in this muck.

As she waited outside the classroom door for Noelle, hunched against the wet snow with the rest of the miserable parents, she told herself she needed to look at the problem from another direction. Was Pam's death the key issue?

At first glance, it looked that way. That her murder was the first of the year meant it was newsworthy, so it wouldn't just disappear. Some reporter would follow up on it when the news cycle was slow and then that person would find out that the victim was Pamela Muir. He'd remember the article about Frank being a bigamist and he'd wonder why she was in the parking garage of the Jamieson Ice Cream Building, a building that held the Jamieson Trust offices, at nine o'clock in the morning.

That connection was what Christy was dreading. The combination of the words murder, bigamy, and long-lost heir would send Joan Shively an adrenaline rush that would have her rubbing her hands with glee.

The door opened and Noelle skipped out. There was a big grin on her face. "Mom! Lindsay invited Erin and Mary Petrofsky and me over to her house to play. Can I go?"

"Sure," she said, then added, "if it's okay with Lindsay's mom."

Noelle nodded, still beaming.

Lindsay and Erin came out of classroom together, just as the red-haired woman who was Lindsay's mother hurried across the courtyard toward them. Christy had met Suzanne the previous December. A graphic designer who worked from home, she'd hosted a Christmas party for Lindsay and all of her friends. Christy liked her, and her daughter and Noelle got along well. With Mary Petrofsky now in the friendship mix, Christy figured she'd be seeing and hearing more of Lindsay and her best friend Erin in the months to come.

Lindsay danced over to her mother and bounced up and down, talking in an animated way. Suzanne looked around, caught sight of Christy, and smiled. Taking Lindsay's hand, she walked briskly over. "I understand my daughter invited yours to our place for the afternoon."

Christy smiled. "The plan must have been hatched during the school day."

Suzanne nodded. "First I've heard of it." Then she smiled. "I'm okay with it, though. I like Lindsay having her friends over."

"Then I'm okay with it, too," Christy said, smiling in return.

The three girls, who were clustered around, cheered. "Let's go get Mary Petrofsky," Lindsay said, her voice at high volume.

The three girls rushed off. Christy and Suzanne followed more slowly.

"Lindsay told me Noelle and Mary Petrofsky are a duo," Suzanne said. "One doesn't go anywhere without the other."

"Mary is Noelle's best, best friend, ever," Christy said. "The school admin put them into different classes in the hope they'd make other friends, besides each other. It took a long time, but they seem to have widened their social network."

Suzanne laughed. "I'm glad it worked. Noelle is a sweetie and I like Mary. More importantly, so does Lindsay."

They turned the corner and followed the three girls to the open classroom door where Mary and Rebecca Petrofsky waited. Rebecca gave her permission once she had Suzanne's confirmation she didn't mind her house invaded for the afternoon by three extra girls. At that point, they parted, Lindsay's party going in one direction, Rebecca and Christy in the other.

When they reached their street, Christy said good-bye to Rebecca. She had unlocked her door and was about to go inside when she wondered if Roy was immersed in his writing or if he was free to talk.

He had a great way of brainstorming and focusing in on an issue. She could use his help.

She sent him a text and he replied immediately, inviting her for coffee. She collected Frank and Stormy the Cat and headed over. When they were settled at his kitchen table with cups of coffee, it didn't take her long to explain her problem.

He rubbed his chin. "Seems to me the story you need to get ahead of is Muir's involvement with the Jamieson Trust."

She had no involvement with the Trust. We were never married and the kid isn't mine.

Roy shot the cat a disapproving look. "Easy for you to say, Frank, but it's not proof."

You don't believe me?

"It doesn't matter if we believe you or not," Roy said impatiently. "If Christy tells some reporter her dead husband refutes Muir's claims, she'll be in an even deeper mess than she is now." He tapped his finger on the rim of his sturdy white mug and stared at over Christy's shoulder at the cupboards behind her. Finally, he said, "Who was this woman, anyway? Why would she think she could get away with pawning some other guy's kid off on the Jamieson Trust?"

She liked to hang out with guys who had influence and money. Even if she thought they were stupid.

Christy frowned at the cat, who was crouched on the tabletop. "She didn't like your crowd?"

She told me once the girls were catty. There was a pause. *Sorry, bud, didn't mean anything by it.*

Roy laughed and after a minute, so did Christy. She scratched Stormy's neck and he preened against her hand.

She said Aaron was playing the girls against each other, and he was. She thought he liked the drama. I think he liked the control.

Since Aaron DeBolt had been part of the conspiracy that ultimately ended Frank's life, Christy wasn't surprised by the comment.

"There you have it," Roy said. "Pam Muir liked men of power and influence. That's probably who the father is, some guy with a wife and three other kids who can't afford to admit he had an affair." He pursed his lips and nodded thoughtfully. "He's not going to come forward voluntarily."

"No." Christy stared into her coffee. After a moment she looked up. "Then we have to find him. How do we do that?"

"Someone who knew her?"

They both looked at the cat, who hunched into an even smaller size and glared at them. *I've told you what I know! We weren't close.*

Roy sighed in a theatrical way. "Unfortunate. Who then? She has parents, doesn't she? Though I doubt it's a good idea for someone from the Trust to be talking to them right now."

"Mallory knew her," Christy said.

Roy's brows met over his nose. "Mallory Tait, the lawyer?"

Christy nodded. "They were friends. A long time ago now, but it's a start."

Roy nodded. "Tait might have done some digging too, when Muir approached the Trust with her claims."

"I'll talk to her. I don't know why I didn't think of it before. Thank you, Roy."

Hey! What about me? I helped.

"Not enough," Roy said. He wagged his finger at the glaring cat. "You need to think harder."

The cat leapt off the table and trotted across the floor, his tail high. *I'll do what I can.*

"That's what I'm afraid of," Roy muttered.

Christy laughed.

CHAPTER 9

As always, Mallory Tait made her trim business suit look not only fashionable, but coolly, icily, sexy. How she did it was a puzzle to Christy. Her hair was pinned up in a severe bun that allowed not a loose strand and the pencil skirt finished below her knees. Perhaps it was the four-inch needle heels that made her ankles and calves appear so slender, or the sway of her hips as she maneuvered her way though the crowded tables of the same family restaurant they'd met at before.

Then again, it might be the challenging look in her very fine eyes as she surveyed the room around her as she walked. Whatever it was, Mallory Tait was a formidable woman, one in charge of any situation she was in. As Christy watched her approach, she had the feeling Mallory had only accepted this face-to-face because the Trust was an important client of McCullagh, McCullagh, and Walker.

It was possible, of course, that she was making too much of what was just an impression on her part, but Christy didn't think so. When she'd called that morning to ask for a meeting, Mallory had made excuses. That was unusual. Prior to this, the woman had been both accommodating and flexible. If Christy said she needed a meeting, Mallory agreed instantly and found an opening without hesitation.

So why was she so reluctant this morning? Pam Muir might be dead, but the parentage of her son, and her accusation that she'd been Frank's first and still wife, continued to blight Frank's name and hang over the Trust. The chapter wasn't closed and wouldn't be until the boy's real father was found.

Mallory reached the table. "Christy." She pulled out a chair and eased into it in a smooth movement.

Christy smiled at her. Mallory might be turning on the feminine power, but Christy refused to be intimidated. "Mallory. Thank you for finding a way to fit me in today."

Mallory nodded and spread her napkin over her lap. "Of course. It's my pleasure."

Sure it is, Christy thought, not believing her for a moment. Mallory Tait didn't want to be here. Christy's mind sought answers, even as she smiled acknowledgement of the woman's social lie. "As you predicted, the police came to the office yesterday."

Mallory nodded and scanned the lunch items on the menu, not making eye contact. "You didn't call me, so I hope the questions were relatively simple."

Christy put her hand on the edge of her menu, but she didn't pick it up. Instead, she watched Mallory as she said, "They wanted to know why we were meeting with Pam. I saw no reason not to tell them."

Mallory's head jerked up. Their eyes met. "They, them. It wasn't just the obnoxious Detective Jones, then? There was more than one of them?"

"There were two, your Jones and Detective Patterson." She almost said my Detective Patterson but choked off the word at the last moment. As their server approached the table, Christy took a quick look at the menu, made her decision, and closed it. She smiled at the server as she gave her order and surrendered her menu, then waited for Mallory to do the same.

"Patterson," Mallory said in a musing voice after the server was gone. "She must be called in to sort out all the screw ups."

Christy laughed, assuming the woman was referring to the unfortunate incidents during the investigation into the death of Fred Jarvis. Another officer, by the name of Inspector Fortier, had arrested Tamara Ahern for the crime, even though Patterson didn't believe she was guilty. Mallory had defended Tamara, but it had been Christy, with the help of Quinn and the others, who uncovered the real killer and Patterson who made the arrest.

"Anything else?" Mallory asked. She drummed the tabletop with her fingers.

A gesture of impatience? Or was she working through thoughts? "Patterson told me they wouldn't be releasing Pam's name to the press, but if a reporter decides to dig into the story, they won't suppress it."

The drumming stopped. Mallory's gaze sharpened. "That could be a problem."

"I agree. That's why I asked to meet with you today. I think we need to find out who the father of Pam Muir's son was. You knew her. What can you tell me about her?"

Mallory raised her water glass and sipped. She made eye contact, then looked away. "Not much. It was a long time ago and I didn't know her well."

Not helpful. Christy cast Mallory a fulminating look. "All right. What do you know about her? Where did she work, for instance?"

"She was unemployed."

Christy waited for more, but Mallory didn't augment her brief, uninformative statement. Keeping a firm grasp on her temper, Christy said with careful precision, "I know that, but she must have worked somewhere, at some point."

Mallory tilted her head and nodded in a thoughtful way. "I see what you mean. Yes, you're right. She worked in the local film industry, on a show called *Blood Wars*, I believe."

"The one about vampires?"

"I guess so," Mallory said. She waved her hand in a dismissive way. "Not my kind of thing."

Nor was it Christy's, but she did know the show had a huge following and when the series wrapped many of the actors had gone on to other, more important roles. "Do you know what she did?"

Mallory shook her head. "She worked on the production side, I guess. I know she wasn't one of the actresses on the show."

"The show last aired a year ago. It must have finished filming months before. That's a long time to be out of work."

Mallory shrugged. "She may have found work on another production that didn't get picked up by a network. All I know is that she was currently out of work and had been for a few months."

Christy found Mallory's vagueness and her unhelpful manner odd, perhaps even suspicious. Before Pam's death she had the impression that Mallory was digging into the woman's past, searching for the kind of details that would prove Muir was neither Frank's wife nor the mother of Frank's baby. Why was she suddenly so unhelpful? "Is there something I should know about your relationship with Pam Muir?"

Mallory raised her brows. "I didn't have a relationship with Pam Muir. We weren't friends. Nor were we business associates. I've never represented her in litigation of any kind. In fact, I didn't meet her until she came to my office to provide her poorly reproduced fake documents. She's someone whose name I knew many years ago. That's all."

Christy eyed her in a considering way, wondering whether to accept the explanation. During their last meeting, she'd formed the impression that Mallory not only knew Pam Muir, but that they shared a past. Like her impression earlier, she could have overreacted, however. "No wonder you know very little about her."

Mallory nodded. Relief flickered in her eyes.

Christy caught the expression and annoyance flared. She said crisply, "The problem remains, we need to know who the father is. What do you suggest?"

Conversation halted when their lunches arrived and were placed before them. When the server had gone, Mallory said, "If I can push the petition to dismiss the Child Services case forward, and get it resolved, the identity of the father becomes less critical."

"I still want to know who the father is. And the Trust still needs proof that Frank was the boy's father or that he was not."

"Agreed. We can work on that later, though. For the moment, I plan to focus on the Child Services suit."

"I'll see what I can dig up about Pam's time on *Blood Wars*."

Mallory raised her brows. Her expression was skeptical. "Really?"

Don't underestimate me, Mallory Tait, Christy thought, thoroughly annoyed. "Really. You'll be surprised at what I can find out."

CHAPTER 10

"Frank! We need to talk." Roy stood in the center of his living room and shouted the words. He had no idea where the cat was currently located, but he hoped he was in the house and not outside.

Now? The Cat wants a nap.

"Yes, now!" It was two o'clock in the afternoon and Roy had lost track of time. He'd planned to tackle Frank much earlier in the day, but he'd been in the middle of a scene and the words were flowing nicely. Time had become an unimportant construct.

He heard the sounds of pounding cat paws upstairs as Stormy abandoned whatever bed he was sleeping on—probably Quinn's, just because Frank liked to mess with him—and answered Roy's call. Christy had told him that thunderous steps indicated strong emotion on the cat's part, so Roy figured Stormy was annoyed at having his nap interrupted.

Tough. It was Friday afternoon and he wanted to have this conversation with Frank while Christy wasn't around, which meant now, before she returned from the Trust's office and before the weekend took over all their lives.

Stormy appeared on the landing and paused at the top of the last flight of stairs. *The Cat's paws are cold and he wants to curl up and tuck them under him until they are warm again. Can't this wait?*

"No, it can't." Complaints about the weather had become an everyday occurrence. Vancouver's climate was more temperate than the rest of Canada's, but like other parts of the country, January was cold and precipitation could come in the form of snow. The wet, slushy muck that had stopped traffic and caused innumerable accidents the other day was mostly gone, but patches remained and the ground was cold. Worse, the forecast called for more snow and the temperature had plummeted.

Roy didn't have a lot of sympathy for Stormy's cold paws, though, because the cat insisted on spending a portion of every day outside, winter chill or not. That was why he was at Roy's townhouse instead of Christy's. Roy could let him in and out through the day, so he wasn't cooped up inside.

Stormy slowly thumped down the stairs. When he reached the bottom, Roy pointed toward the picture window that looked out on the small back garden. An upholstered and well-padded chair was positioned beside a couch that stretched the length of the window. "Tell Stormy he can curl up on the chair. I'll take the couch."

Why doesn't he get the couch? Why the chair?

Roy groaned and rolled his eyes skyward. "He can have the couch! I don't care. I though he could make more of a nest for himself on the chair. That's all."

The cat sat at his feet and glared up. *No need to be so testy.*

Roy thought there was every need to be grumpy, considering his heating bill had gone up since he'd set up his cat daycare at the beginning of December. He had to leave his front door ajar while the cat was out, and he had to scoop a litter box regularly because Stormy did not like using the outside when it was cold and damp. Resisting the urge to sigh, he gestured to the furniture. "Shall we?"

After a moment, the cat trotted over to the chair and hopped up. He then circled the seat, searching for the best, most comfortable spot. When he and finally settled down, he curled into a ball with his tail wrapped around his cold paws.

Roy sat on the couch and made eye contact. "I want to talk about Pam Muir."

That's why you interrupted the Cat's nap? I've already told you everything I know about her.

"I bet there's more."

The cat stared at him, eyes wide, expression uninformative. Frank didn't speak.

"Ah-ha!" Roy pointed his finger at the Cat and waggled it. "I was right. There is more."

You're crazy, old man.

"You're not denying it. I figure you don't want to talk about Muir in front of Christy because the woman is part of your romantic past."

She's not! We were friends, nothing more.

Roy waggled his finger back and forth. He figured it would annoy Frank and fascinate Stormy. Indeed, he could see the cat's eyes following his finger with the same intensity cats had when they were stalking some small, hapless creature. Frank had been complaining all month that the squirrels and birds were lying low and that Stormy had no one to play with. The cat was probably desperate for something to pounce on.

"You were what? Nineteen or twenty? I know young males that age. Sex is always on their minds. And with a woman like the one Christy described? Pam Muir was probably a walking sex bombshell."

She was gorgeous.

The statement was made reluctantly, the tone almost a trance-like monotone. Roy kept his finger moving and said nothing.

You're right. She came on to me. She came on to Aaron and the others too. I didn't want to share.

"So, you didn't get together, not once, even though she hung around with your gang for a couple of summers?"

He kept his finger moving. The cat's eyes followed it intently.

We talked. She liked to complain.

Getting information out of Frank was worse than trying to find out what had happened during Quinn's school day when he was a pre-teen. But he'd pried details out of his son all those years ago and he could do it with Frank now. "What did she complain about?"

Stuff.

He was kidding, right? Roy kept his finger moving as he waited for more, even though he wanted to throw up his hands, roll his eyes and demand a full and detailed explanation. After a moment, his patience was rewarded.

She was older. She graduated the summer after my second year. She wanted to go to grad school.

"I'm sensing a but," Roy said, when the memory dwindled away.

She said the dean of her faculty came on to her and when she wouldn't have sex with him, he made sure none of the programs she'd applied to accepted her.

"What?" Roy was so surprised he let his finger drop.

Stormy shifted his paws more comfortably under him and put his head down on the chair cushion, preparing to snooze.

In Roy's mind, he heard Frank yawn. "Wait! You can't go to sleep now."

Stormy shifted and yawned too.

"What university did she go to?"

I don't know. The tone was an impatient shrug. *Somewhere local. English Bay, I think.*

"What faculty was she in?"

I don't remember.

Stormy stood up, arched, then circled again. This time he stretched out on his side, a prelude to sleep.

Getting desperate, Roy said urgently, "Did she complain about anyone else? Or anything else?"

Maybe. I think she said some of her profs also propositioned her. She was mad the only jobs she could get after graduation were clerical ones. She thought she deserved better. We saw her a lot that first summer and at the beginning of the second, but after she got a permanent job she didn't come round much, even though it was clerical too.

In his mind, the voice sighed. Roy sensed sleep would soon overcome Frank as he surrendered to Stormy's lethargy. He guessed he had one question left before the pair of them were fast asleep. "What about the summer before you met her? Do you know what she was doing then?"

Another sigh. *She had a job, I think, an internship.*

"Do you know the name of the company she worked for?"

There was no answer. Roy had a sense of deep breathing. Frank and Stormy were asleep.

Roy glared at the snoozing cat. He could wake Frank up, of course, but he doubted he'd get much else out of him. To be honest, he'd already obtained more than he expected, Frank being rather cagey about his past.

He reviewed the conversation. He had two good clues about Pam Muir they didn't have before. Her university career had ended badly, which she resented, and she had a job she thought was beneath her.

That had happened during the second summer Frank had known her, a crucial time, because it was then she claimed she'd married Frank and started a family with him. Yet, according to Frank, he'd barely seen her that year and by August, before he'd returned to university back East where he would meet Christy and fall in love, Pam Muir was almost nowhere to be seen.

Those details were significant. As the summer waned was Pam

already pregnant and feeling the first physical effects, making partying and socializing less appealing to her? Or was she deeply involved with a man outside Frank's social circle, and so cutting her ties with Frank and the others because she'd found someone more to her taste?

A lot of questions and no answers. Frank had given him a string to pull though. He'd start with English Bay University and see what he could find out about Pam Muir and the dean of her faculty who apparently ruined her career.

Deliberately.

While the cat slept in the living room, Roy returned to his laptop in the kitchen and got to work. He discovered that English Bay University did not make it easy to access information about their grads online. Their website had lots of trifling data about their alumni—how many had graduated over the life of the university (187,345), how many were from the United States (6,589), East Asia (2,368) and Europe (534), and what provinces were represented (all ten!). Roy gave up in disgust as the stats went on to identify which Canadian provinces were most represented, and what cities had the greatest number of grads.

The website was getting him nowhere. Time to talk to a person. He found the department's number and dialed it at three-thirty on Friday afternoon. His call was answered by an automated system that offered him five choices, none of which included talking to a person. As the canned voice ran through the options and offered to start over because he hadn't made one, he pounded the zero button on his landline. The voice kept talking. Years ago, he'd heard that if you punched zero three times the recorded system would automatically transfer you to an operator. That wasn't happening, but he really wanted it to, so he tried again. And again.

The automated system hung up on him.

He phoned again. This time, he chose upcoming alumni events

from the menu and keyed in the number. That led him to another list of options that included several cities and one that promised to itemize all events for the next three months.

This time he hung up.

He dialed again and selected employment opportunities. That turned out to be a way for alumni to access a job board. By four o'clock, he'd gone through all the options and decided there were no live people working in the alumni office at English Bay University. He envisioned a giant bank of computers inhabiting prime university office space, their flashing lights creating a malevolent, leering face that laughed at the stupidity of mere humans who were foolish enough to believe they were at the core of the university experience.

He firmed his jaw and narrowed his eyes. He wouldn't be beaten by an inanimate machine, no matter how much data it contained and how quickly it could process that data. After digging through the website, he found the number for the university's switchboard and phoned it.

A canned voice, remarkably like the one on the alumni system, answered. It directed him to state the name of the person he wished to reach or to type the person's name using the numbers on his telephone keypad.

He held the phone in front of him and fumed. Then he said, "Alumni director."

"I'm sorry," the melodious female voice said. "I do not understand your request. Please try again."

He typed in the words, slowly, laboriously, on the telephone keypad.

"I'm sorry. Your request cannot be fulfilled at this time. Please call again." The machine hung up on him.

The bank of computers he'd been imagining after his attempt to connect with the alumni department mutated into a whole family of giant computers, all grinning with malicious pleasure.

Roy's determination not to be beaten by a machine had him gritting his teeth and phoning the main switchboard again. This time, he asked for the president's office. The same thing happened. He went back to the website and did a search for the name of the university's president. What came up was a page that included the names of several programs and of a dozen A to Z directory listings that did not include the president's name or his (or her) office phone number. It did, however, provide listings for three vice presidents, which wasn't what he asked for.

The final group of listings was for news stories. There he struck gold. The second item was a recent press release announcing that the president had been appointed to a second term. He clicked on the article.

What came up was an image of a smiling middle-aged woman pasted overtop of a panorama of EBU buildings. To fit as many buildings into the photo as possible, the image size had been reduced, making them appear to be far distant from the woman. The sky was deep blue, the grass behind the woman was a deep green, and the miniature neo-gothic buildings in the background were stately gray stone. It would have been an effective scene had the photo manipulation been done well. As it was, the president's image was obviously a late addition, added through photo manipulation. She looked absurd.

He stared at the picture, marveling that a large institution like EBU didn't have a graphic designer capable of creating an image that didn't make the poor president look like a giant cardboard cutout. Or better yet, they could have employed a real live human photographer who scouted the perfect location, then took the president there to shoot a photo that made her appear both professional and approachable. It was possible to do. He knew it because he'd had it done to him. All it took was a human with a little bit of creativity and the willingness of the organization to spend a few extra bucks on said human.

Clearly, EBU was more about automation than it was people, and wasn't about to fork out the dollars for something as trivial as getting it right. Still, he finally had a name. He scrolled down to the bottom of the website and found that there was a link to the A-to-Z directory in the footer. He clicked it and typed in the president's name. The directory coughed up a link that led to the webpages for the office of the president. Along with her bio—a truly formidable page listing her publications that seemed to scroll down forever—her priorities for the university, events she'd be speaking at, her awards, and her annual expense reports—what the heck was that?—he discovered a contact page.

Now, he thought, he was getting somewhere. He clicked on the link.

Maybe, maybe not. The page opened to a list of people who worked in the president's office. There were sixteen of them, because all the managers had coordinators and some of those had assistants. None of the people cited seemed to have any relationship with the alumni office, so he selected the least senior person in the bunch, who happened to be the receptionist, and phoned the listed number.

The melodious female voice he'd encountered earlier offered him seven options and invited him to press the appropriate number. He pressed the one for the president's executive assistant. It rang through. Optimism flared in Roy. He held his breath, hoping.

A recorded voice, male and a human one this time, said that the office of the president of EBU was now closed. It then listed office hours. It didn't offer the opportunity to leave a message before it disconnected.

Roy glanced at his watch. He was one minute and thirty seconds beyond the stated quitting time. Clearly, the staff at EBU took their office hours seriously.

He'd have to call back on Monday—early, he thought with disgust, because it would probably take him all day to find someone who answered his or her phone. Even then he doubted he'd have much success if he managed to connect with a real, living, breathing human. If the university was this cagey about publishing the president's name and number, they'd probably refuse to give him any information about an alumna, citing privacy issues.

He rubbed his chin, wondering where else he might find information on Pam Muir. He'd located her on social media when Christy had first found out her name from Frank, but this time he did a general Google search. He scrolled down the page and paused at a LinkedIn reference. Everyone who had a job had a LinkedIn page, didn't they? He clicked on the link and discovered a long list of Pam Muirs. He scrolled through and finally got results. There she was, Pamela Muir, graduate of English Bay University and currently employed at P. Muir Consulting. An email address was listed, but no website.

Great. Another dead end. He pushed his chair back with more force than necessary and went back into the living room. There he prodded the cat awake. Stormy yawned and Frank grunted.

"I've hit a wall," Roy said. "I need more details. Where did Pam work after she graduated? And what was the name of the company she got the permanent job with?"

I don't know! It was a long time ago.

"Think," Roy said, all the frustration of the last couple of hours welling up and bubbling over.

The cat stared at him, before he stood and arched up into a stretch. Then he sat down and wrapped his tail tidily around his paws. *The cat's paws are warm again and he's hungry.*

"Great and too bad."

Stormy stared at Roy, who stared back. After a moment, the cat stood, then rubbed his cheek against Roy's leg. "I know," Roy said. "You're not to blame, Cat. You're stalling, Frank."

Stormy rubbed his whole body against Roy, who reached down to stroke his back. "Well, what's the answer, Frank?"

I'm thinking!

"Think faster."

The cat jumped down off the chair and trotted across the living room.

Roy followed. "I'm serious, Frank. I want an answer."

Stormy hopped down the stairs but paused at the bottom and looked up. Roy thought he could see an apology in the green eyes but told himself he was reading too much into the glance. He doubted Frank was apologizing and the cat... well, the cat was a cat, after all.

All right, all right! She had a degree in computer science, but the only jobs she could get were clerical ones that had something to do with a summer job she once had.

Outraged, Roy watched the cat slip through the partially open door. He ran down the stairs and shouted, "That's it? You can't do any better than that?"

There was no answer. Frank was silent and the cat was gone.

CHAPTER 11

Christy sat on the stairs leading down to the big, open playroom on the bottom floor of her townhouse. In the middle of the spacious area, Noelle and Mary Petrofsky were setting up a tent.

The instruction booklet was on the floor beside them and every item on the list was read and discussed before they attempted to implement it. That made their process slow and lengthy, but it was also remarkably harmonious.

It would have been easier—and far faster—if she'd controlled the instruction booklet and gave each of the girls tasks to do. She put her elbows on her knees and set her chin in her hands. She was sitting here on the stairs because she had expected that letting the girls run the whole process themselves—the hard way—would end up with squabbles of frustration, but really, she wasn't needed.

Stormy's input was also adding to the ponderous pace as he pounced on the booklet and chased the poles around as the girls fitted the pieces together. That resulted in gales of laughter from both children and more time spent on entertaining the cat. Frank encouraged this, of course, making the whole activity a game. Christy had a sense he was enjoying himself as much as the kids were.

As much as she was, Christy admitted to herself. She wasn't surprised Noelle and Mary were working easily together. Not only were they avowed best, best friends ever, but, for the most part, Noelle was an even-tempered kid and Mary had one of the sunniest personalities of anyone Christy had ever met.

Finally, the tent was erected, and it was time to blow up the air mattresses. Noelle plugged in the air pump and said, "Stormy, you should go upstairs." She waggled the air pump in the air. "This makes a lot of noise you don't like."

Stormy, who was sitting on the instruction booklet, attacked the cord before he rubbed against Noelle in an affectionate departure. Then he sauntered across the room, tail high. *We'll be back when you're done.* He rubbed against Christy as he passed, then trotted regally up the stairs.

Noelle started the air pump while Mary held the mattress. No one talked. It took the girls a couple of tries to successfully insert the stopper before too much air escaped, but eventually they did. Lugging the mattresses into the tent and laying out their sleeping bags was a snap after the rest of the tasks.

"We did it, Mom. We did it! All by ourselves," Noelle said as she emerged from the tent. Mary followed. There was a big grin on her face.

"Well done, ladies. Give me a high-five," Christy said. Both girls bounced over, pleased with themselves, and they all high-fived. "Okay," Christy said, glancing at her watch. "It's eight o'clock. I want you to get ready for bed now. You can stay up for an hour and read, or talk, or play with your dolls, but it's lights out at nine. Understood?"

They both nodded.

Christy stood. "I'll be back down at nine to say goodnight."

Upstairs, she settled down with a book while she waited for the house to quiet. Stormy went downstairs now that the evil air pump had been put away. It wasn't long before the sounds from below quieted to the odd giggle and by nine, when she went down to say goodnight, both girls were tucked up in their sleeping bags with the lights out and nothing more than a flashlight on. Stormy was curled between them and already asleep. Christy was pretty sure the girls wouldn't be far behind.

She returned to the kitchen where she poured a glass of wine. She smiled faintly to herself as she lifted the glass. Mary had come at midday and the two girls had played happily together all afternoon. From time to time, they drew Christy into their activities, but for the most part she'd just been aware of a low buzz of cheerful noise from the two of them. They'd helped her make spaghetti and meat sauce for dinner and had filled the dishwasher afterward. All together, it had been a good day and heaven knew, after the week she'd had, she appreciated the mellow goodwill.

The day was about to get better, too, even though it was almost over, because she would soon be talking to Quinn in Toronto. She was looking forward to it.

She stretched out on the couch, her iPad on her lap to make the call.

Quinn responded immediately. "Hi beautiful," he said when he came online.

"Hi yourself," she said. She couldn't help smiling. His dark hair fell over his forehead in a way that said he'd been running his fingers through it. He looked tired, not surprising since it was after midnight in Toronto, but his gaze was steady. She missed him more than she'd expected and, while video calls like this helped, she'd rather have him home in Vancouver. "How's it going?"

His mouth tipped up into a rueful smile and she could see relief in his eyes. "I think we have an agreement. I had dinner with my agent tonight and she told me there were a couple of minor clauses she wanted changed, but she didn't think they'd be an issue. The revised contract might be signed as soon as tomorrow."

"On a Sunday?"

"If business needs to be done, the film industry never sleeps." He shook his head. "Once the contract is signed, we can start work on the treatment. I'm hoping it won't be too much longer before I'm on a plane for Vancouver."

"I'll pick you up at the airport," she said.

He laughed. "I'm looking forward to it already."

Christy laughed too. She told him about Noelle and Mary's tent-building project. He let her describe the story her way, smiling and nodding as he listened without interruption. His interest warmed Christy, because Noelle was the center of her life and knowing Quinn cared about her too made him all the more special to her.

She ended by saying, "I went downstairs and peeked into the tent before I called you. They're both sound asleep. I expected them to be whispering secrets for a while longer, but I think they were tuckered out."

"How about you?" Quinn asked. "You've had a long week."

"I was tired but talking to you chases it all away." She enjoyed his quick smile in response then said, "I found out a bit more about Pam Muir from Mallory Tait."

"They were friends at one point, right?"

Christy shifted. "That's what Mallory said at first, but when I talked to her yesterday, she claimed Pam was little more than the name of someone she knew about. An acquaintance, I suppose." She hesitated, then said, "Quinn, I have this feeling there's more between Mallory and Pam. That Mallory is hiding something."

"Like what?"

She shrugged. "That's just it. I don't know. Before Pam died, Mallory was all over proving Pam was never married to Frank and finding out who the father was. Now that the cops are involved, she doesn't want to bother. And she claimed she and Pam were friends, then suddenly they aren't. It doesn't ring true."

Quinn was quiet for a moment, then he said, "What if there was bad blood between them and now that Pam is dead Mallory is worried the police will discover it and make her a suspect?"

Christy blew out a gusty sigh. "Wouldn't that be just perfect? The Trust's lawyer becomes a suspect in a murder that already involves the Trust?" She rubbed her forehead. "It would almost incline me to investigate Pam's murder on my own." She drew a deep breath. "But I'm not going to do that. I'm going to discover who the real father is, but that's it."

Quinn laughed. "And I'll do what I can to help. What have you got to start with?"

"Mallory did give me a small tidbit. I think she figured I wouldn't leave her alone until she produced something. Anyway, according to Mallory, Pam worked on the production side of a cable show called *Blood Wars*."

"*Blood Wars*? That was a series made in Vancouver, wasn't it?"

"That's the one," Christy said. "I did some basic research on it this afternoon. It ran for five years before it was cancelled. The first couple of years it was pretty successful because it was new and fresh, then other shows moved into its genre and the plot lines became more and more ridiculous and it lost audience."

"Hence the cancellation," Quinn said. He looked thoughtful. "The people involved with a successful show probably had no problem landing positions on to other productions."

Christy nodded. "That's what I thought, too, except I don't know how to find out the names of the people she worked with, or even what shows she herself was associated with after *Blood Wars* closed down."

Quinn grinned. "Leave that with me. I'll see what I can dig up. Toronto and Vancouver are the big production centers in Canada, and people tend to move around. I may be able to find someone here who worked on *Blood Wars*, or who knows someone who did."

"Awesome," Christy said. She smiled and added, "I have to admit I was hoping you'd offer to do something like this."

He laughed. "Helping you out will be more fun than trying to make my documentary run smoothly. Give me a couple of days and I'll see what I can come up with."

A rush of emotion washed over Christy. "Thank you so much."

"I wish I was there," he said quietly. "This being three thousand kilometers away grates on me."

"I miss you," she whispered.

"Me too." He hesitated, then said, "Talk soon?"

"Soon," she agreed, and then he was gone. She sighed and put down the tablet. Toronto was a long way away.

CHAPTER 12

After his frustrating Friday afternoon, Roy took a break. He fully intended to get back to his research on Saturday, but inspiration grabbed him in the middle of breakfast as he was crunching his way through a bowl of cereal.

While his mind played with the idea, his spoon hovered over the bowl, slowly dripping milk until all that was left was soggy puffed rice. He put the spoon in his mouth and chewed, didn't notice the taste or that he'd finished chewing and had swallowed. He dropped the spoon into the bowl, which he pushed aside so he could replace it with his laptop. Hours later, he surfaced for a bathroom break and a cup of coffee. Then he was back at it, typing furiously, deep into the lives of the characters in his current work in progress.

The night was upon him when he finally sat back and stretched. He realized his shoulders were stiff and his back ached. That usually happened when he'd been writing for a long time, sitting in one place, and not moving around. Yawning, he closed the laptop and stood. He'd have dinner, then get back to the research he'd put off earlier in the day.

He poked around in the fridge. Finding some leftover stew he'd made a few days before, he slopped it onto a plate. As he pulled open the door to the microwave, the illuminated clock caught his eye. Three forty-five. Odd, the clock said it was the middle of the afternoon, but it was full dark...

With sudden clarity, he realized it was almost four in the morning, not the afternoon. He'd worked through the day. His gaze sharpened and he noticed the bowl sitting on the table beside his laptop. He'd forgotten to eat his breakfast, to have lunch, to make himself dinner at a normal hour. He shrugged. No matter. He'd eat now, but maybe he'd put off doing that research until tomorrow.

When he finally sat down to see what else he could find on Pam Muir, it was late Sunday afternoon. If Frank remembered correctly, she graduated with a degree in computer science. That meant the dean who had interfered with her attempts to enroll in graduate school would have been the Dean of Science at EBU. He'd start there.

The website was no easier to navigate on Sunday than it had been on Friday, but Roy knew where to look now, so it didn't take him long to find a link to the office of the Dean of Science. He clicked and a suite of pages organized much like the president's popped up. To his great disappointment, the bio of the current incumbent stated that he had been appointed three years before, long after Pam Muir had graduated and moved on. Though Roy clicked through all the pages, he couldn't find one that listed past deans.

He propped his elbow on the table and put his chin on his hand as he considered his next move. What did deans do when they left office? Retire? Move on to a higher position? Return to faculty? None of the above? All the above?

If the individual who'd messed with Pam Muir had retired or left academic life, Roy was out of luck because he had no idea of the man's name. Of course, he could call the dean of science's office on Monday and ask—provided he could get hold of a person, and that person had been around long enough to know who held the office twelve or thirteen years ago.

Another of the options—a return to faculty—was more promising. It would be frustrating, slow work, but he could go through all the bios of the professors teaching in the science department. Surely, if an individual had once been the dean of the faculty, he or she would note that in their curriculum vitae.

Then there was the promotion option. He'd have to follow the same process as for a return to faculty, but there were fewer vice presidents than there were professors. Of course, the dean might have moved to another university, which would mean his search of EBU's website would be fruitless. Still, why not try?

So he did ... and hit the jackpot on his first attempt.

The page for the office of the vice president academic, whose official title was the provost, indicated the current incumbent was one Ronald Gallagher. He clicked on the man's bio and discovered that Gallagher had become Provost four years before, leaving his position as Dean of Science at EBU, which he'd held for two five-year terms.

Bingo! This, then, must be the guy Pam Muir had complained about. Roy studied the bio, looking for more dates and details. Gallagher had been new to the job of Dean of Science when Pam Muir was studying in one of his programs. He'd been young too. Roy estimated he must have been in his late thirties at the time. So he was something of a high flier.

He contemplated Gallagher's photograph. The man was standing, leaning against his desk, looking relaxed and happy. He was smiling, of course. Photographers and directors of communications always had you smile when they took an official portrait. It made you look more approachable, showed you were a fun guy. He couldn't tell if Ronald Gallagher was approachable or not, but he was certainly a good-looking fellow. His dark hair was thick, his face unlined, his features chiseled, his body trim.

As he stared at the picture, ideas began to leap around in Roy's head. Ideas he had to tamp down, at least until he'd talked to the man.

He found the contact information page and blinked. Gallagher had half a dozen vice provosts to help him manage his empire and they in turn had directors who reported to them. Fortunately, Gallagher's name was at the top of the list and along with it both a telephone number and an email address.

Roy thought about his options. He could wait until tomorrow, then phone and probably talk to an assistant provost—or an assistant to an assistant—and be asked his business, then be transferred to someone who would stonewall him.

Or he could write an email to Gallagher now and see if he got an answer. The email option appealed to him more than another fight with the telephone system, so he wrote a message that had sufficient information to let the man know what he wanted. The result was cryptic enough not to give too much away, in case one of the assistants opened it before Gallagher got to it. Then he pressed send and went off to make dinner.

A reply came in at eight o'clock that evening. It was even briefer than Roy's had been. It read: Six-thirty AM Monday. My office.

Roy stared at the screen. The word *clandestine* leapt into his mind and had those earlier ideas bouncing around his brain and getting bigger by the moment. What was going on here?

On Monday morning, still grumpy from rising unreasonably early, he decided that a six-thirty meeting did have its benefits. The drive from Burnaby to EBU took half the usual time, because there was hardly any traffic, then finding a parking spot at a university that limited its parking area to discourage cars on campus was a breeze.

As Roy exited the car rain poured down, making the pre-dawn darkness thicker and somehow blacker. He hunched his shoulders against the icy sleet and hurried to the gray stone Gothic Revival building that housed the offices of the senior executives who ran EBU. The heavy wooden door that guarded the entrance was unlocked. He pulled it open and hustled inside. After brushing the moisture from his jacket, he discovered the old building, stately and magisterial on the outside, was a maze of small offices packed together along intersecting hallways with minimal signage. He figured he'd get lost for sure, and probably be late for the meeting, but by some fluke he managed to arrive at the provost's suite three minutes before the designated time. He went inside.

Gallagher's personal office was located down a hallway and around a corner. Roy was detecting a pattern here. Whoever had laid out this space was probably working with the same mindset as the one who had designed the telephone system.

The door to the inner sanctum was closed. He stared at it. Was Gallagher expecting him to knock, like some disobedient student or underperforming academic called on the carpet? If he was, too bad.

Roy pushed the door open and marched inside. Ronald Gallagher was sitting at his desk, the same heavy Victorian antique he was leaning against in his promo photo. Unlike the photo, where the desk was clear, now it was littered with paper, and despite the early hour, it was evident Gallagher was hard at work. Roy studied him for a moment. The photograph on the website didn't do the man justice. He brimmed with vitality and as he looked up, Roy saw a quick intelligence in his eyes that was appealing. It was allied with an intensity that sucked you in.

Pam Muir must have been mesmerized.

Surprise flickered in Gallagher's eyes. "You're Roy Armstrong, the writer!"

Roy nodded. His mind was still reeling with the direction his impressions were taking him, so he didn't bother asking whom exactly Gallagher thought he was when he agreed to this meeting.

Gallagher narrowed his eyes. "What's your relationship to Pam Muir?"

"What's yours?" Roy retorted.

Gallagher's lips firmed and he thrust out his chin. His eyes narrowed. "I never had a relationship with her."

Roy wondered if that was true or a self-serving denial. He shoved his hands into the pockets of his jeans and tilted his head to one side. "That's not what she says."

Gallagher sucked in his breath. "You're a novelist, Armstrong. I've read your books. What does Pam Muir have to do with you?"

Roy wasn't about to explain. Instead, he said, "Twelve years ago, Pam Muir graduated from the department of computer science at this university. She tried to get into grad school, but her applications were denied because the then Dean of Science—you—made sure she didn't receive any references."

"Pam's been talking to you, hasn't she? Stringing you along with fine stories about how she was harassed?" Gallagher's expression relaxed a little. "She has no proof of that. *You* have no proof of that."

Roy took note of the man's relief and nodded. "You covered your tracks, I expect. No matter. That you're not denying the accusation tells me it's true."

Expression hardening again, Gallagher said, "What do you want?"

Roy smiled. "I think I know why, but I want to hear it from you."

Expressionless, Gallagher studied him, then his features lit and his eyes widened. He pointed an accusing forefinger at Roy. "You're writing mysteries now. You've heard Pam's lies. I bet you think they'd make a great story, and you plan to use them in one of your novels where real proof doesn't matter. She fed them to you to humiliate me, didn't she?"

Roy blinked. Gallagher was jumping to a lot of conclusions, which was interesting, and, in its way, helpful. It implied he had a guilty conscience, which would mean he had something to cover up. Or he might be a smart guy who understood how rumor and innuendo could be as damaging as hard facts.

He was certainly good at twisting the conversation away from the subject. Roy sighed. "I guess we'll have to do this the hard way. How about this? I'll tell you what I think. You shake your head once for yes, twice for no."

That had Gallagher's eyes blazing with temper. "Idiot."

"Maybe, but I think I'm looking at a man who was a year or so into a big job with lots of new responsibilities when a pretty, somewhat predatory, young co-ed sashays into his life and turns it upside down. Having an affair with a student is never a good idea, but for a dean it's even worse. Not to mention what it can do to a marriage. And you were married at the time, weren't you?"

"I didn't have an affair with Pamela Muir," Gallagher ground out. "She was a promising student and I mentored her. As was my policy through my tenure as dean of science, I had a female member of her faculty included in all our meetings."

Roy raised his brows and fixed a skeptical expression on his face. "Really? Every meeting? Or just those that occurred after she turned you down?"

"She didn't turn me down! It was the other—" He broke off abruptly, but not before Roy caught his meaning. Taking a deep breath he said, "As it happened, she was a good student and studied hard, but she had an average mind, not an innovative one. She wasn't the caliber of student I could comfortably recommend to any postgraduate program. Now, you have your answer. Get out."

Roy stood his ground. "Pam Muir graduated twelve years ago, yet you were quick to grant me an interview. I think you've seen her much more recently than that."

Gallagher's eyes burned. "I've told you all I'm going to tell you. Now, are you going to leave, or do I have to call security?"

Roy threw up his hands. "I'm leaving." He smiled at the provost.

"But think about this, Gallagher. You arranged to meet me when no one else was around. That's as eloquent as a long dissertation. I know what you're hiding. If you want to come clean with the details, you have my email." He turned for the door.

"Fat chance of that," Gallagher said to his back.

Roy laughed.

CHAPTER 13

The situation in Vancouver bothered Quinn. He didn't like being in Toronto when Christy was involved in a murder, even peripherally. He also worried about the threat Pam Muir had made against the Jamieson Trust. It was his rather grim assessment that the danger wasn't over just because she was dead. He agreed with Christy—unless the real father was discovered, the possibility that Pam Muir's son was also Frank Jamieson's would hang over the Trust forever. So, he got to work researching crew and cast of *Blood Wars*, and by Monday he knew that Pamela Muir had worked on the show from its inception. She'd begun as a production assistant, then moved up to become a line producer during the show's second season.

The number of people who worked on a television production over a five-year period was daunting, so he focused on those people who, like Pam, had been with the show for its whole run, or who worked in the same department she did. His goal was to find people who knew her reasonably well who could encapsulate what kind of woman she was. Perhaps, if he was lucky, he might also track down someone who knew who the father of her son was.

He found two individuals now living in Toronto who had worked on the show. One was an actor whose character on *Blood Wars* had grown from a guest role to a series regular who was now the lead in a romantic drama filmed in Toronto. The other was a production manager who'd become the executive producer on another show being made in Toronto. Quinn took note of the names of the two series and prepared to use his journalistic credentials to get into see both men.

He started with the producer. His name was Isaac Holley and he'd left *Blood Wars* midway through the second season. Quinn thought the timing was interesting—Pam Muir had moved up to line producer about the time Holley had left. He arranged to meet with the man on Monday afternoon at, of all places, Toronto's Union Station.

Quinn arrived early for the meeting. He didn't know the building and he wanted to be sure he found the spot Holley suggested. Union Station had been built in the nineteen twenties, when train travel in Canada was a popular means of transportation. To Quinn, the station's imposing design owed more to an architect's image of a Roman bath or basilica than it did to modern architecture. The great hall that opened from the main doors soared to an impressive height and was built of warm golden stone. At one end, a huge, rounded window rose several stories to the high, barrel ceiling, allowing natural light to flood the concourse. Additional light was provided by clerestory windows that pierced the long walls.

He paused for a moment, getting his bearings. Holley had reacted positively when Quinn called and introduced himself. He suggested Quinn come to his office that afternoon. Then he discovered Pam Muir was the reason for the interview. His initial warmth was replaced by arctic cool and for a time Quinn wondered if Holley would refuse to talk to him. It had taken all of Quinn's skill to persuade him to meet. When he finally agreed, his office was out and a bench in the center of this enormous, impersonal space replaced it.

The man had something to hide. Quinn planned to discover what it was.

He noticed a staircase going down to the train platform on the level below and saw an empty bench beside it. As he strode toward it, the heels of his boots clicked on the marble floor, the sound echoing through the massive structure.

Great. He'd planned to tape the interview, but the acoustics would be terrible. He'd have to go the old-fashioned route and use paper and pen.

He parked himself on the bench and watched the people streaming through the giant concourse. Most were clearly office drones, men in suits and overcoats, women in heeled boots and fashionable coats to their knees. Few people wore hats, despite the damp cold, but everybody had gloves. Everybody rushed too, as if getting to their commuter train on time was the most important task in their day.

Idly, he wondered which of the men in overcoats might be Isaac Holley. He ignored the ones with suitcases, who were probably travelling somewhere, rather than simply commuting, but didn't discount those carrying briefcases. He also didn't think the man would be wearing a down jacket as Quinn himself was, but you never knew. It was damn cold in Toronto in the middle of January.

As it turned out, he was right to look for a topcoat over a business suit. The one that headed his way was a serviceable dark blue wool with large buttons down the front. The coat belonged to a still trim middle-aged man with dark blond hair receding at the temples and glasses with heavy black frames. Quinn stood as the man neared.

"Quinn Armstrong?" he asked. His voice was deeper than it had sounded on the phone, but Quinn still recognized it.

He nodded.

The man stripped off a black leather glove, then thrust out his hand. "Isaac Holley. I have exactly ten minutes before I catch my train. You wanted to know about Pam Muir."

Quinn nodded again.

"She was a nasty homewrecker who thought I could provide her with a meal ticket." He glanced at his watch. "Now, is there anything else?"

Quinn resisted the urge to laugh. With an opening like that, of course he wanted more. "But you didn't provide the meal ticket."

"No." Holley studied him for a moment. "Look, what do you want to know about Pam? She's not one of my favorite people."

"I guessed." Quinn had a sense that if he was careful, he might get a whole lot more out of Isaac Holley than the man had originally planned to divulge. "Pamela Muir had a son—"

Holley held up his hand. "I'm not the father."

Quinn raised his brows. "I didn't think you were. However, she's dead and the police have labeled her death as suspicious. I want to know her background, who she was, why someone would kill her."

Enlightenment dawned on Holley's face and with it, relief. He nodded. "You're doing a story on the murder."

Quinn didn't agree or disagree. He waited silently as Holley rattled on, his voice becoming more excited as he created what he thought was the rational behind Quinn's desire for information on Pam Muir.

"The police aren't giving you much, are they?" He shook his head. "They can be mighty closemouthed when they want to be. So, you have to find context to keep the story going until there's a break in the case."

From what Quinn had learned of Isaac Holley before he came to this meeting, the man had a head for numbers and an orderly disposition, making him very good at keeping a film production running on, or under, budget. Years of working with creative types must have rubbed off on him, though, because right now he was attributing motives to Quinn that had more to do with series TV than real life.

Quinn let him run on. Whatever Holley wanted to believe was fine with him.

"Well, you're on the right track. There's plenty of scandal in Pam Muir's life," Holley said, rather gleefully. "Enough to keep your readers entertained for days."

Quinn allowed himself to smile in a predatory way. Let Holley think he had him hooked. "Tell me more."

Holley glanced at his watch again, then said in a rush, "That kid of hers. No father in the picture, at least not when I worked with her on *Blood Wars*. She liked to hint that the dad was some big shot, but she never said who."

Great. Not exactly what Christy would want to hear. "No clues? Were the hints broad enough to give you an idea who it might be?"

Holley shook his head. "I don't think it was someone in the business. Though I'm not entirely sure about that. Pam was beautiful, and hot, and she liked to flaunt herself. There are plenty of men high up in the chain who are willing to take advantage of what's offered. But..." Holley shook his head again. "Pam worked on an internet series with Marenda Riddle before Marenda came over to *Blood Wars*. She brought Pam with her. The series was Pam's first job in the business and from the age of her kid, I think he must've been born before she started there."

Quinn made a note of the woman Holley had mentioned, then said, "So Pam worked for this Marenda Riddle until she because a line producer herself?"

"Pam was my assistant," Holley said. His jaw hardened. He looked at his watch again, this time, Quinn thought, to use the time as his excuse to leave.

Quinn's reporter's sixth sense told him he was close to getting the information he needed. All he had to do was word his question the right way and Holley would spill. He studied the man's face. "When did she come on to you?"

Shock widened Holley's eyes. It was followed by horrified dismay, then something like relief as he wrestled with himself, clearly wanting to tell all, but afraid of the repercussions. Finally, he said, "From the beginning. At first, it was flirtatious looks, then suggestive moves, touching, comments I couldn't misunderstand." He shrugged. "It escalated from there."

"How long did the affair last?"

After another glance at his watch, Holley said with obvious derision, "Long enough for her to start fantasizing that I'd divorce my wife and marry her. She had impressive plans, Pam did. Along with divorce, she wanted me to head to Hollywood and the big time. When she started talking about my getting to know her kid so I could become his daddy, I broke it off." He shook his head. "I had two teenagers who were almost out of the house, what did I want with a kid in grade school?"

Quinn didn't comment, but sympathy for Pamela Muir began to sneak up on him. "What happened after you ended it?"

"She went to my wife and almost ruined my marriage, then she got me fired." Bitterness resonated through his voice.

The sneaking sympathy evaporated. Pam Muir had been quite capable of taking care of herself. "How did she get you fired?"

"She undermined everything I did. She had a great way with numbers—she claimed it was because she worked for a bank during the summer while she was in university. I think there was more to it than that. Some people just understand numbers and accounting systems and how to manipulate data. She was one of them. She realized she could make little changes that would cascade into big problems. Before I knew it, I was out, and she had my job."

"Is that why you ended up here in Toronto? You couldn't find another position in Vancouver?"

"She made sure everyone knew I'd been sleeping with her. When I broke it off, she cried big, salty tears and claimed I'd been using her.

That I threatened her and made her fear for her job—which, she said, she needed to support herself and her kid." He consulted his watch again and said, "Look, I've got to go, and I've said enough anyway. Good luck with your research."

"Thanks for talking to me," Quinn said, meaning it.

Holley nodded and turned away. Before he left, he looked over his shoulder and said, "One more thing. If you learn anything positive about Pam Muir, consider it carefully. Odds are the person didn't know her very well or she had something on them." He hurried away, dodging through the crowd as he headed for the train he didn't want to miss.

Quinn watched him go. Isaac Holley had given him some clues to work with and a great deal to think about.

CHAPTER 14

Quinn's second contact was Jeremiah Brownrigg, an actor whose star was on the rise. Photographs showed a handsome man in his late twenties, with thick hair—blond when he worked on *Blood Wars*, but now dark brown. His eyes were a warm brown with thick, dark, lashes. His nose was chiseled, his square jaw jutted just enough to give him an excellent profile, and his mouth was perpetually set in a sensual pout.

As Quinn's purpose had nothing to do with building Brownrigg's career or promoting the show he was now lead actor on, he didn't want to go through the man's agent or the show's producers to book an interview. Instead, he contacted Brownrigg directly. The actor immediately agreed to speak to him, either because he liked to operate on his own, or because he assumed any press would be good press.

That was why Quinn was sitting in an upscale bar at the most secluded table available, watching Jeremiah Brownrigg make an entrance, swaggering through the doorway as if he expected all eyes to be on him. Quinn had found references describing the actor as a heartthrob and if all that counted were facial features, Quinn figured the description fit. Body wise, however, he reserved judgment. The man barely topped five eight and at best his physique could be called wiry.

Brownrigg paused to survey the assembled company, and probably to figure out where Quinn was sitting. His head was tilted to show off his excellent profile, and his lustrous dark hair fell over his forehead, tousled just enough to indicate this wasn't a formal meeting. He was off duty, here in a private capacity. His clothes confirmed the image—designer jeans, snug and slung low over slim hips, a fashionable jacket of first quality leather, a silk and wool black sweater beneath. Outside, it had started to snow. Although the bar didn't extend to windows, Quinn knew, because Brownrigg casually brushed flakes from the arm of his leather jacket, using the moment to extend his time in the spotlight. With some amusement, Quinn noticed the actor's boots were regular soled black leather. Evidently, clunky snow boots weren't his style.

Quinn stood as the man strutted through the restaurant toward him. He held out his hand. "Quinn Armstrong. Thank you for agreeing to see me, Mr. Brownrigg."

The actor shook his hand. "My pleasure, Quinn. Call me Jeremiah."

Quinn nodded, indicated a chair, and they both sat. He pulled out his phone. "Do you mind if I record our conversation?"

Brownrigg eyed the phone, his expression disclosing nothing. He nodded agreement. "Tell me, what publication are you writing for?"

"I haven't placed the article yet. I'm researching the people who worked on *Blood Wars*."

"*Blood Wars*? But that show wrapped a couple of years ago." Brownrigg's tone said, 'who cares about *Blood Wars* now? It's over, done!'

Quinn knew he'd lose the actor if he wasn't careful. Time to stroke the man's ego. "*Blood Wars* is a Canadian success story. Not only was it a hit in Canada, it was sold into the US market and has had incredible reach worldwide."

Brownrigg brightened. The show's success emphasized his success. He looked interested now. Quinn pressed on. "Members of its cast and crew have seen their careers rise because of the popularity of the show."

By the time he finished speaking, Brownrigg was nodding. "Like myself, you mean."

"Exactly."

Smiling, Brownrigg said, "Though I only had a minor part in season one, the producers thought my work was exemplary. They enlarged the role in season two and gave the character more scope to showcase my talents."

He nodded as if to confirm this statement to be the truth. And maybe it was.

"I went from *Blood Wars* to my current show, *State Secrets*, without a hiatus. The producers were so anxious to have me as their lead character, my agent was able to write my own ticket."

The man's self confidence edged into arrogance. Quinn wondered if beneath that smug self-assurance there was even the hint of self-doubt. "Impressive. My research tells me *State Secrets* has excellent ratings." In the Canadian market, that was true. It sold internationally as well, but it had never been picked up in the US, so it wasn't quite as big a hit as *Blood Wars*.

Brownrigg smiled. "We have a very loyal audience. We've won several awards as well."

But none for acting. Quinn smiled. "Other people associated with *Blood Wars* have moved on to new productions as well." He named several people including Isaac Holley, then he said, "Pam Muir, who was on the production side, also did well."

"Pam," Brownrigg said with a sigh. His gaze grew misty. "She could have had more."

Quinn raised his brows and smiled faintly, encouraging confidences. "I don't quite understand what you mean."

Brownrigg leaned forward. "We met on the set of *Blood Wars* and had a relationship during the last couple of years of production. She was gorgeous and soooo sexy, even though she had a little kid, you know?" He paused and shook his head. "She must have been in high school when she had him." Then he shrugged and grinned. "The kid didn't stop her from being a great partier. We had some good times."

Raising his brows and fixing an expression of interest on his face, Quinn encouraged him to continue.

Brownrigg rattled on. "She knew how to make herself look good, you know? When I went to award shows, she was always my date, because, well, all the other guys were envious of me. She was smart, too. Knew what to say to people and when to shut up."

"Arm candy," Quinn said, prodding lightly.

Brownrigg took the bait. He shook his head emphatically. "No, she was more than that. We cared for each other." He paused, hesitated, drummed his fingers on the table, and watched the movement as he made it. When he looked up, the expression in those warm, brown eyes seemed sincere. "I may have started dating her because she looked good and was great in bed, but we were together for two years and, well, I fell for her."

Quinn wasn't sure whether Brownrigg was acting or expressing real emotion. He decided that if it was acting, the man was better at his craft than Quinn thought. "You were in love with her?"

Sadness crept into Brownrigg's eyes as he nodded. "When we were told *Blood Wars* was wrapping, I knew the cast and crew would go their separate ways. I asked Pam to marry me."

"But she didn't."

"No." He sighed. "I got the offer for *State Secrets* and found out it was to be shot here in Toronto. Pam would have to relocate if we married, and she didn't want to uproot her kid." He shrugged. "So we split." Gloom settled over his features. "I wanted to stay in touch, but she said it was too painful. Talking to me, being so far apart, reminded her of everything she'd given up, lost because she always put her boy first."

This sounded farfetched to Quinn. If Pam had cared about Brownrigg, she could easily have relocated to Toronto with him. A year or two earlier, she'd been willing to move to Hollywood with Isaac Holley. In fact, she'd been the one pressing for the transfer and she hadn't been worried about her son then.

Looking past Quinn's shoulder at nothing in particular, but giving Quinn the benefit of his excellent profile, Brownrigg said in a meditative way, "Pam and I made a good team, but our careers were both on the way up. I believe her career was even more important to her than her precious son." He shrugged and his mouth twisted. "Too bad, the way it turned out."

Surprised, Quinn studied him. Had Brownrigg heard Pam had been murdered? Weren't the police keeping it quiet? Or had there been an announcement Quinn had missed? "The way what turned out?"

"The job she got after *Blood Wars* didn't last. She was a full producer, and she was sure the show would be a big success. I could have told her it wouldn't work out. In fact, I did tell her, but she was certain she'd be an executive producer in no time. Instead," and there was bitterness in his voice now, "there were rumors of sexual misbehavior and suddenly she was fired. If she'd stayed with me, we'd be married now, her kid would have a father, and we'd be happy."

The last was said defiantly, as if Brownrigg was trying to convince himself that the life he'd envisioned with Pamela Muir would have been perfection itself.

"Have you heard from her recently?" Quinn asked gently.

Brownrigg shook his head. "Not for over a year. I only know about the scandal because, well, you know, it's a small industry and people talk. I don't have a grudge against her or anything. She made a mistake, but she did what she thought was right. I missed her. I wished it could've been different, but we parted as friends."

"Sad story," Quinn said.

Brownrigg nodded. "Yeah." Then he lifted his shoulders in a what-can-you-do movement.

"Do you get back to Vancouver at all?" Quinn asked in a casual way.

"Sometimes, when we go on hiatus after the season wraps, but not for short visits. We're on a tight schedule and the hours are brutal. I'm in eighty percent of the scenes, so I'm on the set every day. If we aren't shooting, I'm at home vegging, or out promoting the show."

There wasn't much more that Brownrigg could tell him, so Quinn wrapped up the interview soon after. He came away with several impressions. Brownrigg wasn't the father of Pam's child, he truly loved her, and their split had left a residue of unhappiness he still hadn't lost. Quinn also thought Brownrigg had been far more involved with Pam than she had been with him. Then there was the scandal that ended her career in the entertainment industry. That might provide him with more insight as well.

Another string to pull. He had a lot to tell Christy when next they spoke.

CHAPTER 15

Christy stood at the bottom of the staircase leading to the top floor of the townhouse. It was Tuesday, the last day of January, and over three weeks since Pam Muir had sashayed into her life and turned it upside down. She watched the cat descend slowly, as if he was reluctant to be there. "You're coming to the meeting, then?"

Noelle's asleep. Why not?

So casual, as if none of this mattered, when it did. Christy nodded stiffly. "Good. You knew Pam best. We need your input."

Stormy stopped, two stairs from the bottom. *I didn't know her that well!*

"You knew her better than I did, Frank, and Roy and Quinn never met her." She turned away, headed for the kitchen where she'd set up her laptop, primed for a long-distance video meeting.

The cat followed. *You're mad. Why are you mad?*

That pulled Christy up short. Why was she angry with Frank? She believed him when he said he wasn't the father of Pam's child and whatever relationship he'd had with the woman had been over before he ever asked Christy out on a date.

She sat on one of the kitchen chairs and picked up the cat. Holding him in her lap, she stroked his back from ears to tail. "I'm on edge. Pam's parents called the Trust today to ask for an appointment to meet with me. They didn't say why, which worries me. What if they plan to continue Pam's suit against the Trust? I have no idea how to prove you weren't the child's father. The police have made no progress in finding Pam's murderer and what if Shively hears that Pam Muir is Vancouver's first murder victim of the year? She'll connect it with me somehow and decide I'm a suspect. Then everything I've been doing to get free of the woman will be washed away and Noelle will be in danger again."

Stormy began to purr, a loud rumble that had Christy sighing as some of her tension leaked away.

The doorbell rang.

"That will be Roy," she said, putting Stormy on the floor. "I'll go let him in."

It was indeed Roy, without a coat, despite the temperature, which hovered close to the freezing mark, and the misty rain that added to the feeling of cold. It was a good thing his house was close to hers.

"Come on in." She held the door wide.

"Man, it's cold out there," he said as he bustled inside. "I hate January."

Christy laughed. "I've set up my laptop on the kitchen table so we can all see the screen and Quinn can see us. Well..." She looked up at the top of the short flight of stairs where the cat sat watching. "He can see you and me. I don't think he'll mind if Stormy isn't visible."

Roy chuckled. "Probably not."

They all adjourned to the kitchen. Christy provided herself and Roy with a cup of coffee then they settled at the table and Christy contacted Quinn.

Though it was nine o'clock in Vancouver, it was midnight Quinn's time. Despite the hour, he looked wide awake. Christy figured late nights were part of the Armstrong DNA. The previous evening when they'd connected, it had been even later than tonight. As he'd told her what he'd learned, he'd been full of energy, his expression animated and his eyes bright with the excitement of the chase. Before they disconnected, he'd said he expected to learn more the next day, so they'd decided to set up a meeting that included his father this evening.

He smiled at her and said hi to both her and his father. He ignored the cat.

Christy got the information sharing going. "I'll start because I've learned absolutely nothing of value. Mallory Tait has been avoiding me, so either she doesn't have anything new for me, or she's keeping secrets. I contacted Gibson Jessup at Point Grey College—he's the Chair of Theater Arts there. We met him when Karen Beaumont was killed during the At Risk Students Gala, remember?"

Both men nodded.

Christy glanced from Roy to the screen. "He has links to the local entertainment industry, but he's more involved with the actors than he is with the production side. He thought he'd heard of Pamela Muir, but only in a vague way. He said she might have worked on the *Blood Wars* series."

"Which we already knew," Roy said.

"Yeah." Christy grimaced as she nodded. "So, no help there."

"I followed the *Blood Wars* trail out here and had some luck," Quinn said. He looked pleased with himself.

Christy smiled. "Do tell."

He grinned back. "I found two people—a production manager she worked for during the first year of the series, and one of the actors on the show."

"Both of them are working in Toronto now?" Roy asked.

Quinn nodded. "I don't think either of them could be the father, and I doubt if either of them killed her, but they both gave me insight into her character."

"Okay, shoot," Roy said.

Christy smiled in an encouraging way and nodded agreement.

"I'll start with the production manager. His name is Isaac Holley and he's a middle-aged guy, with a couple of kids who are probably young adults now. They were teenagers when he knew Muir."

Roy frowned. "And that's significant?"

"Oh, yeah. Holley claims he and Muir had an affair while she was working for him."

"Bad form," Roy murmured.

Quinn pursed his lips and nodded. "He also claims she originally came on to him, rather than he to her. I can't prove that one way or another, though. Anyway, for Holley it was simple recreational sex, but he said that after a while, Muir decided they were meant for each other and started talking about him being a father to her son and relocating to Hollywood to move into the big time."

"Sounds intense," Christy said.

Quinn laughed. "Holley thought so too. He panicked. He wasn't interested in a second family with a son who was in elementary school, not when his own kids were about to move out. That's a quote, by the way."

Christy wrinkled her nose. "What a jerk. Poor Pam."

"Not quite. According to Holley, she called his wife and told her about the affair, which almost ruined his marriage, then she got him fired from *Blood Wars* in a way that made him look incompetent. He couldn't find work in Vancouver and had to move to Toronto."

Roy laughed. "The lady was tough."

Quinn nodded. "The situation with the actor, whose name is Jeremiah Brownrigg, by the way—"

"The guy who stars in *State Secrets*?" Christy asked, surprised.

Quinn raised his brows. "You know it?"

She nodded. "I've watched it a few times. Rebecca Petrofsky loves the show and some of the moms talk about Jeremiah Brownrigg while we're waiting to pick up our kids after school." She grinned. "He's considered a hunk. Is it all make-up or is he as good looking as he seems on screen?"

"I'm not the best person to ask," Quinn said, dryly.

She laughed. "Good thing too. So, what did Jeremiah have to say?"

"He was in love with her. They had a relationship for the last couple of seasons of *Blood Wars*."

"Was it behind the scenes like the one she had with Holley?" Roy asked.

Quinn shook his head. "Completely in the open. They went to cast parties together, she was his date at award shows, and that kind of thing. Everyone knew about them. When *Blood Wars* wrapped, Brownrigg was offered the role in *State Secrets* soon after and he grabbed it, even though it meant moving to Toronto. He asked Muir to marry him. She declined."

Christy and Roy looked at each other. The surprised look on Roy's face mirrored her own. "Did she give him a reason?"

"Yup. She didn't want to uproot her son. She found work on a new show quickly, as well. Brownrigg tried to stay in touch—I think he's still half in love with her—but she told him she couldn't do it, as she found their break up and separation too painful."

"That's interesting," Christy said. "When you told us about Isaac Holley, I thought perhaps she was looking for someone to provide a father figure for her son, but it sounds like Jeremiah Brownrigg was prepared to do just that, yet she turned him down."

"I'm not sure how good Brownrigg would have been as a father to a stepson. He seemed more interested in Pam and what a pretty couple they made than in making a family. Maybe that's why she refused to marry him."

"Maybe," Christy said. "But neither of these two men sound like they were great father material. What they had in common was success."

Success? The word sounded like a snort of derision. *What's so successful about a second-rate actor and a middle-aged man in a middle level job?*

Christy glared at the cat. "Yes, Frank, success. Or at least the potential to be successful. From the sounds of it, Isaac Holley was well respected on the *Blood Wars* production until Pam decided to ruin him. She believed he had the potential to go further up the ladder if they moved to Hollywood together. Jeremiah Brownrigg's career was on the way up too. His part in *Blood Wars* started small but grew over the run of the series. Pam had every reason to believe he would become a big star. Maybe she figured they'd move to Hollywood too."

She noticed Roy watching her with some amusement and the spurt of temper Frank's jibe had roused evaporated as quickly as it had come. Sheepishly, she ended by saying, "I don't know what Isaac Holley looked like, but when Jeremiah Brownrigg worked on *Blood Wars* he was a gorgeous blond—"

What do his looks have to do with it?

She glared at the cat as her temper rose again. "You knew Pam, Frank. She liked good-looking men."

"Brownrigg is dark haired now. I think he dyed his hair for the *Blood Wars* role," Quinn said, wresting the conversation away from the cat and recapturing Christy's attention. "Holley is a blond as well."

"You think that means something?" Roy said doubtfully.

On the other side of the continent, Quinn shrugged. "It might. Their hair color and their success, or potential for success, seems to be all the two men had in common."

Roy cleared his throat. "I think success was more important than hair color for her. She seems to have had a penchant for men in a position of power."

Quinn's eyes twinkled. "You've found someone interesting."

Roy nodded. His eyes were lit with enthusiasm and there was an expression of almost malicious amusement on his face. "I did some digging into the years before her son was born."

"What did you learn?" Christy asked, intrigued by Roy's air of excitement.

Roy rubbed his chin. "I began by looking into her university career. She went to English Bay U and graduated with a degree in computer science. I was trying to find out more about her time there when I stumbled onto something interesting."

Christy noticed the cat was staring at Roy in a fixed way, eyes wide, body tense. Frank didn't say anything, but she assumed he felt more connected to the Pam Muir who'd just graduated from university, the time when he knew her, than he did to the woman who worked in the local film industry.

Roy stopped for dramatic emphasis.

Quinn raised his eyebrows and said, "We're listening, Dad. Spill."

"The guy who was the Dean of Science when she graduated is now the provost at EBU. Back when he was still the dean, I think either he made a pass at Muir, or she came on to him."

Christy gasped and Quinn frowned. "What makes you think that? Did he admit to anything?"

Roy shook his head. "No, but his response to my simple request for information was to set up at meeting at six-thirty in the morning, well before any of his staff would be in. He admitted to mentoring her when she was a student but said her claims he had deliberately torpedoed her chances to get into grad school were lies."

"How strange," Christy said. She looked at the cat. "Did she ever say anything about that to you, Frank?"

The cat stood and stretched, lazily, then he butted Roy's arm with his head. *She complained a lot. She talked about going to grad school, but I don't remember if she ever went.*

"So Gallagher—that's the provost's name, Ronald Gallagher—he makes a big deal of telling me Pam Muir had a commonplace mind and that he was really disappointed in her. That, he says, is why he couldn't recommend her to any graduate programs."

"Frank," Christy said.

The cat looked at her.

"Try to remember. Think hard. Did Pam have a job when you knew her? Was she looking for a permanent position?"

Stormy sat down and wrapped his tail around his paws. He stared at Christy. Frank was silent.

"Frank?" she said, her voice sharp.

I don't know! She talked about working at a bank, but I don't think it was permanent and I can't remember if it was during the first summer I knew her, or the second. I wasn't listening. I didn't care.

On the computer screen, Quinn raised his brows in a long-suffering way. Christy shook her head and shrugged as she filled Quinn in.

"So, what have we got?" Quinn asked when she was finished. He lifted his hand so it was visible on the screen and ticked the points off on his fingers as he spoke. "An affair that seems to have been part of a quest to find a father for her son. A love relationship that may have started with the same purpose, but, for whatever reason, didn't cut it. A guy who may or might not be a blond, but who is now in a position of considerable influence, who deliberately ruined her chances to continue in an academic career."

"Gallagher's got dark hair," Roy said. "I don't think he's likely to be the father, though. Whatever went on between them, it was over before she ever met Frank."

"I don't think any of them could be the father," Christy said. "She met Brownrigg and Holley after the boy was born."

"So where does that leave us?" Roy asked.

"Looking for more men," Christy said gloomily.

"Brownrigg mentioned she found a position in another series after

Blood Wars wrapped. He said he'd heard rumors she was involved in a scandal there and the executive producer fired her. Isaac Holley mentioned a woman named Marenda Riddle. They apparently worked together before *Blood Wars*. I'll see what I can find out on both," Quinn said.

Relieved they had some leads to follow, Christy said, "Great."

"I'm going to dig around in her university career some more," Roy said. "Who knows? Maybe I can find out something about other students she was close to. I'll try to find some of her professors too. They might know something."

"Ten years is a long time, Dad."

Christy shook her head. "If Pam Muir, the student, was anything like Pam Muir, the woman who came into my office and claimed my husband was her husband and the father of her child, her teachers would remember her. Especially the men."

She was.

Christy glared at the cat. "I thought you said you couldn't remember much about her."

The cat crouched down on the table and didn't meet her gaze. *I don't.*

Christy looked from the cat to Roy, then Quinn. Her brows were raised and her jaw was set. "Looks like I'll be working with Frank to find out more about this bank she worked at." She leveled a stern gaze on the cat. 'You'll do everything you can to help, won't you, Frank?"

There was no reply.

CHAPTER 16

Standing in the hallway, looking through the doorway to the reception area beyond, Christy paused to gather her defenses. In a moment she would have to confront two grieving parents with the news that their recently deceased daughter—their murdered daughter!—had fabricated a twisted tale of love and abandonment for the simple purpose of relieving a prominent family of some of its wealth.

It wasn't a message the Muirs would enjoy hearing. They might not be willing to listen to it at all, which would make for the kind of conflict Christy hated. It was hard being reasonable when the other side was acting out with emotion and anger.

She studied Pam Muir's parents, hoping she was wrong, and they'd be reasonable people who had suffered a loss, but who weren't here to lay blame or find a scapegoat.

The man had broad shoulders and a wide chest. He was running to fat in his midriff area, which the suit he was wearing didn't quite disguise. His hair was thick, and still dark, with only hints of silver at his temples. His face was wide, with a square jaw and a nose that jutted imperiously. He made her think of a bull, oblivious until he wasn't, and dangerous once roused. A shiver slithered down her spine and she had to take a deep breath.

His wife was built more like their daughter. When she'd been Pam's age, she probably would have had a tight body, with slender hips and long legs. Now she had put on weight and was heavier, but even though she was sitting, Christy could see she had a small waist, which the dress she was wearing made the most of. Like the rest of her body, her face was narrow, with high cheekbones, large brown eyes, and a wide, sensual mouth. Pam had inherited many of her mother's features, but her beak of a nose and determined chin had come from her father.

Christy straightened her shoulders and curved her mouth into a pleasant, but impersonal, smile before she walked into the reception area. "Mrs. Muir, Mr. Muir, I'm Christy Jamieson." She held out her hand as the older couple rose from the sofa.

The man was the first to react. "Lincoln Muir." He had a strong grip, and he shook her hand in an energetic way. "Thank you for seeing us."

"Of course," Christy said as she turned to his wife.

"I'm Dawn," Mrs. Muir said, placing a limp hand in Christy's. She didn't smile and her eyes, so very much like her daughter's, were hard.

With the introduction formalities taken care of, Christy said, "Please accept my condolences, and those of everyone at the Jamieson Trust, on the loss of your daughter."

Lincoln Muir nodded abruptly. Dawn pursed her mouth and raised her eyebrows in a sour expression.

Christy took note and armed herself for trouble. "Bonnie, Isabelle and I will be in the conference room with Mr. and Mrs. Muir. Will you bring us refreshments, please?"

"Of course, Mrs. Jamieson." Bonnie smiled at the Muirs and asked if they preferred tea or coffee. Once they'd responded, Christy led the way to the conference room.

Isabelle was already there, her laptop open for note-taking. Lincoln Muir seemed taken aback by the precaution. Dawn's sour expression deepened.

"Lincoln and Dawn Muir, this is Isabelle Pascoe, the manager of the Jamieson Trust. I've asked her to join us today as she's an expert on the history and workings of the Trust."

Lincoln nodded again, while Dawn said coolly, "Hello."

"How nice to meet you, Mr. and Mrs. Muir," Isabelle said. She smiled in a friendly way, but sobered when she added, "Please accept my condolences on the death of your daughter." Lincoln nodded jerkily. Dawn dabbed at her eyes with the tips of her fingers and sniffed, but she too nodded.

Before the meeting, Isabelle and Christy had discussed how best to handle the Muirs. Christy wanted to extract as much information about their daughter as possible, but she had no idea what kind of people the couple were. Eventually, they decided Isabelle would be welcoming and open, Christy reserved and judicial, at least until they could get a read on the pair.

Taking her place at the head of the table, Christy indicated the Muirs should sit to her right, looking toward the spectacular view of the North Shore mountains. Isabelle was already seated to her left, with the wall of windows behind her. His expression wary, Lincoln made sure his wife was comfortable before he took the chair nearest to Christy. As he sat, his every move was cautious and careful, almost defensive. Beside him, Dawn's posture was defiant, her spine straight, her head tilted in an imperious way. Christy wondered if Dawn was the one who had pushed for this meeting, although it had been Lincoln who made the phone call to set it up.

She smiled at them both, but it was Lincoln she addressed. "When you contacted the Trust, Lincoln, I assumed you wanted to discuss your daughter's assertion that my late husband, Frank Jamieson, was her son's father."

"It's not an assertion," Dawn snapped. "He is the father. Pam said so."

Her husband's mouth flattened into a straight line and he nodded.

Well, that made their position clear. Relieved to have the problem in the open, Christy pressed on. "If your grandson is a Jamieson, we will welcome him into the family. We cannot do it, however, until the Trust is provided with the appropriate documents." She kept her expression impassive, but watched the couple for their reactions, which were quick and unexpected.

"That's a lie. Pam told us you'd find someway to weasel out of supporting Carson." Dawn's voice was strident and her sour expression ratcheted up to outrage. Anger flashed from her eyes. She clenched her hand as if it was the only way she could keep herself from pounding on the table.

Isabelle looked up from her screen, her head angled, her brows furrowed.

"I assure you, it's not," Christy said. She couldn't keep a frosty note from her voice, but she did manage to control her facial expression. "If your grandson is a Jamieson, he'll be a recipient of the Trust. There's no question of that. However, for that to happen, proof is necessary."

"Pam already gave you Carson's birth certificate. The night before she died—" Lincoln's voice wavered, and he had to clear his throat before he continued. "She told us getting the Jamieson Trust to pay up was a long shot, because she'd already given you the document, but you claimed it wasn't valid and refused to accept it. She said you'd use your money and power to silence her."

"Turns out you didn't have to," Dawn said, a vicious sneer turning her attractive features hard and ugly. "Someone did it for you."

Christy sucked in a shocked breath. "Are you accusing the Trust of involvement in your daughter's murder?"

Lincoln Muir put his hand over his wife's and they shared a look. Her face crumpled and she shook her head.

Lincoln said heavily, "We're grieving, Mrs. Jamieson, trying to find reasons for our baby's death."

And lashing out at anyone who was in the way, Christy thought. She didn't like it, but she understood. Pam's death was recent and unresolved. There'd been no time for closure and no one to blame. She had a gnawing suspicion there was nothing she could say that would stop these people from believing their grandson was a Jamieson, but she had to try.

Nodding briskly, accepting Lincoln's explanation, she said, "To my knowledge Pam did not supply a birth certificate, or any other form of documentation proving her son was fathered by my husband." When Lincoln opened his mouth to speak, she put up her hand. "However, it doesn't matter whether she did or didn't, because you can still provide us with the documents. I presume you have access to her papers?"

"We do," Lincoln said. His expression didn't appear reassured by Christy's statement. If anything, it was gloomier than before.

Isabelle smiled at him, and said in an encouraging way, "I suggest you gather up everything you have that provides proof that Carson Muir is Frank Jamieson's son. That includes the birth certificate and but also any documents that link Pam to Frank around the time Carson would have been conceived. Photographs of them together, letters from Frank to Pam, emails. The more documentation you have, the stronger your case." She paused, then said carefully, "You do understand that the Trust's lawyer must review all the data you provide, so the more extensive your proof is, the more likely it is that your claim will be accepted."

"Lawyers," said Dawn. Her expression indicated she didn't have a lot of faith in the legal system.

There was a little silence before Christy said, "Did you ever meet Frank?"

The Muirs glanced at each other, then Lincoln asked, "What do you mean?"

Christy shrugged. "Did Pam ever introduce him to you? Bring him home for dinner? That sort of thing."

Another exchanged glance, followed this time by a shrug. "No," Lincoln said.

Christy tried again. "Where did she meet Frank?" She already knew, because Frank had told her, but she was curious to hear what Pam had told her parents.

It was Dawn who answered. "I don't know the exact location, but I do know it was through mutual friends. One of her girlfriends was close to a young man called Aaron DeBolt. She introduced Pam to Aaron, who introduced Pam to his friends, including Frank Jamieson."

"When was that, Dawn?" Christy asked.

"The summer she graduated from university," Dawn said.

This fit with what Christy already knew, but it didn't mean all that much unless Dawn had known about Frank all those years ago. The close ties between Aaron DeBolt and Frank Jamieson had been all over the news last year during and after Frank's disappearance. Then, this past fall Quinn's book describing his and Christy's search to find out Frank's fate had become a bestseller. It would have been easy for Pam to put the details together and create a fictitious history between them.

Smiling sympathetically at Dawn, Christy said, "You and your daughter must have been close."

Dawn's eyes narrowed a little and she shot Christy a sideways look. "You could say that."

Christy nodded encouragingly. "She would have been excited when her friend introduced her to Aaron DeBolt. He's a handsome and charming man." Christy let her smile turn rueful and she shrugged. "And so was Frank, even though I must admit I'm prejudiced toward him."

"I suppose," Dawn said.

"She told us meeting Frank had helped her get through the disappointment of not being accepted to grad school," Lincoln said. He shook his head. "She was so excited when the dean took her under his wing. She thought that meant she was on her way to a career in academia."

"That was her dream, always," Dawn said.

Was there relief in her eyes, Christy wondered, when her husband directed the conversation away from confidences between mother and daughter?

Dawn's gaze turned wistful. "When she was little, she used to say to me, 'I want to be a teacher, Mommy, to help people.'" Lincoln nodded agreement while Dawn fished around in her purse and finally drew out a packet of tissues. "She would've been an excellent teacher," Dawn said, then blew her nose loudly.

"I'm sure she would," Isabelle said.

Her sympathetic expression appeared to spur Dawn on, because she nodded as she put the tissue packet back into her purse. "Not that I would've wanted her to work at a place like EBU. Pam told us the dean didn't support women, which was why he wouldn't give her a recommendation to the grad schools she applied to." She sniffed. "That doesn't surprise me. She had to report Dr. Olynuk too."

"Who's Dr. Olynuk?" Christy asked.

"One of her computer science professors in second year."

"What did she report him for?" Isabelle asked.

Dawn's eyes flashed. "He made sexual advances toward her. He claimed he didn't, and she had to face a tribunal, but in the end, they believed her, and he was fired."

"Not a good idea to mess with my little girl," Lincoln said.

He looked fierce and proud at the same time. Christy figured that if Pam Muir hadn't won her case against Olynuk, Lincoln Muir would have sought the man out and made sure he regretted whatever he'd done to Pam.

Christy made a note of the name but thought it best to move the conversation away from Olynuk and back to what Pam was really up to when she was supposed to be having a relationship with Frank. "When she wasn't accepted to graduate school, what did Pam do?"

"She found a job, of course!" Dawn snapped.

Taken aback, Christy said, "Well, yes, but where?"

"She used the skills she learned when she worked for the bank the summer before. She had an internship there, working for Theo Perkins."

"Who's Theo Perkins?" Christy asked. Talking to these people was bewildering.

"He was manager of loans for the Western Region—then. He's the vice president now," Dawn said. She added, with a sneer in her voice, "With all your fancy friends, we assumed you'd know him."

Taken aback, Christy blinked. The slam had come out of nowhere. Annoyed, her voice was sharp as she said, "We assumed? Do you mean yourself and your husband? Or was Pam the one who made that unpleasant and unnecessary observation?"

Once again, Lincoln Muir patted his wife's hand before he said, "Pam was a smart girl, but she was also a beautiful one. Too many men were more interested in her looks than her brain and that frustrated her." He shook his head, his mouth a grim line. "She learned a lot in that internship. She was good with numbers, and she used those skills after her applications to graduate school were denied."

"One dead-end job after another, until she landed a good job at a manufacturing company," Dawn said. She sounded and looked bitter. "Then your husband got her pregnant and refused to marry her! She lost her job and had to move home until the baby was born. She lived with us until she found work at the TV show. Even then, she brought Carson to me to care for until he started to go to school."

Christy waited until the bitter rant had run its course, then she pounced. "Pam told us she was married to Frank and there was an article in the newspaper that claimed the same thing. How do you explain that difference?"

Dawn colored and Lincoln frowned. "She told us Frank Jamieson refused to acknowledge his son. That's enough for me. I love my little girl, and I trust her word. Now, are you going to right the wrong that was done to her and our grandson?"

"As I said earlier, Mr. Muir, the Jamieson Trust will accept Carson as an heir if you can prove that Frank Jamieson was his father. You must provide the original paper documents, but in light of the discrepancy you just identified, I think a DNA test that links Carson to the Jamieson family is also necessary." She picked up a card from the file folder in front of her. "Please contact the Trust's lawyer, Mallory Tait, to arrange the details. All further communications between the Trust and yourselves will be through Mallory." She slid the card across the table to Lincoln Muir.

He picked it up, frowning. "You don't believe us?"

"Nothing you've said provides solid proof that your daughter had an intimate relationship with Frank," Christy said.

"You think my Pammy was a liar?" Dawn demanded. Her face was twisted into lines of grief and outrage.

"In a situation like this one, the Trust must take every precaution to ensure the information a claimant provides is correct," Isabelle said. Compassion etched her features and her voice was soothing. It didn't have a noticeable impact on Dawn, but Lincoln nodded. "We must involve our lawyer because this is a legal matter."

"You want your grandson's rights protected, now and in the future, do you not?" Christy added. She knew Dawn Muir was spoiling for a fight. Indulging her would do nothing except put Christy and the Trust in the wrong.

"Of course," Lincoln said. Reluctantly, Dawn nodded.

"Then talk to our lawyer. Provide the documents and information she asks for. Take the DNA test. Then we can meet again."

Lincoln looked at Dawn, who drew a breath, then lowered her eyes. Lincoln nodded jerkily. "All right, we'll do it."

"Excellent." Christy stood. "Good day, Mr. and Mrs. Muir." She rounded the table, walking past them on her way out the door, leaving Isabelle to see them out. She didn't say it had been a pleasure meeting them.

CHAPTER 17

Christy closed the door to her office very quietly. She walked over to the window and stared out. There were clouds collecting over the North Shore Mountains, suggesting a storm ahead and to Christy's mind today's meeting was as ominous as those clouds. Deep in her gut, she believed the Muirs were trouble, Dawn particularly. But where Dawn led, Lincoln followed.

Crossing her arms over her chest, she hugged herself and fought to regain her equilibrium. After a moment, she sighed. Staring at the gray clouds rolling in from the ocean and imagining the gathering storm in her own life wasn't helping her marshal her thoughts.

She shivered and turned away from the window. Crossing to her desk, she pulled out a pad to make notes and hopefully create a plan of action.

She'd begin by emailing Mallory Tait to let her know that the Muirs were aggressive, combative, and confrontational—and that they were headed her way.

Her next note read 'Move the investigation forward. Find a resolution sooner rather than later.' Having written the words down, she paused to stare at them. The two short sentences disguised a complex task with endless subheadings. The timing in the second sentence, 'sooner rather than later,' was the critical element that had tied her stomach in knots from the first moment she'd met Dawn and Lincoln Muir.

She had the impression that Pam's parents—Dawn Muir especially—were impatient to see their grandson acknowledged as heir to the Jamieson fortune. She paused to tap her pen against her chin. Grudgingly, she conceded there was no malice in that desire; rather, it was an act of trust for a daughter they loved unconditionally.

She understood love and loyalty to a child. Noelle was the core of her existence and she would do anything to ensure her daughter was safe. The thought of losing Noelle was so awful, she wouldn't even allow herself to imagine her death, so she guessed the Muirs were living a nightmare that would never truly end. It would account for their aggression and their anger and their desire for closure.

After a moment, she added a note to ask Mallory to deal with the Muirs in an empathetic way. She circled it and drew a line up to the email Mallory task. That done, she turned her thoughts back to the Muirs. Was it possible to resolve their issues without a confrontation?

They believed in their daughter. Pam had told them their grandson was a Jamieson, so it was true. Not 'it must be true,' or 'it could be true,' but the absolute—it was true. Pam's last project was to see her son named a Jamieson and Christy suspected the Muirs would go to any lengths to ensure that happened, a final gift from loving parents to their lost child.

She was mulling over that thought when there was a tap and her door opened. She looked up to see Isabelle in the doorway.

"They've gone," Isabelle said, coming into the office.

Christy straightened as she put her pen onto the pad. "Did they say anything I should know about? Threats? Promises? Angry diatribes?"

"Arguments, mostly from Dawn, with Lincoln chiming in from time to time. They think we're being unreasonable. I convinced them that asking for documentation and a DNA test, even dealing with a lawyer rather than the Trust directly, was standard practice for something like this."

Christy nodded. Isabelle had reaffirmed what had been said during the meeting. "Anything else?"

Isabelle hesitated, then said, "I told them if their son was a Jamieson, and that we were absolutely sure he was Frank Jamieson's son, the Trust would defend and protect the boy, but that we had to be certain before we could commit to that."

Christy's mouth compressed into a hard line as she fought down a quick, angry response. Isabelle had no right to make a promise like that to the Muirs. She didn't speak for the Trust and fulsome promises had a way of being misinterpreted. "Probably not the best promise to make."

Isabelle frowned and her eyes flashed. "They're hurting! I was just—"

"Yes and hunting for something—anything!—that rationalizes their daughter's death," Christy snapped. More quietly, she said, "I don't believe Frank was that boy's father, but the Muirs do and I think they'll do whatever's necessary to force the Trust to accept him."

"Like what?"

Christy studied Isabelle. She was truly upset on behalf of the Muirs and that added another problem to the ones Christy already faced. Isabelle was her ally, a trusted employee. If she'd been won over by the Muirs, how easy would it be for the couple to get the public on their side? Isabelle was inside the Trust. She had in-depth information available to her. If she could be convinced by the grieving grandparents, so would others who didn't have her insider knowledge.

"Remember the sensational article that claimed Pam was married to Frank and that he was the father of her son?"

Isabelle nodded.

"It's likely Pam provided the reporter with the information in that article. I'm concerned the Muirs will also try to use the press to make their case if they don't get satisfaction from the Trust."

Denial leapt in Isabelle's eyes, but she took a moment before she replied. "Possibly, but Christy, all they want is the best for their grandson."

Christy nodded. "I agree with you." She sighed. "But I don't believe the boy is Frank's son."

Their gazes met and locked. Christy could see Isabelle was struggling to find a compromise between her sympathy for the grieving couple and her loyalty to Christy and the Trust.

"The only way forward is to prove the boy's parentage one way or the other," Christy said. Her tone was firm and the look she sent Isabelle offered no compromise.

Isabelle pursed her lips and nodded.

Christy tapped the pad she'd been writing on. Her brow furrowed as she thought about the information the Muirs had revealed during the meeting. "Pam had an interesting history with male authority figures in her life. The professor who apparently propositioned her, the dean who refused to endorse her grad school aspirations, the bank executive who was unwilling to hire her after her internship concluded."

"They didn't say that!" Isabelle protested.

"No, but it was implied, don't you think? She was capable, she had a way with numbers, and she was looking for a job after graduation." Christy dropped the pen, then linked her hands together on top of the pad. "Her parents said she had a number of temporary or part-time jobs after her applications to grad school were turned down. If she was looking for work, wouldn't the bank be one of the first places she'd apply to? Her supervisor during her internship was a regional manager. A reference from him would surely go a long way toward getting her hired."

After a moment, Isabelle nodded. "They never did tell us which of the national banks it was."

Christy grinned, a mischievous smile that had Isabelle raising her brows, then smiling in return as Christy said, "No, but they did mention the man's name and the Trust has access to Harry Endicott who knows everything about everybody in Vancouver's financial world." Harry was also one of the four trustees who oversaw the Jamieson Trust, so he would have an interest in resolving the Muir case. "I'll ask him what he knows about—what was the banker's name?"

"Theo Perkins."

Christy nodded. "That's right, Theo Perkins. I bet Harry can tell us what bank he worked for, where he is now, and what his reputation is like, both personal and professional."

Isabelle frowned. "Personal?"

"On the surface, the timing isn't right for him to be the boy's father, but..." She shrugged. "Who knows? Companies have rules about employees engaging in intimate personal relationships. Maybe the reason this Theo Perkins wouldn't put in a good word for Pam was because they were in a relationship and he couldn't."

"I suppose," Isabelle said. "But why wouldn't Pam introduce him to her parents if they were together?"

Christy tapped the pen again. "Because her parents wouldn't approve?"

Isabelle frowned. "Why wouldn't they approve? The man had a good job and he sounds quite respectable."

"Age? He might have been much older than Pam. Personality? Reputation?" Christy flung out her hands and laughed. "That's why I need to find out more about him."

Isabelle laughed too. "Okay, fair enough."

Christy glanced at her watch. "I'll let Mallory know that the Muirs are headed her way, then I'll call Harry and see what he can tell me."

Isabelle nodded and rose, taking the hint that the discussion was over. Christy watched her cross the room. She was more determined than ever to discover the truth behind Pam Muir's claims.

∾

In the end, she arranged to meet Harry Endicott at his office, which was a small suite in an old building not far from the Downtown East Side. The office was a simple space, stuffed full of Harry's enormous partners' desk that could easily have graced the office of some Victorian industrialist, a desk lamp with a green glass shade, a desktop computer, two filing cabinets, a visitor's chair, and an aloe plant.

Harry himself was a large man. He sat on his side of the partners' desk with the window behind him, beaming at Christy as she settled into the visitor's chair. "How lovely to see you, Mrs. Jamieson. How are you today?"

"I'm very well, Harry. How are you?"

Endicott responded in the same way. With the pleasantries taken care of, he said, "When you phoned, you mentioned you'd like to talk to me on a matter of Trust business. I take it you were referring to the woman claiming to be Mrs. Frank Jamieson?"

Harry Endicott had been appointed a trustee in September of the previous year after he'd managed to recover most of the funds that had been embezzled at the time of Frank's death. As Harry saw his role to be the management of the Jamieson fortune, he normally left personal and family matters to Christy and the other trustees. That didn't mean he wasn't aware of what was going on.

Christy nodded. "The woman's name was Pam Muir."

Harry Endicott was quick. He raised his eyebrows as he said, "Was?"

She nodded. "Mallory Tait, the Trust's lawyer, as you know, told her she needed to produce proof of her claims in the form of a birth certificate and a marriage license. We had a meeting scheduled. She never showed."

"I see," Harry said. He clasped his hands in front of him. His expression was worried. He knew that two of the four trustees—Ellen Jamieson and Trevor McCullagh—were out of the country, leaving himself and Roy Armstrong as the two remaining members available. "Do you know why she missed the meeting?"

Christy nodded. "She was murdered."

Horrified shock tightened Harry's round features. "Good heavens!" He thought for a moment. "Was she the first murder of the year? The woman who was killed in a downtown parking garage?"

Christy nodded.

"Oh, dear," Harry said. He rubbed his chin thoughtfully as the shock gradually eased from his features. "Does that mean her claim against the Trust has gone away?"

Christy shook her head.

"Unfortunate," Harry muttered, his hopeful expression giving way to disappointment.

"Yes, it is. Harry, I don't believe Pam Muir was married to Frank. I don't even believe he was the father of her son."

"Of course not," Harry said. He sounded affronted, but he was watching her carefully.

"I have to find out who Pam Muir was, what kind of woman she was, what she did, where she worked. To do that, I need your help."

"You have it, of course, but..." He frowned, disapproval in his voice. "You aren't trying to solve her murder, are you?"

Christy shook her head. "No. Her parents, Dawn and Lincoln Muir, visited the Trust today. They want their grandson established as an heir to the Trust. They were... impatient, even aggressive. I got the sense that they loved their daughter and they trusted her. She told them Frank was the boy's father and to them that means he was."

"Surely, they'll understand that proof must be rendered, DNA testing done, that sort of thing?"

Christy sighed and shook her head. "This was the project their daughter was working on when she died. I think it's a point of loyalty for them to see it through."

"Well, no harm in that. They supply the birth certificate and any background documents that support their claim. We arrange for DNA testing to be done. The experts do their work and make recommendations." He shrugged. "The answer comes back yes, the boy is a Jamieson, or it comes back no, and he is not. Simple."

"I don't think the documentation exists and I'm afraid they'll go to the press just as their daughter did and claim we're trying to keep the boy's heritage from him."

Harry rubbed his chin again as he studied her in a thoughtful way. "What do you need from me?"

"Lincoln Muir said Pam had a summer internship around the time she might have known Frank. It was with one of the national banks, but he didn't say which. He mentioned a name, though, Theo Perkins. He was her supervisor, apparently. At the time, and this must have been thirteen or fourteen years ago, he was the manager of loans, Western Region."

"Indeed, he was," Harry said, his round face suddenly wreathed in smiles. "I know Theo well. He's now the vice president, Western Region at the Bank of Southern Ontario."

Christy leaned forward. "Tell me about him."

"He's done very well at the bank. Increased their revenues by fourteen percent—"

"So, he works hard at what he does. What kind of man is he?"

"How do you mean?"

Harry asked the question cautiously. Christy suspected he knew more about Theo Perkins' business qualifications and successes than he did about the man himself. "Is he married? Was he married fourteen years ago? Does he play around? Would he get involved with an employee?"

Harry frowned. "You're wondering if he's the father."

Christy nodded.

"He's married. The wedding was four, no five years ago, now. He has two children. One's a toddler, the other an infant. His wife is Idriss Young."

"The city counselor?"

Harry nodded. "She's quite a formidable woman. Theo stays in the background, I think, because she wants to forge her own path."

Christy thought about this for a moment, then she said, "Was he single when he knew Pam Muir?"

Sitting back, Harry steepled his fingers over his broad belly and stared at the ceiling. "Let me see. Fourteen years ago…" Finally, he shook his head. "No, I think he was still married to his first wife. The union ended with a nasty divorce." Harry suddenly sat up. "If I remember correctly, his wife claimed he was having an affair with a young woman he met at work. He denied it, of course, and eventually they settled out of court. He was angry about it, for a very long time."

"The young woman was Pam Muir," Christy said.

Harry frowned, then nodded solemnly. "Could be."

"I think I need to speak to Theo Perkins. Can you arrange an introduction for me, Harry?"

"Of course. I'll set up a meeting."

Christy leaned forward. "As soon as possible, if you would. I have a feeling the Muirs won't wait long."

Harry nodded as he pulled out his cell phone. "I'll do it now."

CHAPTER 18

Harry Endicott's relationship with Theo Perkins seemed to be a genial one if his telephone manner was anything to go by. But then Harry himself was an affable fellow whose apparent enjoyment of the human race also included a delighted fascination with those of a criminal bent. After some light banter and chuckles, over what Christy couldn't fathom, a meeting was set up.

As Harry ended the call, he beamed at Christy. "Theo Perkins is a cautious man. He's agreed to speak to you, but not at his office. He wants to meet at a coffee shop on Granville Island at one-thirty." He glanced at his watch. "It's one now. Should be plenty of time for you to get there."

Christy gathered her purse and pushed back her chair. "Thank you, Harry. I appreciate this."

He shook his head and waved a hand modestly. "No problem." He smiled at her. "I'd be interested to hear what you think of him."

Christy cocked her head, not sure what to make of that request, but it was a small price to pay for the introduction, so she said, "Of course. I'll be in touch."

Located under the Granville Bridge, which crossed False Creek connecting the Kitsilano area to the downtown, Granville Island had once been a warehouse and industrial area servicing the logging and fishing sector. By the 1970s, the old industries had moved to other locations and the district was derelict. An urban renewal project transformed the area into a trendy community of shops, theaters, hotels, and an expansive public market selling everything from local seafood and produce to bread and pastries.

The coffee shop Theo Perkins chose for the meeting was decorated in pale blue and cream, with tiny tables sporting repurposed tops paired with scarred and battered chairs of every style and era. A quick scan of the room told Christy that Perkins hadn't arrived, unless he was a long-haired young man wearing jeans and a sweatshirt. As she considered this to be unlikely, she went to the counter at the back of the room to buy a coffee.

She took a moment to study the menu as she inhaled the fragrant aroma of freshly made coffee. While the shop sold a variety of lattes and cappuccinos, their brewed coffee was fair trade, so Christy ordered a simple medium roast and carried it over to a table that had a good view of the door but was away from other customers. She slipped her coat over the back of the chair and settled in to wait.

She'd only taken three sips of her rich, flavorful brew when the door opened, admitting a gust of cold air and a tall man with broad shoulders wearing an expensive wool top coat open over a bespoke dark blue suit.

Like Christy, he paused to inspect the room as the door slowly closed behind him. Christy noted the moment when he saw her. His gaze sharpened and his eyes narrowed. Moments later he was wending his way through the tables to her secluded spot.

"Mrs. Jamieson?" he asked when he reached her.

Christy nodded.

He stuck out his hand. "Theo Perkins." They shook. "Let me pick up a coffee, then we can talk."

It wasn't long before he was back. Unlike Christy, he didn't drape his coat over the back of the chair; he kept it on. As he settled into his seat, he put the heavy earthenware mug onto the table. Christy noted he'd chosen a specialty latte topped with a slowly melting froth of whipped cream.

She smiled in a friendly way. "Thank you for meeting me, Mr. Perkins."

His expression non-committal, he nodded.

Christy estimated Theo Perkins was in his mid-forties, a young age for a man in a senior position at one of Canada's national banks. Excellent grooming made the most of even features, ordinary blue eyes, and abundant brown hair. Though his looks were not extravagant, women would find him attractive, while men would relate to him.

He smiled, obviously aware that Christy was sizing him up. At that moment, she realized that underneath his unthreatening exterior was a man very conscious of himself and the impact he made on those around him. She hastily revised her initial impression of him.

"Harry indicated you wanted to talk to me about a former employee of mine." He said the words evenly, without a hint of reluctance.

Christy nodded. "Pamela Muir."

He nodded. "Lincoln Muir's daughter. She was my intern. It must be fourteen years ago now." He watched Christy's face as he spoke. "May I ask you why you want to know about Pam?"

Christy had a feeling Theo Perkins was on as much of a fact-finding expedition as she was, and that the more information she gave him, the less he'd provide to her, so she said, "How did Pam get the internship at your bank?"

He studied her, not answering immediately. After a moment, he seemed to come to a decision. "Lincoln was a branch manager. The internship was open to the children of bank employees. Pam applied for it and won the competition." He smiled rather nastily. "It was a nice little package. The successful applicant received an honorarium for their summer's employment, plus full payment of their tuition for the next year. It's a pity, but after Pam's summer the program was cancelled."

This man didn't like Pam Muir at all. Christy could see it in the way his mouth twisted into a sneer as he spoke. "What happened?"

"I'll ask you again, Mrs. Jamieson, why are you asking questions about Pam Muir?"

Christy lifted her coffee mug, decorated and shaped differently than Theo's, and sipped, buying time as she decided how much she should reveal. As she put the mug carefully back on the refurbished tabletop as she said, "Pam Muir came to the Jamieson Trust with a farfetched story of a bigamous marriage and a lost heir. I want to know what kind of woman she was."

Amusement leapt into his eyes as she spoke, but when she finished, he frowned. "Was?"

Christy nodded. "Pam was Vancouver's first murder of the year."

His breath escaped in a heartfelt whoosh, and he muttered, "Thank God."

Christy raised her brows and let her expression speak for itself.

"You think that's an inappropriate way to respond to a woman's death." His voice had a hard edge as he spoke.

"I didn't say that," Christy replied, keeping her tone even.

"No, you didn't." His mouth twisted again, this time into a rueful smile. "There was a time when I thought Pam Muir had destroyed my future. My career was on a knife-edge, my marriage disintegrated, my reputation was as dark and dirty as a man's can get. I did not like Pam Muir and I won't pretend to mourn her passing."

Theo Perkins appeared to be admitting a great deal, but he spoke in generalizations. Christy wondered how open he was prepared to be. She moved her coffee cup on the table and said in a conversational way, "Other people I've spoken to claim she had difficulty separating office from personal."

The amusement was back in Perkins' eyes. "It wasn't a problem for her, Mrs. Jamieson. She simply didn't have any boundaries." He stopped, sighed, then leaned forward, resting his elbows on the table. His expression was rueful. "To understand Pam Muir, you have to consider the whole woman. She was gorgeous—sexy figure, beautiful face, great hair—but she was smart, too. Creative, imaginative, terrific with numbers. She out-thought most of the people in my division and she did it without even trying."

He paused to sip his coffee. Christy waited silently for him to continue. As he put his mug back on the table, he made a derisive sound, not quite a laugh, more than a sigh. "At first, her enthusiasm was wonderful, infectious even. And then..." Now he did sigh. "And then she got bored and she started looking around for a playmate."

Playmate. Euphemism for a lover? "I take it she chose you?"

His lip curled. "Pam did like to start at the top."

Christy studied him. She thought his sneering expression was aimed inward, at himself for how he handled a tricky situation with a girl who was probably just out of her teenage years. "Were you lovers?"

He drank coffee again, then shook his head. "We flirted. I took her out for drinks after work a few times." His gaze shifted to study the tabletop. "She kissed me." He looked up, the movement sharp, emphatic. "I didn't kiss her."

Christy raised her eyebrows skeptically. She'd seen Pam Muir in action, a sexy steamroller who ignored the rules, and refused to behave in a way that benefited anyone but herself. Even fourteen years ago, still testing her sexuality, she would have been difficult for a man to resist.

Perkins' jaw worked. "All right, I kissed her back, but she was the one who initiated the kiss."

"You never took it further?"

"No way!" He shut his mouth, his lips a hard line, then he drew a deep breath. "That didn't prevent Pam from implying we did. I caught the first rumor about the end of July, and I called her on it. She sat down on the other side of my desk, smiled at me, and asked me why a rumor mattered." He shook his head. "She was so sweet, so logical, so affectionate. We had a future together, she said. And, after all, today's rumor was tomorrow's truth."

He stopped again, fiddled with the coffee cup, then lifted it to gulp a large mouthful. After, he carefully placed the empty cup on the tabletop and sat back. "I didn't see it coming."

"Didn't see what coming, Mr. Perkins?"

He shrugged and made that little derisive sound again. "I told her there was no 'us.' I was married, happily, and Pam was still an undergrad with the rest of her life and a great career ahead of her." He pursed his lips. "Yeah, that wasn't what she wanted to hear. She took action and being Pam, it was quick, direct, and in her favor."

He paused, his mouth hardening. When he seemed to have fallen into a brooding silence, Christy said, "Let me guess. She contacted your boss and the HR department with accusations of your inappropriate sexual conduct."

He shook his head and in the sideways glance he sent her there was a mordant humor. "No," he said, drawing the word out. "Worse. She went to my wife's workplace and told her all about our so-called affair, in front of her co-workers, and her boss. She also informed my wife that I didn't love her anymore and that she should do the sensible thing and give me up." He stared down into his empty mug for a minute before he looked back at Christy and shrugged. "She did."

"I only met Pam Muir once," Christy said, "but I don't find what you've told me surprising. I'm very sorry you had to go through that."

He shrugged. "It was a long time ago. At one point, when things turned nasty in my divorce, I thought the top brass would get wind of why my marriage had fallen apart, but my wife and I sorted out our differences and there were no repercussions at the bank. I've remarried. I love my wife, she's a great woman. My career is chugging along nicely. What more could I want?"

Christy smiled.

"Now, Mrs. Jamieson, I've told you my story of Pam Muir. I'd like to hear about yours."

His gaze was sharp, assessing. Christy lifted her hands expansively. "Mine starts with a woman who walked into my office and said she married my husband a year before he met me and that she never divorced him, so Frank was a bigamist and legally I wasn't Mrs. Frank Jamieson."

Perkins sat back, his expression incredulous. "Wow. Sounds exactly like the tactics she used on my ex-wife."

"The difference being," Christy said, "your ex-wife bought it. I didn't. I told her to prove it and that she needed to go through the Trust's lawyers."

There was interest in his expression. "What kind of proof did she provide?"

"None. She was murdered before she could supply it."

"So why your interest?" he asked, frowning. "Surely, with her death the problem is solved."

Christy lifted one shoulder. "It's not that simple. She claimed Frank was her son's father. There's a lot of money involved, and her parents have decided to pursue her claim."

His lips pursed in a silent whistle. "That's tough."

Christy nodded. "Tell me, did you ever see her again after that summer?"

His expression shuttered, the openness of a moment before whisked away. "Strangely enough, I did. She came to the bank looking for a loan to buy a new car. She told me she was trying to build a consulting company, but because she no longer had a full-time job her credit rating was bad, and she was having trouble finding someone to give her the loan. She asked for help to rebuild." He shrugged. "I gave it."

"Why?" Christy asked. She thought she knew the answer, but she wasn't sure how much Theo Perkins would admit.

"I don't believe in holding grudges, Mrs. Jamieson," he said. There was a defensiveness in his voice that hadn't been there before.

Christy tilted her head as she met his bland expression. He'd told her all he was going to. She nodded her understanding. "Grudges can be exhausting, can't they?"

"Exactly." He made a point of glancing at his watch, an expensive Rolex. "I'm afraid I do need to get back to the office. It's been very nice meeting you, Mrs. Jamieson. I do hope we'll see each other again in the future."

"I'm sure we will," Christy replied with a smile.

He smiled back. "If you, or the Jamieson Trust, ever has banking needs I can assist you with, please don't hesitate to contact me." With a smooth, practiced motion, he handed her his card.

Christy took it and nodded. "Thank you. I'll keep it in mind."

With a nod, he stood. A moment later, he was striding across the room to the door. Christy sipped the last of her coffee as she watched him go and wondered how much that car loan had been for and if it had come out of Theo Perkins' own pocket.

CHAPTER 19

"Then he says he has to leave, but before he does, he gives me his card and offers me banking services," Christy said, shaking her head. "Even though I assumed he was willing to talk to me because he was interested in the Jamieson account, I didn't expect him to be so blatant about it."

She was sitting with Roy at her kitchen table. Her laptop was open, and they were video conferencing with Quinn in Toronto. It was ten o'clock in the evening. Noelle was in bed sound asleep. The cat was on the table, out of range of the laptop's camera.

Chancer. Frank was in this conversation because they were discussing Pam Muir's past and Christy wanted whatever input he might be able to add to their slender stack of knowledge, but Stormy was used to taking a long nap with Noelle in the evenings and he was tired. Right now, the cat was in a hunched position, his long body compact, his paws folded beneath, his tail tucked tight, the picture of misery.

Roy shrugged. "He's a banker. His purpose is to increase business. Snagging the Trust as a client would be a big deal. Head office would be pleased, and he'd increase his chances to move up the ladder."

"Could be," Quinn said. "Or he might have been hinting that there was a cost for his information."

"I gave you something, now you need to give me something in return," Roy said.

"Yeah," Quinn said.

Christy sighed. "Harry asked me to let him know what I thought of the man. I suspect Perkins has been trying to convince Harry to move the Trust's funds to his bank."

Quinn nodded. "He probably thinks if he has you on his side, it will increase his chance of succeeding."

Christy wrinkled her nose into a grimace. "A problem for another day. Right now, I'm more worried about the Muirs and what they're likely to do."

Normal people would provide their documents, do the sampling, and wait.

"Well, they aren't normal people!" Christy glared at the cat, who stared mournfully back. Sighing, she stroked Stormy apologetically as she said, "Their daughter has died, and the police don't seem to be making any headway in finding her murderer. They want a resolution. Proving their grandson is a Jamieson was important to Pam, so it's important to them."

In Toronto, at the other end of the video call, Quinn wouldn't have heard Frank's comment, but then he couldn't hear the cat when he was in Vancouver sitting around the table with Christy and his father. He was used to ignoring the cat's interjections into their conversations. "Did they tell you anything that might prove useful?"

Christy thought back. "They talked about the dean who mentored her, then refused to recommend her to any grad programs."

"That would've been Ronald Gallagher, the man who is now the provost at EBU."

Christy nodded. "They also mentioned an incident with one of her profs in second year. Dawn Muir said he made improper advances toward Pam and she reported him. He was fired as a result. They gave me a name, a Dr. Olynuk."

"A name gives us a place to start," Quinn said. He smiled at her in a reassuring way.

Christy decided she must look frazzled and upset, which wouldn't surprise her, because today had been one fraught situation after another. She'd been exhausted when she got home and even an afternoon with Noelle hadn't done much to help her unwind. Touched by his concern, she smiled back. "I don't know if finding this Olynuk is worth the bother. Whatever happened between him and Pam, and later with Ronald Gallagher, both relationships are too early for one of the men to be Carson Muir's father."

"Let's look at this in chronological order," Roy said. "Her first year at university seems to have been relatively quiet, but in second year she accuses a professor of sexual misconduct and gets him fired. During the summer between her third and fourth year, she works for Theo Perkins at his bank and breaks up his marriage. At the end of her fourth year, she tries to manipulate the dean of her faculty into recommending her for a graduate program, but it doesn't work."

"When she can't get into grad school and is looking for a job, she takes up with Aaron DeBolt and meets Frank," Christy said, staring at the cat. Frank said nothing, so she continued. "According to Dawn Muir, she had a succession of jobs, but by the next summer, the summer in which she became pregnant, she's working for a manufacturing company. Neither of the Muirs can remember the name of the company, though."

Roy rubbed his chin thoughtfully. "She goes on maternity leave, then the next thing we hear about is that she's working in TV production."

"Where she does well career-wise but seems to be searching for a male who will become a father figure for her son. We know of two, Isaac Holley and Jeremiah Brownrigg. There may have been more," Quinn said.

"I wonder why she didn't go back to the manufacturing company after her maternity leave was over," Christy said. In Canada, employers had to keep a position open for anyone on maternity leave. Pam didn't have to change jobs unless she chose to.

Quinn shrugged. "She wanted better hours? A shorter commute? More money? There could be any number of reasons for the change."

Christy sighed. "Yeah."

"So, we've got a gap between the men she was involved with before she left university and the ones she met in the film industry," Roy said. "The gap is the sweet spot where we find Carson Muir's father."

"And the gap is filled with lots of dead-end jobs and an unidentified manufacturing company about which we have absolutely no information." Frustration had Christy shaking her head. "How do we move forward? Frank, do you have any suggestions?"

No.

She tightened her lips. "That isn't helpful. You're the only one who knew her."

Not well enough to know where she worked. The Pam I knew was only interested in partying and having fun.

Christy relayed what he'd said to Quinn. "Another dead end."

"Then we have to find more people who can tell us about her," Quinn said. There was a light in his eyes that suggested the difficulty was only adding to his enthusiasm. "For instance, Isaac Holley mentioned a woman called Marenda Riddle. We can start with her."

"Then there's Aiden O'Bryan, the fellow who fired her from her last job," Roy said. He was looking happy at the thought of their search. "I don't think he'll be able to give us a lot of information about her employment stats from before her time in the entertainment industry, but it might be worthwhile to find out why he fired her."

"I suppose." Christy resisted the urge to sigh disconsolately, but she was feeling gloomy about the likelihood they'd ever solve this mystery.

Her computer pinged, indicating an email had just arrived. A second later, Roy's phone launched into the opening riffs from *The Letter* by the 60s rock group, The Box Tops. On the other side of the continent, she heard Sledge's voice, supported by Hammer's driving drums, the music Quinn used for his ringtone.

Roy raised his brows as he consulted his phone. "It's from Kim Crosier. I've been invited to a party." He scrolled through the message. "Seems she's hosting a dinner." His brows rose higher. "For Sledge." He chuckled. "He's apparently in town for a flying visit and discussions with Mitch that day." He looked up with a grin. "Poor Sledge. I guess Kim figures he'll need cheering up after Mitch bends his ear for hours."

"I've been invited to the dinner too," Quinn said. "Would you look at the guest list?" He shook his head. "All of them movers and shakers in the entertainment industry."

"I got one too, but mine's a little different," Christy said. "Kim apologies for the last-minute invitation, but Mitch had his assistant organize and confirm the guest list." She choked back a giggle. "She says she can't in good conscience leave Sledge to the mercy of Mitch and his scheming—" Her giggle became a full-blown laugh. "So, she wants us to come and support Sledge."

She's a nice person.

Quinn sighed. "Even for Sledge, I'm not flying across the country for a party."

Christy sighed too, then, as she scanned further, she laughed again. "She says, 'and bring the kitty too. I know he'll have a good time and Mitch likes him.'"

The cat sat up. *I'm invited too? Awesome.*

Roy was frowning. "My invitation only asks me to attend. How come she told you all this extra stuff?"

Still chuckling, Christy said, "Girl to girl talk, I guess. Did you get a guest list like Quinn? She didn't include one in mine."

Roy scrolled down the invitation. "Yeah. Hey, would you look at that. Aiden O'Bryan is one of the guests."

"So is someone called Landon Olynuk," Quinn said. "Do you think he's the professor Pam got fired?"

Roy frowned. "Why would Mitch be inviting a disgraced university professor to his dinner party for Sledge?"

"It might not be the same guy, but Olynuk is an unusual name," Quinn said, shrugging. "Marenda Riddle is also on the list. That's useful."

While the two Armstrong men talked, Christy typed Landon Olynuk's name into her web browser and came up with gold. "Check this out. Landon Olynuk is the founder and CEO of Everything Electronics, the computer game maker."

"Convergence," Roy said gloomily. "That's why Mitch has invited him to his party. He wants to make a deal with Olynuk and bring Everything Electronics into his weird convergence empire."

Christy waved this away. "That doesn't matter, but this does. For three years after he completed his PhD, Landon Olynuk was a professor at EBU." She closed the browser and refocused on the video window. "He's our prof, the one Pam had fired!"

"Olynuk, O'Bryan, and Riddle, all in one place. Looks like you and I are going to a party," Roy said.

The cat batted his arm, claws in. *Don't forget me. I'm invited too.*

CHAPTER 20

The gates to the Crosier mansion closed behind Roy's compact car and Christy saw his hands tighten on the wheel as his jaw clenched. "I haven't been here before," she said to take his mind off whatever was bothering him. "This is a lovely property."

"It's like being in a prison," Roy said through gritted teeth. "People shouldn't have gates and walls around their houses. Not to mention, cameras everywhere and security guys spying on your every move."

The house came into view as the drive curved. Elegant and traditional, it sprawled over a large swathe of acreage. "We had gates, a fence, and security at the Jamieson mansion," Christy said. "Sometimes, you don't have any option but to have them."

As Roy grunted a reluctant agreement, they pulled up in front of the grand portico with its ionic columns and wide porch.

The door flew open. Two uniformed staff appeared. One, wearing winter boots and a coat, hurried out. He opened Christy's door while Ray got out the other side. "Good evening, sir, madam. If you'll leave your keys in the car, I'll take care of the parking."

"Thanks," Roy said, coming round the car. He slipped the valet a bill, then took Christy's arm. Together, they entered the house. The doorman blinked at their appearance.

Roy was wearing a well-cut, dark suit, white shirt, and a dark blue tie decorated with images of assorted animals at risk. His shoulder-length hair was combed and tied back in a queue. Christy guessed his apparel was no stranger than any other man's here tonight. No, it was her the attendant was focused on, and it wasn't the black cocktail dress she wore, or the wool coat over it, that had him gawking. It was the battered, and a little grimy, canvas tote bag she had slung over one shoulder, and the cat whose head appeared just over the bag's rim that was doing it.

The original plan had been to outfit Stormy in the halter and leash he hated, but when the time came, there was no convincing the cat to allow that indignity.

Give the guy a break, Frank had said. *He was invited to the party. This is a special deal for him. Don't humiliate him by making him wear THE LEASH.*

Christy wasn't sure who was more worried about the halter and leash, Stormy or Frank, but in the end, she caved and agreed Stormy should be transported to the party in the tote.

Christy slipped the bag off her shoulder. After giving it to Roy to hold, she shrugged off her coat and surrendered it to the attendant. By that time, Kim had come to greet the latest arrivals. Wearing a spectacular off the shoulder, body-hugging dress in emerald green that sparkled with iridescent glitter and ended mid-thigh, she moved quickly across the floor, obviously well used to walking in sky-high heels. Her polite smile of welcome broadened into one of real warmth. "You're here and you brought the kitty. I'm so glad."

Christy scooped Stormy out of the tote. She handed the cat to Kim and took the now empty tote from Roy to give it to the bemused doorman. "Please keep this with my coat. I'll need it when I go."

Kim was tickling Stormy under the chin. Stormy was purring

loudly, his head tilted upwards, his eyes slitted closed. Kim chuckled. "Let's go find Mitch. He'll be so glad to see you." She turned to move deeper into the house.

Mitch thinks he can own me. Let's find Sledge instead.

Roy touched Christy's shoulder, his head jerking sideways in a gesture indicating she should look over her shoulder. Christy turned and saw that the doorman's eyes had widened, only to narrow into a frown as he noticed he was being observed. Christy stifled a grin. Apparently, he was one of those people who could hear the voice but couldn't figure out where it was coming from. How many others would there be at this party? This could be an interesting night.

They followed Kim through an archway into a large, open living room packed with people. A fair-haired man holding a glass containing two fingers of amber liquid smiled as he saw Kim. She angled his way, her pretty features lit with pleasure.

"Darling!" She leaned forward to do cheek-to-cheek air kisses. "I missed greeting you when you arrived. I'm so sorry!"

Trapped between her body and the man's, Stormy squirmed. *Hey! Watch the cat. You're squishing him.*

Kim jumped back guiltily. The man shook his head and smiled. "That's okay, Kim. Mitch took care of me."

Evidently, he wasn't one of the people who was attuned to Frank's mind-speak. Kim shot a conspiratorial glance at Christy. "I'm so glad," she said, her look turning mischievous as she introduced them. "Aiden O'Bryan, I'd like you to meet Christy Jamieson and Roy Armstrong."

They all murmured polite how-do-you-dos. Christy glanced at Roy, who raised his brows. Neither of them had expected to chance upon one of their targets a few minutes after they'd arrived.

"I'll leave you to chat," Kim said, beaming at all of them. "The kitty wants to find Sledge."

Apart from raising his pale brows, Aiden O'Bryan took this in stride. "Sledge was with Mitch the last time I saw him. They were headed into the music room."

His statement seemed to annoy Kim. He eyebrows flew upwards, and her mouth pursed. "That man!" she said, shaking her head. "I told him Sledge wasn't to do a concert tonight. He's here to have fun, not to be shown off like a prize pig at the fall fair." She glanced at them all in turn. "I'm sorry, darlings, but I must go and rescue him." She darted away, Stormy's head just visible over her shoulder as she departed.

Aiden watched her for a moment, a smile in his eyes, then he turned back to Christy and Roy. "Kim Crosier is a complete flake, but she's a delight. If Mitch hadn't found her first, I'd have snapped her up."

Christy wondered at that statement, but she smiled without comment. A determined-looking woman joined them at that point. Introduced as Laurel Tremblay, she turned out to be the head of the sales agency that worked with Roy's publisher. She'd known Roy for years and drew him away to talk about his latest novel, a murder mystery with thriller undertones that had been released just before Christmas.

After they'd moved off, leaving Christy alone with Aiden O'Bryan she studied him. He was an attractive, well-groomed man. His trim body was clad in a perfectly tailored suit and his highly polished shoes were hand stitched. Silver threaded through his blond hair and there were laugh lines around his eyes. She guessed he was in his mid-forties. "Tell me, Aiden, how do you fit into Mitch's convergence world?"

He raised his brows at that, but he laughed. "So, you know about Mitch's dreams of empire?"

Christy nodded.

"My company produces music videos and other forms of entertainment. We also create material Mitch's artists can use on their social media accounts." He cocked his head. "You're a Jamieson Trust Jamieson, aren't you?"

Since Christy's role was to be the face of the Jamiesons, she smiled and agreed. She had a sense that Aiden O'Bryan was the kind of man who kept abreast of who was who in Vancouver's moneyed society so he could cultivate them for his own benefit.

"Where do you fit in Mitch's world?" he asked, confirming her impression.

Her smile widened into a grin. She couldn't resist saying, "I brought the cat."

He stared at her, speechless, obviously not expecting her answer. She watched as he pulled himself together, then directed his gaze across the room to where Kim was standing with Mitch and Sledge. Sledge was smiling broadly, tickling the cat's chin with his forefinger while Kim laughed at something that had been said, and Mitch looked on, his expression thoughtful.

Aiden dragged his gaze back to Christy. There was a small frown between his brows and he blinked quickly several times. "You're Kim's friend."

He was probably now regretting his earlier remark about Kim being a flake. That was fine with Christy. The longer she kept him off balance, the easier it would be to dig beneath his smooth polish and find out about his relationship with Pam Muir.

She tapped her chin thoughtfully, pretending to ponder his statement. Then she shook her head. "It's more that my cat is Kim's friend," she said, and watched with satisfaction when his frown deepened as he tried to figure out if she was joking or serious.

She didn't wait for him to decide. "You mentioned you're in the film business. Do you know a woman by the name of Pamela Muir?"

He stiffened, suddenly wary. His gaze searched her face before he said cautiously, "I do."

She beamed at him as if she was completely unaware of his

unease. "Wonderful. Would you be willing to tell me what you think of her?"

The guarded expression hardened into suspicion.

Before he could demand an explanation, she waved a hand airily and said, "You know, an impression of her work."

His eyes narrowed. "Why do you ask?"

Christy shrugged. "She approached the Trust about investing in a project of hers." She firmed her expression into one that was at once confiding and disapproving. "I'm not going to authorize anything until I know more about the woman. How reliable she is, if she follows through on her promises, or..." and here Christy spread her hands wide, "if she has bad habits that will end up causing problems."

He stared at her thoughtfully. "The Jamieson Trust is looking to invest in film production?"

Christy noted his cautious statement and the speculative look in his eyes. She guessed he was wondering if the Jamieson Trust might be a new source of funds for his own projects. She smiled and, choosing her words as carefully as he had, said, "The Jamieson Trust is willing to entertain investment proposals in any industry. This is the first time we've been approached by someone involved in TV production."

Apparently satisfied with her answer, his cautious expression eased and he nodded. "Pam Muir," he said, "is very capable, but she's erratic. She tends to be sidetracked by..." Here he hesitated. "By personal matters."

Christy frowned, deliberately leading him on. "You have direct knowledge of that?" She kept her tone more curious than critical.

His expression impassive, he didn't immediately reply, then he said, "I do."

His answer was a direct statement, but it was one filled with ambiguity. Christy tipped her head to one side and said, "I suppose it was her little boy? She put him first and not her work?"

He smiled thinly. "The boy was part of the equation, the cause you might say, but not the reason."

"You intrigue me," Christy said, and waited.

She watched him struggle to find a way to reply without revealing too much. This man was not like Theo Perkins, who opened quickly and without much effort on her part. Aiden O'Bryan was a man who liked to keep his secrets to himself.

Finally, he said, "Have you spoken to anyone else about Pam?"

This, she thought, was the key to unlock him. He wasn't prepared to be the first person making allegations against Pam, but he wouldn't mind supporting the complaints of others. She let a slow smile play on her lips. "Several people."

He inspected her narrowly, then he nodded. "You've probably heard about the scandal then."

She raised her brows but didn't speak.

"When *Blood Wars* folded, I hired Pam to work on a pilot I was doing for one of the US networks. I knew of her work on the show, and she was highly recommended by Marenda Riddle. I thought she'd be a good fit." He shrugged. "I was wrong."

"She wasn't good at her job?"

"She was terrific. She just wanted more."

When he stopped and didn't begin again, Christy said, "Let me guess. She wanted you."

His scowl was quick, perhaps surprised. "Why do you say that?"

"Because you aren't the first man I've talked to that she's chased."

"Hunted, more like," Aiden muttered. He eyed her speculatively. "Why are you really asking about Pam Muir?"

"Pam didn't come to the Trust with a TV project. Her purpose was to claim she was married to my late husband," Christy said.

Aiden lifted his glass and pointed it at her. "I remember now. There was a news report about that."

Christy nodded. "Planted by Pam because she couldn't prove what wasn't true."

"Interesting." He shook his head. "That was Pam all over. If she couldn't get what she wanted in a direct way, she'd go about it in an underhanded one. That's why I fired her from the show. I wanted her out of my life."

"Do you know if she found another job after yours?"

He shook his head. "Not that I've heard of." He hesitated, then added, "The film industry in Vancouver is pretty small. Everyone knows everyone." He shook the glass, making the liquor swirl. "I took a risk when I hired her. She had a rep, but I knew she was coming off a long-term liaison with Jeremiah Brownrigg and I figured she wouldn't be looking for someone new. I was wrong."

"You weren't interested in getting involved with her? She was very beautiful."

"I don't have relationships with the women who work for me," he said stiffly. "It's not a good idea and I don't want to be sued for sexual harassment."

"And, as you say, Pam had a habit of getting what she wanted through fair means or foul."

He eyed her cautiously.

"Did she try to make you change your mind?"

He was slow to reply, clearly deciding how much he wanted to say. "When I terminated her employment, we came to an agreement that neither of us would talk about the reason she was let go."

Christy raised her brows. "And yet, here you are, telling me all about it."

His expression hardened.

Christy didn't think there was much more she could pry out of him, so she smiled and said, "It's been a pleasure chatting with you, Aiden."

CHAPTER 21

Roy accepted the glass of Scotch Laurel Tremblay, the head of the sales agency that represented his publisher, handed him. Laurel was a go-getter, a whirling dynamo of a woman whose hair was a different color every time Roy saw her.

Today, it was a bright, flaming red, a vibrant contrast to the deep black of her cocktail dress. Her shoes were high-heeled and a hot red that was doing its best to out do her hair. He smiled and raised the glass in silent thanks, because Laurel was talking in an animated way that didn't allow for interruption. The Christmas sales numbers were in, and his latest literary offering was a big hit, which had Laurel gushing.

Roy was pleased by the news, but then most of his books were what the Canadian literary community considered "big hits" and actual sales numbers didn't put a lot of money in his pocket. The US market, now, that was a different matter. A big hit there meant huge sales and lots of revenue. He hoped Laurel was talking about his US sales, but she probably wasn't. So, he smiled and nodded and let her prattle on about the benefits of series over single title, long tail marketing, and promo opportunities. He even gave her a brief, high-concept description of the second mystery in the series, which had her face lighting up with excitement.

"You have to talk to Landon," she said, taking his wrist and dragging him in the direction of a youngish man with dark hair flopping over his forehead in a fringe and big soulful dark eyes. He was surrounded by a gaggle of women. They were all dressed in expensive gowns and sparkling jewels, and they appeared to be entranced by whatever the fellow was saying, as if he was a guru.

"Landon!" Laurel said, when she and Roy reached him. As she thrust herself into the circle the nearest woman shifted, shuffling sideways, forcing the people beside her to move as well. The result was a reallocation of space that reminded Roy of a domino chain reaction. Laurel beamed at Landon. "This is Roy Armstrong. The mystery writer."

Roy perked up at her introduction. He'd never been introduced as a mystery writer before. Novelist, yes, and sometimes as "the Canlit novelist," but not as the mystery writer. He rather liked it.

Pulled out of his schmooze with the ladies, Landon blinked and smiled in that vague way people do when they have no idea what you're talking about.

Impatient, Laurel said, "You know, Roy Armstrong! We talked about him earlier. The Vancouver Murders."

The Vancouver Murders was the name his editor had given the series. Or maybe the editorial board had put their heads together and come up with it. In Roy's opinion, it lacked panache, but he had to admit it did the job. The books were set in Vancouver and they were about murders.

Apparently, the name struck a chord with Landon because his eyes brightened and the vague expression disappeared. "So, it is a series? For sure?"

Laurel nodded. "Yes. Roy just filled me in on the next book. It'll be awesome."

Yes, it would, but Laurel was going out on a limb with that statement. The next thing she was going to want to know was when the book would be published, which would be contingent on when he finished writing it. He hoped she wouldn't ask because his only answer would be sometime in the next year. He didn't think that would satisfy her.

Laurel must have understood the creative mind because she didn't ask the question. Or perhaps she didn't have the opportunity as the gaggle of expensively clad women started bombarding him with questions he didn't have the chance to answer.

"You're an author?" one said. She sounded amazed by that, as if it provided him with semi-divine status.

"My book club is planning to read your book! Will you come to talk to us?" That was said by a young woman who was probably older than her wide eyes and baby face gave her credit for.

Beside her, another young woman nodded. "Yes, I adore hearing the scoop behind what's on the page. You must come."

Roy smiled in a vague way, having no idea who these people were. Wives of some of the executives who worked with Mitch? Movers and shakers in their own right? He was certain of one thing—he didn't want to be trapped into a personal appearance with them. He'd done book club meetings before, and the results hadn't always been great. He didn't like talking about his writing and he didn't have a collection of funny stories about his process to entertain an audience. He preferred to let the words on the page speak for him.

Ignoring the women, Landon said, "When will the second book be out?"

Heaving a mental sigh, Roy shrugged and said, "When it's done."

Landon's dark eyes focused intently on Roy's face, making him feel like he was under a spotlight. "Any possibility the book could be out by December?" He glanced at Laurel, then back to Roy. "We could launch the second book in the series along with the computer game. The cross-marketing would send sales through the roof for both."

Evidently, Landon was an enthusiastic member of Mitch's convergence world. Roy eyed him suspiciously. Mitch had already tried to recruit him and it had taken him months to escape the man's toils. "What computer game?"

Landon's expression went from laser sharp to surprised. He turned to Laurel. "Doesn't he know?"

She shook her head. "Negotiations are ongoing."

And they'd be stopped dead when he talked to his agent tomorrow morning. Roy smiled his version of a conversation-stopping vague smile and said, "Is that Sledge over there? I must go over to say hello. Nice to meet you, Landon."

"Wait!" Landon said. "Let me tell you about my company, Everything Electronics."

The name set off a series of alarm bells in Roy's head. "Everything Electronics?"

Landon nodded. His expression was relieved. "We've been in business for fourteen years and we're the largest company in the gaming sector. Our titles are written for all computer and video platforms, and we also have a large online division. Our distribution is worldwide, and our games are regularly bestsellers—"

"You're very enthusiastic. What do you do at Everything Electronics?" Roy didn't care if he was being rude. He didn't think Landon would notice.

Landon didn't, but his gaggle of female fans must have decided the conversation had turned into a business discussion, because the group broke up. A couple of women wandered off, but several others could be heard discussing their current book club selection.

Pride was evident in Landon's smile as he said, "I'm the CEO and CD. I created the company."

Roy knew what a CEO was. CD, in relation to a business, was a mystery. "CD? What's that?"

"Chief Dreamer," Landon said with a grin.

In Roy's opinion, Chief Dreamer sounded like a great job, so he grinned back and nodded in a friendly way. "You set up the company fourteen years ago." He looked Landon up and down. "You must have been just out of university. Or were you one of those computer genius dropouts?"

Landon laughed. "Actually, I was in the beginnings of an academic career when it got derailed. I had to find something to pay the bills. I'd done some game coding for fun while I worked on my grad degrees, so I refocused on that, put together a beta game that went viral, got funding to take it to the next level, and everything fell into place from there."

"What derails an academic career?" Roy asked. He had a pretty good idea it wasn't a what but a who. He wanted to hear Landon's story, told in his own way, though.

For the first time Landon hesitated. "Well..."

Roy raised his brows. "If I'm considering working with a man, I want to know who he is and what made him that way." When Landon's expression continued to be reluctant, he added, "I haven't signed any contracts. Negotiations are, after all, ongoing."

"Landon, what's the problem? It was years ago. He's a man of the world," Laurel said.

Roy wondered briefly if Laurel would receive a finder's fee from Everything Electronics for delivering the elusive Roy Armstrong into their arms. Then Landon sighed and Roy thrust his thought aside for now.

"I was teaching entry-level computer programing to first- and second-year students at EBU. One of them, a young woman, accused me of sexual harassment."

Roy raised his eyebrows and thrust disapproval into his voice. "Was it true?"

Landon hastily shook his head. "She was in one of my lecture classes and enrolment was huge. The students were names to me, not people. There were a few who would linger after class to ask questions, and it turned out she was one of them, but I never thought of her that way."

"So, you never had a sexual relationship with her?"

"Heavens, no!"

By this time, both Landon and Laurel were staring at him with suspicion. That didn't worry Roy. He had what he needed. It had always been unlikely that Olynuk was the father of Pam's child. If what he said was true, he'd have no reason to get involved with her after his academic career tanked. There was a bit more Roy hoped to extract from Landon, however, so he said, "She accused you of sexual harassment. I assume the university terminated your employment as a result?"

Landon nodded, looking relieved. "She actually did me a favor. If she hadn't made the accusation, I'd be living on a professor's salary in a nice townhouse complex in Burnaby, instead of in a multi-million-dollar estate next door to Mitch Crosier."

"If she was little more than an eager student, why would this girl accuse you of harassment and why would the university accept the accusation?"

Landon's gaze slid away from Roy's. He stared over Laurel's shoulder as he said, "At the end of the semester, we went for drinks. She'd aced her course work and we both expected her to sail through her exam. She wanted to celebrate." His gaze skittered back to Roy's, then away. "It was the end of the semester. She wasn't really my student anymore." He shrugged. "She was gorgeous, charming, fun. I thought, why not? So, we went to the student pub. People saw us. She had a way of leaning close and looking up into your eyes. I forgot who

I was and who she was." He held up his hand as Roy's brows shot up. "We did not have sex, but... When we left the pub, she glued herself to me. I thought she'd had too much to drink, so I offered to drive her home. She accepted and when we got to her apartment, she asked me in. I said no, but she told the review committee I said yes."

"And all the witnesses who saw you together thought you were into her."

He nodded.

"This woman," Roy said. "It was Pam Muir, wasn't it?"

Landon frowned. "Yes. How did you know?"

Roy shrugged. "I've met Ron Gallagher."

Landon nodded. "I heard he had a similar problem."

Roy inspected Landon. "I think she was blackmailing Gallagher. Did she try that on you?"

"Blackmail?" Laurel said on a gasp.

Landon glanced at her, then back to Roy. "No, of course not."

Roy's brows went up. "You never kept in touch, then?"

Landon shrugged. "Not really. She did come to see me a year or so ago. She had a great idea for a video game. I worked with her for a while. I even advanced her funds to help with the development. In the end, the project didn't work out."

"That's too bad," Roy said. "How recently was the end?"

Landon frowned. "What do you mean?"

"When did you stop advancing funds?"

Landon's mouth hardened and he said reluctantly, "Three weeks ago."

CHAPTER 22

As Christy moved away from Aiden O'Bryan, she spotted Sledge. Now holding the cat, he was talking to Kim and a large Black woman. Mitch had disappeared.

As she made her way toward them, she thought about how easily Aiden O'Bryan had revealed what was supposed to be a secret. Did that mean he knew Pam was dead and he no longer had to stay tight-lipped about the reason he fired her? That seemed like the most reasonable answer, but to Christy's knowledge, Patterson hadn't revealed the name of the first murder victim of the year. Did that mean Aiden O'Bryan had something to do with Pam's death?

It was possible, but his statement could also have been a slip of the tongue by a man who had already admitted much. Perhaps he thought it was okay to reveal the information to Christy, a person outside his industry, something he wouldn't normally do when talking to someone within his tight-knit community. Thankfully, since Christy wasn't looking for Pam's killer, just the father of her child, Aiden's motive for releasing the information wasn't a question she'd have to find the answer to.

Sledge noticed her making her way through the crowd and flashed his trademark grin at her. The two women with him turned to look. Kim smiled too. The Black woman's expression was mildly curious.

Hey, babe! Sledge was telling us about his adventures in Hollywood.

Sledge rolled his eyes and Kim chuckled as she ruffled the fur behind Stormy's ears. The Black woman didn't react, which meant she wasn't one of those people who could hear Frank's mind-speak.

Christy reached them and rose on her tiptoes to give Sledge a kiss on the cheek. He turned his head and their lips connected for a short minute. The kiss left Christy feeling nothing but mild annoyance. She liked Sledge, with his cocky smile and free-spirited ways, but she was committed to Quinn and Sledge knew it.

He grinned at her, not at all dismayed by her lack of reaction. "Maybe someone snapped a photo that will go viral and break the Internet." The grin turned cheekier and his eyes gleamed with amusement. "Have to keep our wandering reporter on his toes."

"You expect someone to take a picture of you and Christy? At my party?" Kim said with indignation. "Sledge, you should know better. No one would dare."

Way to go, girl. You tell him.

Sledge raised his brows at that, and Christy rolled her eyes heavenward.

The Black woman laughed. "Kim, my dear, these days phones are lethal weapons even you can't control."

Kim pouted and introduced her to Christy. "Marenda Riddle, this is Christy Jamieson."

Marenda raised the glass she was holding in a salute. "Nice to meet you, Christy." She drank, then held the glass clasped in both hands in front of her.

Kim slipped her hand into the crook of Marenda's arm in an affectionate way. She smiled broadly. "Marenda did some record videos for Mitch way back when, and we've been friends ever since."

Marenda Riddle raised a sculpted brow. She was tall and curvy, and the silk evening trousers and jacket she wore flowed lovingly over her figure. Her hair curled wildly around narrow, sharply intelligent features. She laughed, clearly willing to tease. "The best thing about working for Mitch was meeting you, honey child."

"Marenda is a friend of Hammer and his family," Sledge added.

"Where is Hammer?" Christy asked. "Are he and Jahlina back from their travels yet?"

Sledge nodded. "Just. They flew in from China a couple of days ago. He was here this afternoon, meeting with Mitch and me about the future of the band."

After the murder of SledgeHammer's long-time manager, Hammer and Sledge had put the band on hiatus and Hammer and his girlfriend, Jahlina, had traveled to the Far East, to trace Jahlina's family roots. As the days and weeks turned into months, Mitch became increasingly anxious about SledgeHammer's future, pressing Sledge on numerous occasions to provide him with a commitment to move forward. The talks today must have been emotional and demanding ones.

Christy searched Sledge's expression, looking for shadows that might suggest the meetings had not gone well, but she saw only Sledge's usual confident amusement. Whatever had been decided, there had been no immediate crisis to unsettle him.

"Hammer was supposed to stay for the party," and here Sledge grinned. "But Jahlina came and rescued him before it began. They were expected at a family thing."

"Hammer was perfectly happy to be dragged away," Marenda said with a chuckle. "He hates these kinds of events."

Sledge, who thrived on them, nodded. "He does prefer to let me do the dirty work."

Hey! There's nothing wrong with this party. I'm having a great time.

Kim smiled and scratched Stormy under the chin. The cat began to purr.

"Do you still do music videos for Mitch?" Christy asked Marenda, leaving Sledge and Kim to fuss over the cat.

Marenda's smile was world-weary. "Occasionally. I work from project to project. Mitch asks, and if I can, I fit him in." She shook her head. "Honestly, working with Mitch can be a relief. He expects a good product, but he's willing to provide a decent budget to get it. And," she added, nodding for emphasis, "he lets the professionals do the work. He doesn't look over your shoulder, second-guessing every decision you make—unlike some I could mention."

The thought of a laid-back Mitch leaving the decision-making to the pros was so foreign to Christy's image of the man all she could say was, "I had no idea."

Sledge said gloomily, "When it comes to career direction, Mitch is very hands-on."

"My Mitch cares," Kim said. She stroked Stormy, who was still purring madly.

Marenda nodded and took a moment to tickle Stormy under the chin. "That he does."

Mitch didn't know Pam Muir, did he?

Sledge and Kim frowned. Neither had been filled in on the Jamieson Trust crisis Pam had initiated, or that she'd been Vancouver's first murder victim of the year. "Pam Muir?" Sledge asked.

"Oh, do you know Pam?" Marenda asked.

Sledge shot Christy a questioning look, eyebrows raised. Christy shrugged. Marenda kept talking.

"She worked with me on *Blood Wars* for years. She was terrific at keeping the production on schedule and on budget. Her last project didn't work out, which I feel guilty about, but she was an excellent member of my production team."

"Why do you feel guilty?" Kim asked. There was concern in her eyes and worry in her expression.

Marenda shrugged. "I suggested she approach the producer, Aiden O'Bryan. He had a new project I thought had tremendous potential. I knew Pam needed to keep her life as stable as possible, and she wanted continuity, which is hard in this business. I thought Aiden's new show would be a hit and score a long-term run, giving her both." She glanced across the room to where Aiden was standing, now talking to a group of older men wearing expensive suits. Her gaze hardened. "Something happened between them, though, and Aiden let her go. I've recommended Pam for several other positions, but I don't think she's worked since. That's tough when you're a single mom."

Feeling absolutely no remorse at throwing Aiden under the bus, Christy said, "Aiden wasn't hesitant about telling me Pam wanted more than a working relationship with him and that he was concerned she'd accuse him of sexual improprieties when he turned her down."

If he turned her down. The Pam I remember was hot.

Kim turned a searching look at the cat. His brows raised, Sledge mouthed, *The Pam I remember?*

Marenda, unaware, shook her head as she continued to talk. "That's Aiden and Pam in a nutshell. Aiden has always been ultra cautious about how he acts with his employees, to the point of being cold and standoffish. Pam..." She pursed her lips and shook her head again. "Pam was beautiful, and men buzzed around her like she was an exotic flower. She let them, but she was always looking for a certain man—the right man."

She enjoyed pitting guys one against the other.

Christy looked sharply at the cat, who looked back apologetically. Sledge shook his head. There was amusement in his eyes. Christy guessed he figured Frank would be in a lot of trouble after the party was over.

He was right. Frank had claimed he hardly remembered Pam

Muir. Evidently, that was an untruth. Christy wondered how many others he had uttered about the curvy, sexy, gorgeous, Pam Muir.

Kim patted Stormy and the cat began to purr. "It's okay, kitty," she said, making Marenda raise her eyebrows in question.

"I know women like this Pam Muir," Kim said, her hand moving rhythmically along Stormy's back from head to tail. "They're so attractive that all kinds of men, a lot of them just after sex, chase after them, but what they really want is a man to take care of them."

Marenda considered this, then shook her head. "She didn't want to be taken care of herself. She wanted someone to take care of her little boy. It was terribly important to her. There was almost a desperation in the way she cycled through the men around her."

"She and the father split?" Kim asked.

Marenda nodded. "Long before she became part of my team. I think he dumped her while she was still pregnant. She never told me who he was, just that he wasn't in the picture anymore."

"When did you meet her?" Christy asked.

Marenda waved a hand. "When she first came off maternity leave. Her old job had disappeared—I think the company folded, if I remember correctly—so she was looking for work. You know, all the years I've known her, she's been searching for a blond, blue-eyed man." She shrugged. "Carson, her little boy, was a tow-head when he was small. His hair darkened as he grew, but I suspect his father must have been a blond, because Pam herself had such dark hair."

I am not the kid's father!

Kim's eyes popped open wide, and she stopped patting the cat, her hand hovering over his shoulders. Stormy opened pleasure-slitted eyes and meowed accusingly. Kim started patting him again.

Sledge's brows climbed toward his hairline. "Then who is?"

"That's the question," Christy said.

Marenda blinked several times and looked from one to the other. "What question?"

"We were wondering who Carson's father might have been," Kim said. She gestured toward Aiden O'Bryan with her head. "Lots of men could have been the dad, even Aiden. His hair must have been very blond when he was younger."

Marenda shook her head. "The dad wasn't in the film industry. I don't remember exactly where she worked before Carson was born, but I think the company was in product development. When I hired her as an administrative assistant, she was new to the film business, but the job was generic. She had to do the bookkeeping, manage the schedule, keep my appointments in line. These are transferable skills, not industry-specific ones."

Mitch, having circled the room, schmoozing with his guests, joined them. "Marenda!" he said. "So glad you could come." He leaned in, performing ritual air kisses on both cheeks. "SledgeHammer will have a new record coming out in May and they'll need a video."

Sledge's eyes narrowed to slits. "We will? News to me."

Mitch dismissed Sledge's gripe with an airy wave of his hand. "You told me you had a song collection ready for the next album."

"I do, but—"

Are those the songs we wrote over the summer?

"Hammer's back now. Time to lay down the new album so that it's out while your show is going on."

"We can promote the old one," Sledge said through gritted teeth.

"New's better," Mitch said. He turned to Marenda. "What's your schedule like in the next couple of months? I want something that's top-notch." He beamed. "SledgeHammer is about to go up to the next level."

Hey! I helped write the songs. Can I be in the video?

Sledge looked down at the cat in his arms, then over at Christy. He began to laugh. Turning to Marenda, he said, "You have no idea what you're getting into."

CHAPTER 23

Since neither Marenda nor Mitch had any idea that the essence of Frank Jamieson was rooming with Stormy the Cat, Sledge's announcement pushed the conversation away from Pam Muir and it never returned.

The evening proved to be much more fun than Christy had expected. The food was excellent—not unexpected with Kim managing the menu—but the big surprise was that Mitch was an excellent host. Conversation over dinner never lagged, and there was much laughter as everyone joined in. It was late by the time the festivities broke up, but even so, Christy didn't feel tired.

Nor did Frank. He was riding a high and wanted to talk as Roy guided the car through the dark and relatively quiet Vancouver streets. Stormy, however, had had enough of people for the moment and just wanted to curl up in the back seat and go to sleep. The result was a rather chaotic conversation, punctuated by deep yawns and pauses when Frank's voice simply stopped, only to suddenly start up again a few moments later.

As it turned out, Frank had been disappointed to discover that

Sledge and Kim were the only other attendees able to hear his mindspeak. He admitted that he'd filled them in on Pam's attempt to scam the Trust. To his satisfaction, both had expressed a willingness to help. At that point, there'd been a pause, and when Frank's voice spoke again, it was on a different subject. Christy didn't attempt to guide him back to the question of Sledge and Kim. She wasn't sure what either could do, though she appreciated their offer.

The next day, she and Roy had a videoconference with Quinn. It was lunchtime in Vancouver, after three in Toronto. Quinn's meetings for the day had ended and he was hopeful he'd soon be able to return home. They talked a little about the documentary, then he asked, "How was the party?"

"The food was delicious, Mitch behaved himself, and Sledge did an impromptu concert, which made Kim mad at Mitch," Christy said.

On the other side of the country, Quinn laughed. "Why was Kim angry at Mitch?"

"According to Frank, she believed Sledge should have a chance to just blend in and enjoy himself," Roy said. He shook his head. "Truth is, I think Sledge was quite happy taking the stage. He turned it into a sing-along and had a houseful of high-powered movers and shakers bellowing out his songs as if they were SledgeHammer super fans at a stadium concert."

Christy laughed. "It was fun. The night ended with everyone on an adrenaline high."

"Well, and maybe a few other things," Roy said.

I missed the concert. The cat is a killjoy.

Stormy had slipped away from Mitch's home theater where the concert was taking place and found a quieter spot to have a snooze. Frank complained about it all morning.

"I'm sorry I missed it," Quinn said. He raised his eyebrows. "Find out anything interesting?"

"Interesting, yes. Helpful, maybe. Definitive, no," Christy said.

Quinn laughed. "Okay. I think I need more details, like who talked to whom?"

"I talked to Aiden O'Bryan and Marenda Riddle..."

I talked to Marenda too. So did Kim and Sledge.

Christy ignored Frank and, with a glance at Roy, added, "Your dad talked to Landon Olynuk."

"I don't think Olynuk is the father," Roy said. "He might be her killer, though."

"Whoa," Quinn said. "What makes you think that?"

Roy shrugged. "She was blackmailing him."

Quinn shook his head. "I checked out his company, Everything Electronics. It's one of the top developers of video games in North America. They currently have four titles in the top ten most popular games and their revenues are in the billions. Even if Pam was milking him for some cash, I think the guy's rich enough that the amount she was demanding wouldn't put a dent in his annual income. What makes you think she was blackmailing him? Did he admit it flat out?"

"No. He said he was funding a game she was developing."

"He could have been doing exactly that," Quinn said.

Roy gave his son a skeptical look. "Yeah, right. The woman who accused him of sexual misconduct and got him fired for it. Why would he want to help her if he didn't have to? Unless she made it clear that if he didn't she'd bring up that old charge."

"He has a lot more to lose now than he did all those years ago," Christy murmured thoughtfully.

"Okay," Quinn said, "I'll give you that. If his transgression came out, it would spread through social media like wildfire. His sales could tank, he might even have to step back from his company. Probably easier to pay up than to risk exposure."

"And safer," Christy said. "The extortion makes him a solid suspect for Pam's murder, but not for being the father of her child."

"What about the other guy, Aiden O'Bryan?" Quinn asked.

"He wasn't the father, either," Christy said. "But then, we'd already assumed that. Turns out, though, he was the reason Pam started her blackmailing activities."

Quinn raised his brows. "Because he fired her?"

"Because he made certain she couldn't get another job in the film industry. I think she needed money and when she realized she was no longer employable, she figured out a way to get it."

"Ronald Gallagher, the dean, basically admitted she was blackmailing him," Roy said, rubbing his chin thoughtfully.

"And then there was the supposed car loan Theo Perkins provided her with," Christy said, nodding. "O'Bryan claimed they came to an agreement when he fired her. The deal was, he wouldn't talk about why he was letting her go, as long as she didn't make accusations against him. I think she knew she wouldn't get anything out of him, but he put the idea into her head, and she decided to give it a try."

"Could be," Quinn said.

"The interesting thing about O'Bryan is that he didn't have any problem telling me all about Pam's attempt to coerce him into a relationship."

Quinn raised his brows. "You think he might be the killer?"

She nodded. "He must know she's dead. Why else would he feel confident enough to break their agreement? Since Patterson hasn't identified Pam as the first murder victim of the year, how would he know, unless he was involved in her death?"

"Possibly," Quinn said. "But information like that has a way of getting around. Maybe he heard it somewhere other than through the cops."

"Maybe, but O'Bryan is interesting for another reason. He's fair-haired and must have been blond as a kid."

"And that's relevant how?" Quinn asked.

Christy smiled triumphantly and told him what Marenda Riddle had said about Pam's preoccupation with blond men and the reason for it.

I am not the kid's father.

Roy and Christy ignored the grumpy comment. Quinn didn't hear it.

Roy said, "So we're looking for a man whose hair is blond or maybe sandy brown in color. That lets out Landon Olynuk and Ronald Gallagher, the dean. Both have very dark hair."

Christy nodded. "Marenda had another bit of information. She said she hired Pam when her maternity leave ended, because the company where Pam worked before the baby was born had gone of business." She looked at Roy and then at Quinn. "I think the man we're looking for was employed at the same company and had blond, or light brown hair. For some reason, Pam didn't want to acknowledge him as the father of her child. That's why she was searching for a man with the right coloring as a stepdad for her son. She didn't want people to guess he wasn't the boy's biological father."

"Isaac Holley has sandy blond hair," Quinn said, then he shook his head. "But Jeremiah Brownrigg doesn't."

"He did in *Blood Wars*," Roy said.

"A dye job," Quinn said.

Roy nodded. "A pretty good one, too. Looked natural in the pictures I found."

Quinn frowned. "You think she bought into Brownrigg being a blond, then dumped him when she discovered he wasn't?"

Roy shrugged. "As good a reason as any. Maybe better than her excuse that she wanted to stay in Vancouver for her kid and her career."

"Maybe," Quinn said. He sounded thoughtful. "Why would a woman want to hide her child from his biological father?"

Pam was possessive.

"Was she?" Christy looked at the cat skeptically. "Another interesting detail about a woman you hardly knew."

"Christy?" said Quinn through the screen.

"Sorry. Frank just said Pam was possessive. I don't think that was her reason, but I suppose, if the father was powerful or well-known, she might have been afraid he would take the boy away from her." She shrugged. "Then again, she might have disliked the man for some reason and not wanted him to influence her child. There are lots of reasons a woman might be reluctant to allow her child to have a relationship with his biological father."

"Including abuse," Roy said.

"Or maybe she became pregnant through artificial insemination and didn't want her kid asking questions about who his father was," Quinn suggested.

Roy brightened. "Now that adds an interesting dimension. Isn't the identity of sperm donors secret?"

"It was at one point," Quinn said. "These days, clinics have to keep a sibling registry that includes the father's identity. Too many chances of children who are close relatives becoming involved with each other."

"Isn't artificial insemination expensive?" Christy asked.

Quinn nodded.

"I doubt that was the route Pam took." She paused then said, "Let's find the name of the company Pam worked for before the baby was born. If there's nothing there, then we move on and look at other possibilities. But maybe we'll get lucky."

The men nodded.

"I'll see what I can dig up," Quinn said.

Christy shot him a relieved smile. "Great. In the meantime, I'll update Patterson and see if she has any information we can use."

Quinn's phone beeped and he glanced away to check it. "Sorry. I've got to take this."

She nodded. "Talk to you tomorrow."

～

The next day, Christy walked into the bare-bones diner near Patterson's station. She was wearing jeans, flat-soled suede boots lined with lamb's wool, and a dark blue fleece jacket over a cowl neck cashmere sweater in a rich burgundy color. The outfit was designed to look casual and be comfortable in the damp cold of a Vancouver winter, but it was also stylish and fit her perfectly. As she crossed the room to the booth Patterson had staked out, she drew the gazes of cops clustered around the small tables enjoying a cup of coffee and shooting the breeze with their associates.

As usual, Patterson sat with her back to the wall and her eyes on the doorway. Like Christy, she was dressed for the cold in a high-necked sweater. Her long hair was braided and twisted into a knot at her nape. She had a cup in front of her filled with coffee, indicating she'd been here for a while. Opposite her, on the other side of the table, was a menu in a brown plasticized folder. Christy took the chair in front of the menu, which she pushed aside. She wasn't here to eat.

"You have something for me?" Patterson said.

Christy resisted the urge to say, 'And it's good to see you too, Detective.' Instead, she nodded. There was an urgency in the way Patterson asked her question that had Christy wondering if the detective had other critical interviews she needed to be doing.

"I—" She broke off as a server holding a pot of coffee stopped by. The woman offered Patterson a refill, took Christy's order for a cup of coffee, and disappeared. When they were alone again, Patterson raised her brows and waited.

Christy took a deep breath. She had information to give to Patterson, but she also wanted information in return. "As you know, Pam

Muir claimed to be married to Frank. She also maintained that Frank was the father of her son."

Patterson nodded.

"Before she died, she didn't provide proof of any kind for either of those assertions. I decided I'd continue to look into the possibility that Frank might have been the boy's father, even though I believe it to be quite unlikely. Then I had a visit from her parents a few days ago."

"The Muirs are very angry people," Patterson murmured.

Christy nodded. "They loved their daughter and believed in her—still believe in her. She told them the boy was Frank's, so for them he is. They want the child acknowledged as the Jamieson heir. It was Pam's project and now it's theirs."

Patterson nodded, then took a moment to scan the room. "I was aware of this. Mrs. Jamieson, why are you here?"

Patterson was rarely abrupt. She tended to listen, probe gently, and coax information from people as they talked in an unguarded way. Whatever it was, something was nagging at her. Time to get to the point. "I need to find out who the real father was. Roy and Quinn and I have been doing some digging. We've found a number of people he probably wasn't, but there's a hole in her life no one seems to know much about, and I think the father can be found there."

Patterson studied her. "Okay. What's the timeline for this hole?"

Their server dropped by at that point with a mug of coffee for Christy, who waited until the woman was gone before she said, "Twelve to fourteen years ago, she had a job in a company that manufactures things. I think the father might have worked for that company or have been involved with it in some way. I think that's where she met him and for some reason has kept his son secret ever since."

Patterson raised her coffee cup and stared at Christy over the edge. "Why would you think that?"

"Because the boy is fair-haired and she's been dating blond or light-haired men ever since he was born. I think she was searching for a man who looked like her son, so people would assume he was the child's biological father."

Patterson sipped her coffee. "Maybe she just preferred blonds."

Christy wrapped her hands around her mug. "I don't think she had a preference. The men we know she dated before she became pregnant were dark-haired. One person I talked to described the way she pursued blond men as almost desperate. That person also said Pam ignored dark-haired men who came on to her."

Patterson put her cup back on the table and tapped her finger on the side as she considered Christy's comments. "It's possible. I suppose you want the name of the company she worked for."

Christy nodded. "Fourteen years is a long time ago. If the Muirs know it, they won't tell me and no one else remembers. The only clue I have is that the company seems to have gone out of business before she returned from maternity leave, which was why she ended up working in the film industry. She needed a new job and a position was available."

"Okay. I don't have anything now, but if I find something out, I'll let you know."

"Thank you." Christy knew that was the best Patterson could do and she trusted the detective to follow through on her promise.

Patterson nodded, scanning the room again. Apparently satisfied, she brought her attention back to Christy, who said, "While we were searching for the father, we noticed a pattern I think might be relevant to your investigation."

Patterson raised her brows, lifting her coffee cup to her mouth as she waited for Christy to continue.

"I think Pam was blackmailing three very powerful men."

Patterson sat up straight. Her cup landed on the tabletop with a thump. "Who are we talking about?"

"Landon Olynuk, who owns Everything Electronic. Theodore

Perkins, the regional vice president at the Bank of Southern Ontario, and Ronald Gallagher, the provost at EBU."

Expression incredulous, Patterson said, "Seriously?"

Christy nodded. "I think she may have also tried to blackmail Aiden O'Bryan, the TV producer who fired her."

Patterson shook her head. "And you know this because…"

Christy laughed. "They told me."

"Of course they did," Patterson muttered. "Okay, what exactly did they say?"

"Landon Olynuk claimed she came to him with an idea for a new video game and he was funding the development. Theo Perkins said he'd helped her with a car loan. Ron Gallagher admitted nothing, but he arranged to meet Roy at six-thirty in the morning when no one was around. He then admitted Pam wanted to have a relationship with him."

Patterson said, "The car loan and the development money could have been the real reasons money changed hands. The provost never admitted anything. Roy's assumption was pure speculation—which he's very good at."

"Could be, but Olynuk was a professor at EBU and Pam was his student. She took him before an internal ethics committee and claimed sexual harassment against him. There wasn't enough proof to have him charged, but he was fired from his job. She also claimed sexual impropriety against Ronald Gallagher, but this time it didn't stick. Gallagher had been at EBU when she made the accusation against Olynuk. He knew what she was capable of, so he took precautions. Still, he has a more senior position now and social attitudes to sexual improprieties have changed. He wouldn't want even the hint of a scandal like that in his past, true or not."

Patterson lifted her hand to her face, touching the scar that ran down the side of her jaw. Her expression was thoughtful. Christy took heart and continued.

"Theo Perkins was involved with Pam when she worked as a summer intern for him. He claims it was flirting and kisses, but nothing more. When he realized rumors were starting to spread about them, he called a halt, but Pam wouldn't let go. She walked into the wife's office and told her about his infidelity in front of her colleagues, causing the woman to divorce Theo. He was a regional loans manager then. Now he's a senior vice president. I don't think he wants people at head office to know he was stupid enough to get involved with an employee who was also the daughter of one of the company's bank managers."

Having delivered her information and laid out her theories, Christy sipped her coffee and waited while Patterson considered. She rubbed the scar, a sure sign she was thinking deeply. Finally, she shrugged. "Reputation can be a powerful motivator. Okay, I'll investigate these guys. Thanks for the tip."

"There's one other man I think you should check out—Aiden O'Bryan."

"Why? O'Bryan was the guy who fired her and resisted her extortion, wasn't he? Why look at him?"

"Because he and Pam had an agreement that he wouldn't badmouth her and she wouldn't accuse him of sexual misconduct."

Patterson shrugged. "So?"

"He told me all about her reputation for sleeping around, about her attempt to proposition him, then her threat to destroy his reputation, and his decision to fire her."

Patterson's eyes gleamed with amusement. "You have a way of coaxing secrets out of people, Mrs. Jamieson. Maybe the guy was just smitten with big eyes and a pretty face and was doing a little bragging."

Christy blushed at the comment, but she raised her brows, refusing to let it derail her. "Or maybe he knew Pam Muir was dead and he no longer had to worry about their little agreement."

Patterson sucked in her breath. "Maybe. Okay, I'll add him to my list."

Voices sounded as a group of men crowded through the door together. Patterson glanced over and swore. Christy followed her gaze and saw that one of the men was the second policeman who had come to the Trust's offices to interview her. What was his name? Jones or something, she thought.

As soon as he noticed Patterson, he detached himself from the group and strode across the room. His eyes were narrowed and his mouth pursed. He stopped at the edge of the booth and pointed to Christy, though he spoke to Patterson. "I thought you said she wasn't a suspect."

"She's not," Patterson said.

Jones raised his brows and nodded his head aggressively. "Why is she here then?"

Christy pushed back her chair. "I'm looking for the father of Pam Muir's son. Along the way, I found out some interesting things that might help you find her murderer." As she stood, she smiled at Jones' disapproving and, yes, disbelieving, expression. "Maybe if you're polite to Detective Patterson, she'll fill you in."

She dropped some bills on the table and walked away without a backward glance.

CHAPTER 24

Christy looked at the reminder she'd put into her day planner and frowned. She picked up her phone and dialed Isabelle Pascoe's extension. "Isabelle, have you heard anything from Mallory Tait on the status of the Muirs' claim?"

"Not a thing. I have a note to phone her this morning to check in."

"Do that," Christy said. "Let me know what she says."

"Of course," Isabelle replied.

Christy tapped her desk with her pen and stared at her screen. It had been a week since the Muirs came to the Trust demanding their grandson be instated as a Jamieson heir. Plenty of time for them to provide the boy's birth certificate and time, as well, for him to be DNA tested, if they'd agreed to the procedure. Mallory should have been in contact before now.

Christy shrugged. Whatever the status of the claim, Isabelle would find out when she talked to Mallory. In the meantime, her task this morning was to create a file on Pam Muir. In it, she'd gather all of the information they'd discovered so far. None of it proved Frank wasn't Carson Muir's father, but then, nothing proved he was, either. The

DNA test would be a key piece of evidence and should settle the matter, but she couldn't shake an uneasy feeling that the Muirs wouldn't give up easily. It was best to be prepared for all contingencies.

She was working on that document when Isabelle walked into her office and flopped down onto one of her visitor chairs. Christy looked up in surprise. "Isabelle, what's the matter?"

Frowning, Isabelle shook her head as if she didn't quite believe what she was about to say. "Mallory Tait has taken a leave of absence from McCullagh, McCullagh, and Walker. Her clients have been distributed to other lawyers in the firm. The Trust has been assigned Nolan Walker."

Christy had met Nolan Walker several times over the previous few months. He was silver-haired, wore perfectly cut, expensive suits, and had a smooth, polished manner. "I think we're in safe hands. Did you happen to speak to him?"

Isabelle shook her head. "He was in a meeting when I called. The secretary promised to have him contact me as soon as he was able."

Christy drummed her fingers on the desk as she considered next steps. "Did they tell you why Mallory requested a leave of absence? She isn't ill, is she?"

"No, it definitely wasn't health related. I asked the same question and I was told she's fine. But when I followed up with the obvious question—then why?—her secretary became cagey. She said it was a personal matter and wouldn't say anything else."

"Were you told when she'd return?"

Isabelle shook her head.

Sitting back, Christy thought about that for a minute. Mallory's sudden departure didn't make any sense to her, but there was nothing she could do about it for now. "Okay, I'm going to assume we'll be working with Nolan Walker while we sort out the Muirs' claim. I think it's best for me to talk to him to see what he knows about the situation and how he thinks we should handle it."

Isabelle nodded. "Good idea. I'll put him through to you when he calls."

Christy stared at her as she thought over that option. Finally, she said, "No, I prefer a face-to-face conversation." Nolan Walker was old school. Smooth and charming, he was lovely to meet on a social basis, but there was a hint of paternalism in his manner that she thought would come out in a business situation. "I want to know we can work together."

Isabelle tilted her head. "Would you like me to set up a meeting? Or is that something you'd rather do as part of your testing process?"

Christy smiled. "Part of the process. Let's see how he reacts when Christy Jamieson calls him."

"You don't think he was in a meeting."

Christy said, "Mallory's departure must be recent, so everyone assigned her cases is probably scrambling right now trying to come up to speed, Nolan Walker included."

Isabelle stood. "I'll leave you to it, then."

When Isabelle left, Christy paused for a moment to ask herself why she felt so uneasy about the change in representation. Was it because she didn't like the idea of being passed off to another lawyer? Or was it because the change was happening in the middle of the contentious Muir case? Then again, was it Nolan Walker himself? He was a full partner in McCullagh, McCullagh, and Walker, and he'd worked with Trevor McCullagh for years. Yet, when Trevor was arranging legal representation for the Trust he'd gone to Mallory Tait, not Nolan Walker. Trevor was one of the Jamieson trustees and she had faith in his judgment. Was Nolan more talk than walk?

She drummed her fingers on the desktop for a moment, then shrugged and picked up the phone.

"McCullagh, McCullagh, and Walker. Nolan Walker's line. How may I help you?" a pleasing female voice said.

"Nolan Walker, please," Christy replied.

"Who may I say is calling?"

Christy swiveled her chair and stared out the window at the North Shore Mountains. "Christy Jamieson."

"One moment, Mrs. Jamieson."

Less than thirty seconds later, Christy heard Nolan Walker's melodious tones in her ear. "Mrs. Jamieson, a pleasure to speak to you." There was warmth in his voice, but Christy wasn't sure if it was real or not.

"And to you," she replied. "I understand we'll be working together in the future."

"Yes." Nolan's voice lowered, and a distinctly soothing note crept into it. "I assure you we'll sort out this nasty Muir business. I wouldn't worry about it."

Christy wondered if he'd have told a man not to worry about an issue that could have serious personal and financial repercussions. She doubted it and she certainly didn't want to leave him with the impression she was willing to accept it. "But I am worried about it, Nolan. I want the issue resolved. I'd like to meet with you to discuss strategies. Are you free this morning?"

"I'm free right now. I'd be happy to go over the details with you." The prompt response was issued in that annoying warm soothing tone.

"No. I'd like to meet face to face. At the Cypress View Restaurant, in say, an hour?" Choosing a neutral location, neither her office nor his, was deliberate. The restaurant was closer to her location than his, allowing Christy to imply they were equals in this partnership, but that she had no intention of letting him think he had the upper hand.

There was a pause, then Walker said crisply, "Very well. In one hour."

Christy smiled when she put down the phone.

She was two minutes late. That too was deliberate. Not long enough to be rude, but enough for her to arrive after him if he was on time.

He was. He rose as she crossed the dining room. The table was by the window and had a spectacular view of the snow-covered peak that gave the restaurant its name. She smiled warmly, holding out her hand as she neared. They shook and settled opposite each other. Nolan gestured to the beaker of coffee on the table and asked her if she'd like a cup.

Christy nodded. As she watched him pour, she said, "Thank you for meeting me this morning."

Nolan nodded and smiled. "My pleasure."

"I was surprised to learn Mallory has taken a leave of absence." Christy picked up her cup. "I've been working closely with her on Pamela Muir's allegation that her son is a Jamieson. She gave me no indication she was planning to take time off." Sipping her coffee, Christy watched Nolan fiddle with the handle of his cup.

"I believe her decision was quite sudden," he said.

He spoke slowly, almost cautiously. She had a sense he'd chosen his words carefully.

More briskly, he said, "Now, about the Muirs. They have not provided the required birth certificate for their grandson Carson. Nor have they yet agreed to a DNA test for the boy." He smiled at Christy in a way that was meant to inspire confidence. "I believe they will do neither of these things. I think our best strategy is to do nothing—"

"And wait for the problem to go away?" Christy said. She shook her head. "No, that's not what we're going to do."

He frowned.

She said impatiently, "You know that Pam Muir was murdered, don't you?"

He froze, a sudden moment of stillness that had Christy narrowing her eyes. "Yes," he said. "What has that to do with the grandparents' demands?"

"It's an active case, the first murder of the year in Vancouver. When the police find out who killed Pam and make an arrest, the media will jump on it. They'll rehash everything she was doing before her death, including her claim she was Frank Jamieson's wife and he was the father of her child."

"Mrs. Jamieson, you're overreacting." Nolan's tone was smooth and unctuous, designed to soothe. It didn't work.

Christy gave him a perfunctory smile and said, "No, I'm not. We need to prove the boy is not Frank's son and we have to find out who the father actually was."

Nolan studied her for a minute. When he spoke again, his voice was still smooth, but the smug note was gone. "DNA testing will prove your husband wasn't the father."

"Only if the boy submits to a DNA test," Christy said impatiently.

Nolan smiled. "I'm sure the family will agree to it."

The avuncular smile had Christy fuming. "Mallory wasn't as confident as you are. And she knew Pam Muir. I expect—" She frowned as Walker froze again. "What are you not telling me, Nolan?"

He picked up his coffee cup and sipped. Giving himself time, Christy thought, and waited.

He put the cup back into the saucer with a sharp, determined movement, his decision made. "Mallory Tait has been designated a person of interest in the death of Pam Muir. She's being questioned by the police as we speak."

It was Christy's turn to use her coffee cup to give herself a moment to order her thoughts. She sipped as she scrutinized Nolan's face. Lowering the cup, she said, "Why do the police suspect her?"

Nolan Walker's expression indicated an internal fight as he decided whether to provide her with more details. In the end, he said reluctantly, "Pam Muir was blackmailing her."

"My question is, what would Pam Muir possibly know about Mallory Tait that she could use to blackmail her? Nolan Walker—annoying man!—refused to tell me."

On the screen of her tablet, Quinn chuckled. It was late and around Christy the house was quiet, with Noelle sound asleep in her room. She should have been enjoying a quiet conversation with Quinn and mellowing out from her day. Instead, she was still steaming from her conversation with Nolan Walker.

"We need to figure out how their lives intersected," he said. "Didn't you tell me Mallory said she'd known Pam a long time ago?"

Christy thought back. "I think she said Pam was a friend of a friend and that she didn't know her well." She sighed. "That's why I was so surprised when Walker announced Pam was blackmailing Mallory. How do you blackmail a friend of a friend?"

"By being a confidant of the friend who was Mallory's friend," Quinn said.

Christy sucked in her breath. "A man!"

Quinn nodded. "That's my thought. Pam Muir either dated a man Mallory once dated or Mallory took the man away from Pam."

"Okay, but dating a guy isn't a crime. What would Mallory have to hide that would make her vulnerable to blackmail?"

Quinn shrugged. "Maybe the guy was married, or someone well-known. Or both."

"Like Fredrick Jarvis," Christy murmured, and Quinn nodded. Jarvis had been a prominent politician whose death exposed a complex web of relationships he'd hidden throughout his public life.

"But why would Mallory be so worried about revealing she'd had a relationship with a married man years ago that she'd allow herself to be blackmailed?"

"What if she slept with him to get ahead? Or to pass her bar exam?

Or if he was an opposing council and she leaked confidential information to him?" Quinn suggested.

"So, we're looking for another lawyer? Or perhaps one of her law professors?"

"Could be."

Christy thought about that. "But... How would Pam have become involved with the man, then?"

Quinn considered that. "If it was another lawyer, he might have been a consultant providing legal advice on one of the shows she worked on. Or he could have been the lawyer for the production company. Something like that."

"Could be." But somehow, that didn't seem to be right. If Pam met the guy when she was working on *Blood Wars,* why would Mallory's name come up?

"From your expression and the enthusiasm in your voice, I can see I haven't persuaded you."

Quinn was smiling ruefully, and Christy shook her head. "I wish Trevor was here. I could just ask him what was going on."

"You could call him," Quinn said.

"No," Christy said firmly. "He and Ellen are on holiday and I'm not going to bother them. We'll have to find the reason ourselves."

"I'll do some digging, then," Quinn said. "Once we have more information, the answer might pop right up."

Christy smiled at him. "I hope so. In the meantime, I'll see if I can get in touch with Mallory. There hasn't been an announcement of her arrest, so Patterson may just be questioning her."

But Mallory Tait wasn't answering her personal number when Christy tried calling her the next morning. Nor did she answer in the afternoon. It wasn't until Christy's last attempt, after she'd cleared the dinner dishes away and Noelle was watching a favorite TV show before bed, that she picked up.

"Are you okay?" Christy asked.

"They haven't arrested me yet, if that's what you mean." Mallory sounded tired and the crisp, decisive note usually in her voice was absent.

"Why do they suspect you?"

It was an abrupt question and intrusive. Christy wasn't surprised when Mallory said, "Mrs. Jamieson, I don't think this is your problem."

"You're right," Christy said. "It's not, but Pam Muir is. She lied and had a warped moral compass, but she was smart, and she understood what made people vulnerable. What did she know about you?"

Mallory sighed and said, "I was young and stupid." She rallied a bit and added, "And that's all I'm going to tell you, Mrs. Jamieson."

Young and stupid. Well, that provided a timeline of sorts. "What made the police decide to focus on you?"

Another sigh came through the phone line, then Mallory said, "They found out Pam was blackmailing several people, so they requested her parents allow them to search her personal effects. The Muirs agreed and the cops discovered a journal in which she kept detailed records about the people she was extorting, including payments. Once they had that information, they accessed her bank records, which corroborated the journal entries."

"And they found your name there," Christy said, stating a fact, not asking a question.

Mallory hesitated, then said, "Yes."

"Did the journal include the reason behind the blackmail?"

Mallory laughed. The sound was bitter, not happy. "Are you worried she itemized her scheme to have herself and her son made recipients of the Jamieson Trust?"

"I was hoping," Christy said. "If she outlined the scheme on paper, it would be clear her claim wasn't true."

"Sorry. I can't help you on that. Patterson only told me what the cops had on me. I have no idea who the other people were she targeted, or what she knew about them."

"They wanted to keep you in the dark so you'd confess."

"I didn't kill Pam Muir. I hated her, I wished she'd go away, but I didn't kill her." There was exhaustion in Mallory's voice, but not defeat and her statement rang true.

"What happens now?" Christy asked.

"I go to bed. I get a good night's sleep. In the morning I hire the best defense lawyer in Vancouver. I'm still a person of interest, but I'm not under arrest and I intend to keep it that way."

"Is there anything I can do to help?" Christy asked.

"Thank you, Mrs. Jamieson, but no. I realize you've had some success finding murderers in the past, but this case is complicated and figuring it out is best left to the professionals."

Staring across her table into the darkness beyond her kitchen window, Christy thought with wry amusement that she'd just been put firmly in her place by a woman who probably figured she'd hit rock bottom. "I'll wish you the best then."

"Thanks," Mallory said. "Good night, Mrs. Jamieson."

The line went dead. Christy sat for a minute staring out into the darkness, thinking about a young and stupid Mallory Tait and how her life might have intersected with Pam Muir's.

Quinn was right. It had to have been over a man and very probably sex had come into the equation. Young and stupid. When was that? Most likely before she started with McCullagh, McCullagh, and Walker.

Time to do a little research into Mallory Tait's career.

CHAPTER 25

Christy waited until Noelle was safely tucked up in bed with her lights out before she called Quinn. "Hi. Do you have time to talk?"

"Always," he said. "What's up?"

"I finally got hold of Mallory Tait. She didn't give me much, but I may have the timing for whatever happened that Pam was blackmailing her about." Curled up on the sofa, with Quinn's reassuring features on the iPad screen, she felt better than she had when Mallory abruptly dismissed her earlier that evening.

As usual, Quinn had been busy. "Good," he said. "I constructed a basic career outline for her. Let's see if we can pinpoint the causal incident."

Christy heard Mallory's voice in her head, the hint of remorse, perhaps even of shame. "Whatever happened, it goes way back. Mallory referred herself as 'young and stupid'. My take is that something happened early on in her career."

There was a minute of silence as Quinn checked his notes, then he said, "Crown vs Austin Tohme and Future Pharmaceutical Solutions,

Inc., also called FPS. She was an articling student at the firm representing Tohme."

Christy sat up. Her instinct was telling her they were on the right path. "When was the trial?"

Quinn gazed off to the side of the screen. He must have been reviewing a document, for after a minute he said, "Tohme was arrested and charged eleven years ago. The trial took place over four years later, which is odd. Hang on a sec while I see if I can find out why the delay."

She heard the clatter of computer keys being struck, then quiet broken by the odd tap. "Well, that's interesting. The initial trial date was set for two years after his arrest, but his lawyers kept finding reasons for postponing the trial."

"Why would they do that?" Christy asked. "It doesn't make sense to me."

On the other side of the country, Quinn smiled rather grimly. "His law team must have thought they were going to lose the case. Tohme was out on bail for most of the time. They were probably maximizing his freedom while they desperately searched for a loophole that would get him off."

Christy did some quick math in her head. "Carson Muir is eleven years old, which means Pam must have been pregnant when the investigation into FPS and Tohme was going on. I wonder if she knew him?"

Quinn raised his brows. "It's possible she was employed by FPS. Weren't her parents vague about where she worked before Carson was born?"

"Yeah, they were."

"Don't you think that's odd?" Quinn asked. "Parents usually pay attention to where their kids work. Unless Pam was somehow involved with the case, why would they want to hide it?"

Christy considered that. "Maybe it was because of what the investigation was about? Did the information you found on Mallory provide any details?"

"The reference was in an article on her. She said the case helped her decide what form of law she wanted to specialize in."

"Do you know any of the details?" Christy asked.

"I'm doing a quick search now."

Christy watched him frown at his screen, then he whistled. "FPS was developing a new drug they claimed would cure cerebral palsy. The initial trials showed amazing results, and the company's shares skyrocketed. But the fantastic results failed to pass peer review once the data was published. Later, it came out that the company falsified the results. Austin Tohme, who was the head of research, was charged with fraud and insider trading. He wasn't the only one. The full executive team was as well. As a result of the scandal, the company went out of business not long after the arrests were made."

"Insider trading? How does that fit with falsifying test results? What exactly did they do?"

Quinn was reading his screen again, then he said, "Tohme and other members of the executive team were awarded stock options in lieu of an annual bonus. When the initial results for the drug were so positive, they used the information to convince a great many people to invest in the company, running up the stock price. Just days before the peer review was released, they each exercised their options, selling the stock at a huge profit."

"Did Tohme and the others lose the case?"

Quinn nodded. "Tohme and each member of the executive team were convicted and sentenced to jail."

Excitement had Christy's heart beating faster. "I bet FPS was the company Pam worked for. She wasn't mentioned as one of the people involved, was she?"

Quinn did some more quick digging, then shook his head. "I can't find any connection." He looked up, his gaze meeting Christy's through the screen. "It's not surprising. She was only a couple of years out of university. Even if she worked on the project in some capacity, her position would have been a junior one."

Christy tapped her chin. "She might have used her computer expertise, or perhaps the accounting skills she developed working for the bank. Her position could have been in an organizational department."

Quinn nodded. "Whatever her role, it's unlikely the prosecutors were interested in her. It was the higher-ups who put the scam together they were after."

"So, she wasn't involved in the trial. Then how did she meet Mallory and discover a secret big enough that Mallory would allow herself to be blackmailed?"

"That brings us back to what it was Mallory did. I think it has to be something to do with the people involved in the trial," he said.

"And it probably had something to do with her career." Christy thought about the mistakes a young law student might make on her first big case. "Maybe she leaked confidential information to the press, or perhaps to the prosecution for some reason?"

"Or maybe she failed to produce an important bit of case law that might have kept Austin Tohme from going to jail?" Quinn suggested, though his expression said he thought this was a long shot.

Christy shook her head. "Why would she mention it in an interview, then? The firm she worked for lost the case. If they lost because of her, she'd never reference it at all."

"Okay. Maybe she had a relationship with one of the senior lawyers on Tohme's defense team."

Christy nodded. "Could be. If we're considering relationships, what about one of the FPS executives? Or even Austin Tohme himself? Is it a breach of ethics to be involved with your client?"

"I don't know," Quinn said. "Even if it wasn't an ethical issue, it probably wouldn't be a smart idea."

"Young and stupid," Christy murmured, hearing Mallory's voice in her head again.

Quinn laughed. "Okay. Let me do some deep digging into Austin Tohme's trial. I'll give you a call when I have something, probably in twenty minutes or half an hour." He smiled at her, that slow sexy smile that always made her insides melt. "I'll talk to you later."

His image disappeared and Christy was left staring at her own face. She disconnected and gazed off into space.

Her goal was to find out who Carson Muir's father was. Would discovering why Mallory Tait was willing to submit to blackmail provide the answer? She sighed. Probably not directly, but it might provide them with a clue. Certain that was the best she could hope for, she settled down to wait.

It wasn't long before Quinn was back.

"I've hit the mother lode," he said by way of greeting when they were once again connected on screen.

His wide grin and sparkling eyes told her he was very pleased with himself. Christy raised her brows. "Do tell."

"I'm sending you an email. Open it and tell me what you see."

"Okay." Her email pinged. Inside, she found a professional headshot of a man who appeared to be in his mid-thirties. He had a round face with even features and a wide smile showing strong white teeth. An attractive face, though not a remarkable one, Christy thought. If it weren't for his thick, lustrous hair, she would have wondered why Quinn sent the photo. But the hair said it all. It was blond, a few shades darker than Frank's had been.

She dragged her gaze away from the photo and looked at Quinn. "This is one of the executives, isn't it? Which one?"

"Austin Tohme, the head of research."

"Oh, my," Christy said. "He's blond."

"Yeah, interesting, isn't it? The same hair color as all the guys Pam tried to coax into marriage after her baby was born."

"Do you think he's the boy's father?" Christy whispered.

"Why not?" Quinn said. "From what you told me about Pam Muir, she was gorgeous and not afraid to flaunt it. FPS was a medium-sized pharmaceutical. The staff would know all the executives and Pam had a way of making herself noticeable. It's not a huge stretch to believe that if Pam worked for the company, she and Austin could have hooked up."

Christy thought about what Austin Tohme meant to Pam Muir. If the man was the father of her child, she must have been pregnant when the investigation began. Then, when he was arrested she would have wondered what she should do. Should she distance herself from a man who was now disgraced? She must have asked herself what kind of role model a man accused of fraud would be for her unborn child and wondered if she wanted her baby to know his father. And always, there'd be the daunting question of whether or not she could cope with raising her baby on her own.

But she did cope. With typical Pam Muir style, she set out to find a man with money, prestige, and the same coloring as Austin Tohme.

With a sigh, Christy said, "This is only speculation. How do we prove he's the father?"

Quinn rubbed his chin, his excitement easing into thoughtfulness. "If Pam wasn't a witness, the trial records won't provide any information. What we need is an organizational chart for the company, or a list of employee names. I'll see what I can dig up, but since FPS is out of business, it may be difficult to find."

"Maybe not," Christy said. "The cops would probably have that kind of info. I'll ask Patterson."

∽

At eleven AM on a weekday in early February, the Pacific Centre Mall was quiet. The stores were open, but customers were absent. That made it an excellent place for a discrete, unofficial meeting. Christy found Patterson standing in front of a shoe store gazing at the window display of suede boots with high, thin heels. Fashion boots, not practical winter ones designed to deal with the slushy muck somewhere between snow and sleet that was currently inundating Vancouver.

"West Coast winter," Christy murmured, as she came up beside Patterson. "Most of the time these would be fine, but—"

"But not today," Patterson said, agreeing. There was regret in her voice.

Christy laughed. "Luckily we don't get a lot of weather like today's. Are you going to splurge?"

"Yeah," Patterson said, "but later. Right now, I'm on duty. I'm also here to tell you about an investigation into Austin Tohme eleven years ago."

"You were able to access the files?" Christy could hear the excitement in her voice. If Patterson confirmed that Pam Muir worked for FPS it was a link to Austin Tohme and would be a viable reason to seek out the man and discover if he could possibly be Carson Muir's father.

Still staring at the boots, Patterson nodded.

"And?" Christy asked when the detective didn't continue. "Did Pam Muir work at FPS?"

Patterson turned from the window and started wandering down the hall, her gaze focused on the storefronts as if she was window-shopping. Christy followed. After a moment, Patterson glanced her way and said, "Pam Muir was Tohme's accounting clerk."

"Oh! She knew him and worked closely with him. Even better." Christy clapped her hands together and did a quick two-step. When Patterson eyed her with amusement, Christy laughed and said, "The time Pam spent at FPS was a missing piece of her history. We've managed to find out about her university years, what she was doing when Frank knew her, whom she knew and where she worked after her son was born, but the crucial months when she was pregnant were a mystery. It's exciting to have confirmation of what Quinn and I suspected."

"Tell me again why you think Austin Tohme could be the kid's father?"

They reached a bench and sat down. Christy angled her position so she could look at Patterson more easily. "Pam Muir had gorgeous thick, dark brown hair, almost black. Her son is a blond. All the men she dated after Carson was born were blonds or had light, sandy brown hair. I think Carson's natural father was a blond and she wanted a man who had the boy's coloring as a stepfather for Carson." She dug into her purse and pulled out her phone. Finding the photo of Austin Tohme, she showed it to Patterson. "When she couldn't bring any of the men she dated up to scratch, she remembered Frank, who was blond, rich, and not around to disagree with her. That's when she decided to try her luck claiming that Carson was Frank's son."

Frowning, Patterson handed the phone back to Christy. "I get that Austin Tohme was a blond and so could have been the kid's father, but it's a stretch, Mrs. Jamieson. If Tohme was the father, why not acknowledge him?"

"He's in jail," Christy said.

Patterson narrowed her eyes. "You think Muir was trying to hide the man's son from him because he was a convicted criminal?"

Christy nodded.

"That's deplorable," Patterson said, her voice snapping with disapproval. "The man has the right to a relationship with his own son. It doesn't matter if he served time or not. And by the way, Tohme has paid his debt to society. His sentence ended just over a year ago."

"He's free? Do you know where he is? Can I get his address so I can I talk to him?" This was better than she expected.

Patterson stared at her in an absentminded way. "He's living with his family. How did you find out about the Tohme trial, anyway?"

"I talked to Mallory Tait. When I asked her what Pam blackmailed her about, all she would tell me was that it had happened when she was 'young and stupid.' That gave me a timeframe to work with."

"Okay, but why the Tohme case specifically?"

"Mallory was an articled student working for the firm that represented Tohme. That says young, and we're all stupid and make mistakes when we start out. I put the pieces together and they told me Pam was somehow involved with Austin Tohme. Before his illegal activities were exposed, Tohme was exactly the kind of man Pam liked. He was attractive, a little older, successful, and still on the rise." She shrugged. "I assumed she met him at work, in a casual way, you know?"

Patterson nodded.

"But now that I know she worked directly for him, I think it's even more likely he's the father. Developing a relationship with the man in charge was part of her pattern. She did it before she became pregnant, and she continued to do it after her son was born."

"Could be," Patterson said. "Why were you talking to Tait about the blackmail? You're not trying to solve the murder, are you?"

Patterson was staring at her with penetrating, rather disapproving, but all-seeing eyes. Christy was glad to be able to say, "No, I'm not. When I learned you were questioning Mallory because she was one of the people Pam was blackmailing—"

"How did you discover that?" Patterson demanded, her voice sharp. When Christy frowned, Patterson added less aggressively, "Who told you?"

"Oh, one of the partners at McCullagh, McCullagh, and Walker."

Patterson stared at her for a moment then she grunted, the sound one of accepting disapproval. "Go on."

"Well, I asked Quinn to look into Mallory's career and he found out about the Tohme trial. Was Pam Muir ever one of the suspects in case?"

Patterson shook her head. "She was questioned, of course, but she was never a suspect."

"Did the detective who questioned her mention she was pregnant by any chance?" Christy asked hopefully.

"No. He only noted down his questions and her responses."

Christy sighed. "Too bad."

Patterson glanced at her watch, then stood. "I hope this helps you prove your late husband wasn't the father of Pam Muir's child."

"Thank you, Detective." Christy rose as well.

"It won't change anything with Mallory Tait," Patterson said, fixing Christy with a firm glance. "She's still under suspicion."

"I understand."

Patterson nodded, then began to walk.

Christy followed. "I realize Mallory did something terrible during that trial, but I don't see how she could be Pam's killer. She was with us when it happened."

Patterson shook her head. "No, she wasn't. She arrived at your office at quarter to ten. Pam could have been dead by that time. Mallory's alibi doesn't stand up."

They reached the exit that led to the parkade where they parted. Patterson headed down to retrieve her car while Christy ambled along the gallery to the Georgia Street exit since she was walking back to the Trust's office. It wasn't until she was out in the bleak, cold February day that she realized Patterson had never given her Austin Tohme's address.

CHAPTER 26

Not having Tohme's address proved to be a minor glitch Quinn rectified via an email that included both street address and cell phone number.

After a discussion between Quinn, Roy, and Christy, it was decided Christy and Roy would interview Tohme together, if he agreed to talk to them. No one knew what kind of man he was, or how his years in prison might have changed him. Christy was adamant, though, that she, as the head of the Jamiesons, would be the one to approach him.

He proved to be willing to talk to them, but scheduling was tricky as he worked an eight-hour shift that ended at three-thirty and he preferred not to have the meeting in the evening. In the end, Christy suggested they get together at the Trust's office at five one afternoon and Tohme agreed.

Having made the appointment, she had to scramble to organize a sitter for Noelle. Fortunately, Rebecca Petrofsky was home that afternoon and was happy to keep an eye on her. With Noelle's care arranged, Christy sat down at her kitchen table, a pad of lined paper in front of her and a disposable ballpoint pen in her hand. She was ruefully aware of the difference between her writing materials and the fountain pens and fine paper Ellen used whenever they were working on a case, but it didn't matter. Her goal now was to prioritize what she wanted to ask Austin Tohme when she met him.

And that was when Frank got involved.

I'm coming with you.

Christy eyed the cat, who had hopped up onto the kitchen table. He had effectively stopped her musing by sitting squarely on top of her pad. "No, you're not."

She claimed the kid was mine. I want to know who the real father is.

Christy stared into the wide green eyes. "I'll tell you if he actually is the dad when I get back from the interview."

I want to meet him.

"Taking a cat to an interview isn't professional."

The glare she got from Stormy told her what Frank thought of that. *Where are you meeting him?*

She answered reluctantly. "At the Trust." There was no real reason why she couldn't take Stormy to the office. Bonnie and Isabelle would be gone by five and Stormy could find a place to hide where he was invisible and Frank could hear the conversation. Tohme need never know he was there.

Frank gleefully pointed that out.

Cornered, she said, "All right, but you have to behave like a cat and make yourself scarce."

Stormy blinked at her. Frank didn't reply.

"I mean it, Frank. No hijinks."

Stormy crouched down, further covering the pad. *Would I ever do anything to embarrass you, Chris?*

She glared at the cat. "Embarrassing me isn't the problem. Causing trouble is. What if Tohme is one of the people who can hear you?"

All the better. I can help make him talk.

Christy had to concede Frank had been successful at coaxing

confessions out of people in the past. "Okay, you can come. Now, clear off my paper and let me put my thoughts in order."

Stormy stood, rubbed his cheek against Christy, then jumped down to the floor. He trotted over to his bowl in a vain hope more food had somehow materialized there, even though he'd already consumed his dinner. After a brief, despairing sniff, he knocked the bowl away with his front paw and marched disdainfully out of the kitchen.

Christy went back to her list of questions.

On the day of the interview, Roy and Stormy made the journey into town together, a mutually enjoyable experience. Christy greeted them in the reception area when they arrived fifteen minutes early. While Stormy snooped around the office checking out the smells and making himself comfortable, Christy and Roy set up the conference room and speculated on what Austin Tohme would tell them.

At precisely five o'clock, Christy heard the exterior door opening. "Show time," she said to Roy and strode from the conference room.

She entered the reception area to find a tall man, well muscled, standing in the center of the space. His dark blond hair was thick and combed back from a face with more angles than the one in the photographs she'd seen. There were wrinkles at the corners of his eyes, but over all the man had aged well over the past eleven years.

He was staring at Bonnie's reception desk, which was at the rear of the room. On it sat Stormy, crouched sphinx-like and glaring at Tohme with the cold, judgmental stare of an unimpressed cat.

He's not bad looking for an old guy. Could have been hot when Pam knew him.

Aghast, Christy looked over at Roy, who had followed her into the room. A smile twitched at the corner of his mouth and there was a distinct twinkle in his eyes. No help there, she thought, thoroughly annoyed with Frank. Her gaze travelled to Austin Tohme. Fortunately, he didn't appear to be disconcerted by the presence of a cat. Maybe she'd get lucky and he wouldn't hear Frank. That, she thought, could be important, because she had a feeling Frank wasn't going to sit in the corner and stay quiet.

"Mr. Tohme?" she said, advancing toward him with her hand held out.

He nodded and they shook.

"I'm Christy Jamieson." She turned, indicating Roy. "This is Roy Armstrong. He's one of the trustees for the Jamieson Trust. If you'll come with me, the conference room is this way. I have some coffee and pastries, if you would like a refreshment."

He followed her down the hallway to the conference room with Roy bringing up the rear. Stormy twined around his legs along the way. Christy wondered if the poor cat was embarrassed at being co-opted into Frank's hijacking scheme.

In the conference room, she poured coffee from the beaker for all of them and passed around the plate of pastries while they made small talk. Stormy jumped on to the table and settled in front of Tohme, again crouched sphinx-like and glowering.

"I hope you're not allergic to cats, Mr. Tohme. I can shut him in my office if he's bothering you."

You wouldn't!

Watch me, Christy thought, enjoying Frank's consternation.

Tohme reached out to scratch Stormy behind the ears. He glanced over at Christy and smiled. It wasn't a broad smile, showing lots of teeth. In fact, it was just a glimmer, twitching the corners of his rather thin lips, but it reached his eyes and transformed his face. With a jolt, Christy thought she understood why Pam Muir, so attractive to men, would be interested in this one.

"Call me Austin," Tohme said. "I don't mind if this little fellow stays here. I like cats. I had a Persian before I went to prison. The most cantankerous creature you can imagine, but he was my pal. He was dead by the time I got out."

Huh.

It sounded like Frank was softening toward Austin Tohme. Since Christy didn't know whether she should offer condolences to the man on the loss of his pet, she simply smiled and said, "And I'm Christy."

"Roy," said Roy, chiming in.

Austin's fingers slipped down to Stormy's chin and tickled him gently. The cat lifted his head, slitted his eyes, and began to purr. Smiling at the cat's enjoyment, Austin said, "Why does Christy Jamieson of the Jamieson Trust want to talk to me about Pam Muir?"

Since Tohme was comfortable going straight to the matter at hand, Christy was equally blunt. "Are you the father of Carson Muir, Pam's son?"

Surprised widened his eyes. He lost his relaxed posture and his hand fell away from the cat. "Why are you asking?"

"Because Pam claimed my late husband Frank was the father. I married Frank after Carson was born and Frank never mentioned Pam or her son. I don't believe he was the father, but I don't know for certain."

Austin Tohme was quick. It didn't take him long to work out why Pam Muir would suggest her son was part of the Jamieson family. "She wants to get onto the gravy train." He shook his head. "Sounds like Pam."

Roy raised his brows. "Not a particularly warm endorsement for a woman you had a relationship with."

Since Tohme hadn't yet admitted he was the father, he shot Roy an amused look. "Making assumptions, aren't you, Roy?" There was a challenge and an edge to his tone that suggested he wasn't easily intimidated. Then he shrugged. "Well, you're right. Pam and I did have a relationship all those years ago."

"What happened?" Christy asked gently.

She dumped him, what else? He didn't respect her.

Tohme picked up his coffee cup and sipped. "The house of cards fell down and I was arrested. She wanted nothing more to do with me from the moment she realized I not only wouldn't be fabulously wealthy, but that I'd been caught out as a player in a scam of major proportions."

Looking intrigued, Roy said, "Was everything that was written about the fraud and your trial really true? Did you try to pass off a non-performing drug as a miracle cure?"

Tohme nodded.

"Must have taken some effort," Roy said.

"It did." Tohme was silent for a moment, then he said, "Once we—that is the executive team, including myself—realized the formula was a dud, we knew we couldn't release the news, or the company would go bankrupt. We'd raised huge amounts of investment money based on the success of that drug. If it wasn't real, we had nothing else to replace it with. The money would dry up and we'd be out of business."

Roy shrugged. "It happens."

"Yeah, it does. But when part of those investment dollars came from your own pocket and you know you'll never get them back, well, it changes things." He drank again, then put his cup on the saucer with careful precision. "We'd all sunk our savings into the company, all of us on the executive team. We decided we'd try for one last score to recoup our investments, before the real results had to be released. We hoped we'd be able to keep those results under wraps until we could make it look as if the final trials had exposed a major flaw. That way, it would appear that we didn't have prior knowledge and the failure would just be another in a long line of drugs that never made it into production."

"Was it Pam who leaked the information?" Christy asked.

He shook his head. "I doubt it. She liked the idea of being rich too much."

Hoping for a bigger return than just your savings, weren't you, Tohme?

Roy's mouth twitched and Christy couldn't help but agree with

Frank. The fraud wasn't just about saving the family fortunes. It was about profits, and big ones.

"Pam was in on it, then," Roy said.

"Of course." There was impatience in Tohme's voice. "I'd been wining and dining her for months. She was pregnant with my child. I'd asked her to marry me. Of course she knew. We had no secrets."

Christy thought that probably wasn't quite true. Austin might not have had secrets from Pam, but she wasn't the kind of woman who laid her heart bare to a man. "Did she accept your proposal?"

Regret flashed across Tohme's features. "No. Once the securities commission and then the cops started sniffing around, she made it clear she wanted no part of me."

"You're sure you're the boy's father?" Roy asked sharply.

Tohme slid him a look, then nodded. "Pam and I didn't talk once the investigation got going, but I knew about Carson."

How?

A good question. Christy said, "How did you find out?"

He shrugged. "I was out on bail when he was born. My lawyers thought it best I didn't contact anyone from FPS, so my parents kept an eye on Pam. They desperately want a grandchild and I know that after the trial, while I was in prison, my dad tried several times to convince her to let them get to know Carson. She wouldn't talk to him though. In fact, she refused to admit Carson was their grandson, but my parents knew. Dad said he could see a family resemblance to his own father. In the end, they watched from afar and kept me updated."

Christy placed her hands together on the table. "So, you knew about Carson, but you were also aware that Pam refused to acknowledge you as his father. That must have frustrated you."

Tohme shot her a level look. "There's one thing you learn in prison. When you're inside, things don't happen on your schedule. I knew there was no way of forcing Pam to admit Carson's paternity until I'd finished my sentence. When I was paroled, I contacted her and told her I'd be seeking parenting rights as Carson's father. She told me to go to hell. So, I contacted my lawyer. He told me to get settled, find a job, and make something of myself that a judge would respect."

"Prove you were a reformed character," Roy said.

Yeah, like that's going to happen.

Tohme nodded. "Once I'd done that, he said he could start proceedings against her." He drew a deep breath. "So that's what I did. I got a job in a warehouse. It's steady work and the pay is good. I'm living with my parents, who are getting on, helping them with the mortgage and keeping the house up. It's nothing like the life I had before, but it's a decent one and I think my son can be proud of me."

There was something about that statement that alerted Christy. "You asked your lawyer to start the proceedings."

He nodded.

Roy shared a glance with Christy. "When?"

"The beginning of January." Tohme looked from one to the other. "Why?"

"Pam contacted us the second week of January," Christy said.

Tohme's face hardened. "She wants to have your late husband recognized as Carson's father before my case goes to court. Well, it's not going to happen. The next time she approaches you, you can tell her Carson is mine and there's no way I'll let him go."

"You don't have him," Roy said. There was a gleam in his eye that told Christy he was up to mischief.

"Not yet," Tohme said grimly. "But I will." He pointed to Christy. "I assume you've asked for a DNA test for Carson?"

Christy nodded.

Tohme leaned forward. His expression was angry, determined. Stormy butted his head against his hand, looking for affection. The movement startled Tohme, then after a moment he smiled and relaxed. He stroked the cat as he said, "Make an appointment for me with the tech you're using to do the DNA test. I'll willingly donate mine to be compared with Carson's. You'll find it's a match." He looked down at the cat, who looked back with wide eyes as he stroked him head to tail. He was smiling when his gaze once more met Christy's. "Once I have the DNA proof, Pam won't have a chance of denying me my rights. I want to thank you, Christy. You've saved me an expensive legal bill."

Frowning, Christy said, "You don't know, do you?"

"Don't know what?"

"Pam is dead."

"Dead? But... That's crazy. She's young, healthy. How could she die?"

"Someone killed her," Roy said.

"She was Vancouver's first murder of the year," Christy added. From the shocked look on Tohme's face, she believed he hadn't been aware Pam Muir was no longer alive.

Roy appeared to have a different opinion. "Someone wasn't happy she was trying to pass off her kid as a Jamieson." He raised a brow. "Any idea who that might be?"

Abandoning Stormy, Tohme surged to his feet. "Now just a minute. You can't accuse me of killing the mother of my son. I may be an ex-con, but I'm not a murderer."

"Prove it to us then," Roy said. His tone was mild, his eyes watchful.

"Why should I?"

"Because you're going to have to prove it to the cops anyway," Roy said with a shrug.

"Why should the cops come after me?" Tohme asked.

"Trust me," Christy said. "They will."

"So, tell us where you were the morning of Wednesday, January eighteenth?" Roy demanded.

"I was at work." Tohme all but snarled the words.

"You can prove that?" Roy said.

"I start at seven-thirty and I work till three-thirty, Monday to Friday. I get a break at ten-fifteen, which I took in the staff room in the warehouse, and a half hour lunch at eleven-thirty. I took that in the staff room too. I clocked out at three-thirty, as usual."

Roy narrowed his eyes. "And you have witnesses who will swear you never left the building?"

"Yes," Tohme ground out.

Roy beamed at him and Tohme blinked. "Good. Then you have nothing to worry about." He waved a hand. "It was probably just some low life who did it."

"Who the hell do you think—"

"We'll be in touch about the DNA test," Roy interrupted breezily.

"You can forget about that," Tohme said. "I don't need it now. I'm Carson's only surviving parent. He's mine by right."

"Pam's parents have continued Pam's suit against the Jamieson Trust," Christy said gently. "They believe Frank was Carson's father and they intend to prove it."

Tohme sat down abruptly. "This can't be happening."

"Did you ever meet the Muirs when you were dating?" Christy asked.

He shook his head. "Pam said they disapproved of her and she wasn't talking to them. I figured once we were engaged, I'd try to bring them all back together, so I didn't push it. Then..." He waved one hand in a vague, dismissive way. "It was too late."

Her expression serious, Christy said, "Get the DNA test. Prove you're Carson's dad. The Muirs loved their daughter and I'm sure they love their grandson. You're going to have to find a compromise with them, but it will be easier if they accept your paternity."

He studied her, then slowly bowed his head. When he looked up, there was finality in his voice as he said, "Let me know where and when and I'll do it."

CHAPTER 27

Christy walked Tohme to the door, locking it behind him after he'd exited. She stood for a moment, her back against the door, and thought about the ramifications of Austin Tohme as Carson Muir's father.

Relief eased tension she'd been trying to ignore ever since Pam Muir had sashayed into her conference room and announced she was Mrs. Frank Jamieson. She blew out a long breath, then pushed away from the door and headed for the conference room where Roy was gathering up plates and cups and the cat was sniffing at a remaining pastry.

Christy pulled the platter out of the way. "Not good for cats."

There was a sigh. *It smells heavenly.*

Roy chuckled. "There's a bag of tuna flavored kitty treats at home. Yum."

Yuck.

"What did you think of Austin Tohme?" Christy asked.

"A smart guy, doing all the right things to make sure he can have access to his kid," Roy said.

Christy sent him a level glance. "Then you think he's the father?"

Yeah.

Roy nodded. "Agreed."

"So do I. I'll phone Nolan Walker to let him know about Tohme and ask him to arrange a DNA test," Christy said.

"Why don't you wait?"

Christy frowned at Roy. "Why?"

Roy rubbed his chin. "Tohme told us he contacted Pam, but we have no idea if she told her parents about him. Maybe she did and they refuse to believe an ex-con might be the father of their grandchild…"

"Or maybe she didn't tell them at all," Christy said, finishing his thought.

Roy nodded.

Pam was never one to give away much.

Christy ignored the remark. She already knew Frank remembered much more about Pam Muir than he cared to let on. "Perhaps if I tell the Muirs what we've learned, they'll agree to cancel their suit against the Trust."

Roy gathered up the plates and coffee mugs and headed for the door. "It would save everyone a lot of trouble and Nolan Walker could go back to being smug with his old boy corporate clients."

Following with the coffee urn, Christy laughed. "That would make me very happy. I'll call the Muirs now and see if I can book an appointment."

She expected them to try to put her off, but Lincoln suggested they meet the next morning at ten o'clock at the Muirs' Surrey home. The choice of location surprised her, but she agreed.

The next morning, Christy parked on the street in front of the house. They lived in a mid-century brick bungalow on a large lot in one of the better parts of Surrey. Evergreen hedges surrounded the property on either side and the front walk was lined with flower borders, now dormant. Christy could imagine them bright with color in the summer months, vibrant and welcoming. An enormous tree, its branches bare of leaves, stood in the middle of the large front lawn. In the summer, it would shade the house and provide a little privacy for the big plate glass window in what must be the living room. Now it just looked tired and desolate. She sighed as she walked up the path to the front door and rang the bell.

Lincoln Muir opened the door seconds later, almost as if he was waiting nearby, and invited her in. He led her into a large room, which, sure enough, contained a big picture window. Sheers covered the window, shielding the beige wall-to-wall Berber carpet from the sunlight that poured through the glass. Narrow polyester drapes in a soft peach framed the window. Two chairs upholstered in hard-wearing taupe microfiber, a square oak table between them, were positioned in front of the window. A sofa, covered in the same fabric, had been placed at right angles to one of the chairs and pushed back against the wall.

Dawn Muir was sitting on the sofa. Lincoln sat down beside her. Christy took the nearby chair.

"Thank you for seeing me today, Mr. and Mrs. Muir," she said as she perched on the edge of the chair.

"Would you like a coffee?" Dawn Muir asked, making no effort to rise, and sounding as if she hoped Christy would decline.

On the glass-topped coffee table in front of the sofa were two coffee mugs, half-full Christy noted. Obviously, the Muirs had been drinking from them while they waited for Christy to arrive. Equally obvious was Dawn's reluctance to welcome her. Best get this over with and be on her way.

Christy shook her head. "No, thank you."

Dawn nodded. She picked up her mug and sipped as she watched Christy warily.

Christy smiled as reassuringly as she could and said, "I've learned new information about your grandson's parentage that I believe you should know."

"Trying to exclude our Carson from you fancy Trust, are you?" Dawn said. The mug clattered as the ceramic hit the glass top of the coffee table. There was a sneer in her voice, but there was aggression too. She was ready for trouble.

"No," Christy said carefully. "If Carson is Frank's son, he will be welcomed into the Jamieson family and will be a full recipient of the Trust."

The expression on Dawn's face was disbelieving. Lincoln's features exposed nothing of what he was thinking.

"I've been in contact with a man by the name of Austin Tohme—"

"Him!" Dawn said. The word came out as an angry explosion. "That lying cheat. I suppose he told you he was Carson's father?"

Christy nodded. Dawn's reaction told her that she and Roy had been wrong—the Muirs knew all about Austin Tohme. She wondered if they'd learned of his assertion that he was Carson's father from Pam or Austin himself.

"Yes, of course, he did," Dawn said. Her lip curled and her tone was contemptuous. "Well, don't you believe him, because he's not. Pam told us about him years ago when he was charged with that despicable crime and out on bail. That was when his father first started sniffing around, claiming that Carson was his grandson. She said Austin Tohme wasn't Carson's father and we should never allow any Tohme near our boy."

"Was that when she told you Frank was Carson's dad?" If Pam had identified Frank so early in Carson's life Christy couldn't see the Muirs keeping silent all this time, but she asked the question anyway.

Dawn narrowed her eyes. "No. She said his father wasn't someone she wanted Carson to know, at least not while he was growing up. Once he was an adult, she'd let him make up his own mind whether he wanted to meet his father or not."

Frank had loved Noelle with all his heart. Christy was sure that if he'd had a son, he'd have loved the boy equally strongly, no matter who the mother was. She would have embraced the child as well, as a brother to Noelle and as another loving parent for Carson. If Frank really had been the boy's father, Pam's decision to keep him in ignorance would have been selfish and unkind for both man and boy.

"When did she tell you my late husband Frank was Carson's father?" Christy asked.

"Last September, when you were involved in that murder at MacLagen House." Dawn managed to look down her nose at Christy, even though she didn't move and their heads were at the same level. Apparently, involvement in a high-society party that included a murder pushed Christy down to the level of a woman of ill repute in Dawn's eyes.

That didn't bother Christy. Dawn Muir was entitled to her position, whether it was based on fact or speculation. Her assertion confirmed what Christy had suspected, however. Last fall there'd been a lot of press about the shocking return of the Jamieson fortune, and the Jamieson involvement in murder. Pam must have seen the articles and remembered that she'd known the late Frank Jamieson years before. Christy wondered when Pam decided that a dead man would make a good surrogate father for her son and began planning her scam. It was unlikely she'd ever know and really, did it matter? The important part was that Pam had her plan well organized and already in place by the turn of the year.

She eyed Dawn in a considering way. "Austin Tohme seemed pretty sure that Carson was his son. Why would—"

Dawn sniffed disdainfully. "You're not listening. Pam told us he wasn't the father. She was pregnant when she met him, but Austin wanted to believe the baby was his." With a little shrug and arched eyebrows, Dawn said, "What could she do? Our Pam was beautiful, and the man was obsessed with her. She knew from the beginning that he wasn't to be trusted so she humored him."

"Let him believe what he wanted to believe." Nodding, Lincoln Muir joined in for the first time. "Best thing to do when the man is your boss and can make trouble for you if you flout him."

There was so much that was wrong packed into both those statements that Christy wasn't sure how to formulate a reply. There was a big difference between having a disagreement with your boss over work decisions and having sexual relations with him that resulted in a question over a pregnancy.

Dawn, however, nodded her agreement to her husband's comment, then she added earnestly, "Pam was his assistant, an important job. She had no idea what he was up to, of course. Tohme was a secretive fellow. All con artists are, I suppose. They have to be, don't they, to pull off their scams."

"I wouldn't know," Christy said. Clearly the Muirs' perception of their daughter was vastly different from her own.

"He pulled the wool over my girl's eyes," Lincoln said. "Nasty piece of work."

"And made a lot of trouble for her," Dawn added. "When the police took over the office building with their search warrant, Pam came home crying. She said they thought she had something to do with that man's criminal scheme. Imagine that! Pam!"

Christy looked at Dawn thoughtfully. She'd known that the Muirs loved their daughter and thought highly of her, but it appeared that where Pam was concerned, critical thinking didn't apply. "Did the police accuse Pam of being part of the fraud?"

Dawn shook her head emphatically. "No, never."

"Of course not," Lincoln said. There was indignation in his voice, but his gaze was wary.

Christy wondered if Lincoln suspected that his daughter knew more than she let on, but she didn't press the point. Pam was dead, the fraud long since dealt with. It did indicate though, that some, if not most, of what Pam told her parents was embellished or completely untrue. For Christy, that gave greater credence to Austin's assertion that he was Carson's father.

"The company folded because of the swindle, which meant Pam had no job to go back to after her maternity leave was over," Dawn said. Her lips tightened into a thin line. "That's down to Austin Tohme too, because if he'd just been a decent, honest man, Pam wouldn't have had to find a job in the entertainment business."

From what Christy had learned, Pam had thrived working on *Blood Wars*. "People I've spoken to said Pam was excellent at her job and happy working on a TV series."

"It's contract work," Lincoln said heavily. "The salary was good, but there were minimal benefits, and no long-term job security. Pam did fine on *Blood Wars*, but it folded after five years and the show she moved to never made it past the proposal stage. She was out of work for months before she decided to contact the Jamieson Trust."

"If Austin Tohme hadn't put the company out of business, Pam would have had a job to go back to after Carson was born and she'd be here, with us, now." There were tears in Dawn's eyes.

Christy sighed. "I am so sorry for your loss. I know you loved Pam deeply. I won't bother you about Austin Tohme any further, except I want you to know that he will be taking a DNA test at the same time as Carson and my daughter are. Carson and Noelle will be compared as siblings, but Austin's test will be a full paternity one. I hope we have an answer to who is Carson's father as a result."

Dawn bristled. "Of course you will. His father is Frank Jamieson."

Christy stood. "Thank you for talking to me today. Nolan Walker from McCullagh, McCullagh, and Walker will be in touch to schedule the DNA tests."

"He already has." Lincoln slapped hand hands on his knees, then rose ponderously. "I don't like the idea of subjecting my grandson to this test."

Christy smiled thinly. "You could drop the suit against the Trust if you want to spare him the ordeal."

"It's his birthright," Dawn snapped. "We are not going to drop the paternity suit."

Christy shrugged. "Then we'll meet again at the Jamieson Trust offices when the DNA results are in."

A few minutes later, as she walked to her car, Christy pulled out her phone and punched in Nolan Walker's number. Time to let him know there was another player in the paternity stakes.

CHAPTER 28

Nolan Walker rustled the papers set out on the conference table in front of him. "This is highly irregular."

Christy resisted the urge to snap. Clasping her hands and placing them in front of her on her own set of papers helped her control her temper. Her voice was even as she said, "I don't expect the Muirs to accept the results of the DNA tests without protest. I thought revealing the information with others around them would help them adjust more easily."

They were in the conference room at the Jamieson Trust. Christy was seated at the head of the table, with Nolan on her left, his back to the windows. To his left, sat Mallory Tait. Isabelle Pascoe was at the other end of the table by the doorway, while Bonnie was still in the reception area, ready to greet guests. Once the participants had arrived, she would join them in the conference room to take notes, even though Christy had stipulated the meeting would be recorded.

The missing participants were Lincoln and Dawn Muir, and Austin Tohme. Frank had also insisted on attending. Now Stormy the

Cat and Roy were both out in the reception area chatting with Bonnie. Well, Roy was chatting. Bonnie couldn't hear the cat.

Walker waved his hand dismissively. "It would have been far better to have invited the Muirs to the McCullagh, McCullagh, and Walker offices and informed them of the results there. It's a more official setting and the witnesses you desire could have been individuals working for the law firm. Having the family come to the Trust's office is far too informal." He paused and pursed his mouth. "Inviting all these extraneous people to attend is not just messy, it is a mistake."

"You would be right, if our goal was only to inform," Christy said in a soothing voice.

Walker frowned. "If that isn't our goal, what is?"

"The Muirs need to understand what the results mean, not just intellectually, but emotionally. As long as they believe that my late husband, Frank, is the father of their grandson, it doesn't matter what the DNA tests reveal."

"I agree," Mallory said. "When I told Pam the Trust would need both certification and DNA proof, she laughed at me. She said that her parents believed unconditionally that Frank Jamieson was Carson's father and they would never stop believing unless she told them it was untrue." She paused to draw a breath and her expression hardened. "She had no intention of doing that, of course. She'd conditioned them for years, with hints that the boy's father was well known, wealthy, and married. She had them imagining that she wouldn't tell them who it was for fear he'd use his influence to take the boy away from her."

Walker shrugged. "What these people think is irrelevant. The DNA tests were done through a reputable lab and the results will be accepted by the courts. It would be sheer stupidity for the Muirs to continue their lawsuit against the Trust."

"Not everybody thinks or acts logically," Mallory said. She didn't look at Walker as she spoke. He was, after all, a partner in the law firm that employed her. If Pam Muir's killer was found, she'd be going back to McCullagh, McCullagh, and Walker. She'd have to work with Nolan Walker.

The sound of voices could be heard in the reception area. Stormy galloped into the conference room and launched himself onto the table, landing neatly in front of Isabelle, who stroked his back.

The Tohmes are here. Not just Austin, but his parents too. What's the deal with that?

Christy frowned. She'd invited Austin only and hadn't expected other members of his family to show up as well. She scanned the table. Yes, there were enough chairs. Good. As the voices neared, she stood to greet them.

Bonnie made the introductions. "The Tohme family, Mrs. Jamieson. Austin Tohme you know." She pointed to Austin, then gestured to each of his parents as she identified them. "His father, Mason, and mother, Elsa." She slipped away, back to her position at the reception desk. Stormy hopped off the table and followed.

Christy hadn't met Mason or Elsa before and now she studied them. Mason was a wiry man, with gray hair thinning at the front. His narrow features were drawn, as if the pressure of this paternity fight was taking its toll on him. Elsa was a small woman, gray-haired like her husband, and chubby, though she disguised it by wearing a loose-fitting jacket over an A-line skirt. Her plump features also showed evidence of strain in the dark circles under her eyes.

Feeling sympathy for the whole Tohme family for whom this dispute must be a nightmare, Christy smiled at them in her most friendly way. "Good morning." She introduced everyone at the table, then said, "Austin and Mason, would you like to sit on the far side of the table, in front of the windows?" The men moved into position. "Thank you. Elsa, perhaps you would sit on the other side, opposite them?"

They all settled into their places, though Elsa was visibly upset at being separated from the two men.

"You said on the phone that the results are back," Austin said, his voice tight.

Christy nodded.

"Well, what do they prove?" he demanded.

"In due time, Mr. Tohme," Walker said. His dry tone suggested he disapproved of Austin's impatience, and he shot Christy an I-told-you-so look.

"I'd like to wait until the Muirs arrive, then we can all hear the results at the same time," Christy said, diffusing the demand with another smile.

Austin sent her a narrow-eyed look, but he nodded.

"Hello, Austin," Mallory said. "It's been a long time."

Austin's gaze turned from Christy to Mallory. He hadn't acknowledged her when Christy introduced everyone, but now that Mallory was confronting him directly, he responded with a smile. His parents eyed her coolly. Christy wasn't surprised. Mallory had been part of his legal team, which had failed to keep Austin from being convicted of the charges against him.

"Mallory Tait," he said. "I thought about you often while I was in prison."

"Good or bad?" she asked, sounding uncertain.

He shrugged, then smiled rather ruefully. "My decisions. Not your fault."

Mallory nodded, then bit her lip.

Christy frowned, wondering about the exchange, and what it really had been about, but her attention was diverted to Mason Tohme who drummed his fingers on the table as he watched the conference room door suspiciously.

Austin put his hand over his father's. "It's okay, Dad. We'll get started soon."

"This is crazy," Mason said. "All we need is the proof that the boy is your son, then we can go. I didn't come here to schmooze with a bunch of strangers and that awful woman's parents."

"You can go now," Nolan Walker said. "The only people who need to be at this meeting are Mr. and Mrs. Muir." He glanced at his watch. "Who are late."

Mallory rolled her eyes and shook her head, but she didn't critique Walker.

At last, another set of voices was heard in the reception area. As before, Stormy brought the news. He leapt up on the table, landed neatly, then walked the length of it to Christy, where he stopped and sat in his tidy way, tail tucked neatly around his paws. *The Muirs are here and they're grouchy. They hate this process and they are not going to give up trying to prove I'm the kid's father.*

This didn't bode well for the coming meeting, but there wasn't much Christy could do about it. She picked Stormy up and twisted to put him onto a chair positioned behind her own. Frank wanted to sit on the table and be part of the action, but Christy had nixed that. She wanted the proceedings to be as professional as possible and having a cat as a table centerpiece wouldn't cut it.

The best option would be for him to be hidden under the table, neither seen nor heard like a Victorian school child, but when Frank protested vehemently against that, she'd come up with the chair option. While it was an imperfect compromise that satisfied neither, she at least had Frank's promise that he'd stay put unless circumstances made it impossible.

At the other end of the table, Mason Tohme was frowning as he watched her with the cat. Along with his narrow-eyed scrutiny, he was still drumming the table with his fingertips. It was annoying.

"Mr. and Mrs. Muir," Bonnie said, standing by the door and waving them inside the conference room.

"Good morning," Christy said, rising again. She made introductions. Mason Tohme stopped his irritating drumming. The Muirs nodded to Nolan Walker and Isabelle but ignored the Tohmes.

While they were settling into the two chairs closest to Christy's right, Roy sauntered into the conference room. "I've locked the door so Bonnie can sit in," he said cheerfully. His eyebrows rose when he saw that the one remaining chair was between Lincoln Muir and Elsa Tohme. He sat down, presumably having introduced himself to both groups as they arrived.

Bonnie hustled in, carrying a large tray with a coffee beaker, cream and sugar, and ten cups and saucers. The set was Wedgewood bone china, part of the Jamieson collection that had survived the drastic reductions that followed Frank's disappearance and the embezzlement of most of the Jamieson fortune. Christy had decided to use it to make a statement, but when she noticed Dawn Muir eying it enviously and Nolan Walker with approval, she wondered if she should have gone with the mismatched collection of mugs that were the usual office fare.

After off-loading the coffee set, Bonnie disappeared again, returning soon after with a plate of pastries. She set these down, then handed each person a side plate and a neatly folded linen napkin. That done, she retreated to her chair, which was positioned behind Isabelle's. Christy poured.

As she handed out cups, Roy passed around the pastries. Once everyone had something before them, Christy smiled and said, "Thank you all for coming this morning."

"Can we get on with this?" Mason Tohme said around a mouthful of cinnamon bun.

"Dad!" Austin protested.

"Honestly," said Dawn Muir, her disapproval close to a sneer.

"Not a bad idea," her husband, Lincoln, said, nodding approvingly.

Christy put her hands together on top of the folder that held the results of the DNA tests. "All right. Here's the situation as it currently stands. Austin Tohme is claiming he's the father of Pam Muir's son, Carson. He was given a paternity DNA test, which is considered conclusive in proving whether an individual is the father or not. In fact, the lab asserts their testing is ninety-nine percent accurate."

The Muirs stared across the table at Austin Tohme, Dawn with pursed lips and narrowed eyes. Lincoln was more circumspect, but his hard expression told a story.

Christy hurried on before either could speak. "Because my husband, Frank Jamieson, is dead, Carson's DNA had to be compared to that of my daughter, Noelle, in a sibling comparison test. The sibling test is not as accurate as a paternity test, but it can predict if two people are likely to be half-siblings."

She paused. The Muirs now gazed at her with the same intensity with which they'd studied the Tohmes. Austin and his father were both staring at her with expressions of impatience, but Elsa simply looked sad. Nolan Walker, who knew the answer to the DNA puzzle, was eating his blueberry Danish with neat precision, while Mallory was studiously avoiding looking at anyone. Isabelle was doodling on a pad and Roy was glancing from face to face, drinking in their reactions. He caught Christy's eye and winked.

Chris, you're killing me with the dramatics. Can you get on with it?

When the results of the DNA tests had come in, Christy had deliberately not included Frank in those she told. She was still annoyed with him over the way he'd prevaricated throughout the search for the father of Pam's child.

She drew out photocopies of the test results and handed them to Nolan and Lincoln to pass around the table. Nolan took a copy and handed the pile to Mallory. Lincoln kept hold of his, reading the document.

As the papers circulated, Christy said, "The results of the tests are conclusive—"

"No!" Lincoln bellowed. "This is a fraud!"

"Let me see!" screeched Dawn, clawing at the stack in her husband's hand.

By this time the pile on Nolan's side of the table had reached Austin and Mason Tohme. Austin grinned as he read. "I am Carson's dad. I knew I was."

Good. We're done. Let's split this scene.

"You are not!" Lincoln roared. "Frank Jamieson is. The sibling test means nothing."

Dawn nodded, her features twisting into a spiteful sneer. She pointed to Christy. "All this proves is that your brat isn't a Jamieson at all." The sneer widened into an evil grin. "All the more for our Carson, since your kid will be out of the Trust."

Christy stared at her with amazement. This was a direction she hadn't even considered when she'd agreed to allow Noelle's DNA to be used as the Jamieson baseline.

Nolan dusted his hands on his napkin. In an impersonal, almost bored voice, he said, "Christy and Frank Jamieson were lawfully married when Noelle Jamieson was conceived and when she was born."

As he spoke, Stormy the Cat leapt from his chair to Christy's shoulder then onto the table where he bounded over to stand directly in front of Dawn Muir.

Stormy's sudden appearance and the violence implied in his swift movement widened Nolan eyes. For a moment, his mouth opened, but no sound emerged. Then he cleared his throat and said, "In the law that makes the girl a Jamieson, no matter what her DNA profile indicates." His voice rose to a shocked squeak as the cat arched, fluffed his tail and back fur, and hissed.

Dawn leaned back in her chair, her expression horrified. "Rabid cat! Get it away from me."

Noelle's my daughter. Mine! Christy was faithful to me all my life, which is more than I deserved. Back off you evil harpy!

Roy had frowned at Dawn's accusation, shooting her a disapproving look. Now he nodded at Frank's defense of Christy. "Well said."

Lincoln nodded, too, but he was agreeing with his wife. "You bet." He made a grab for Stormy, who shot him a disdainful look and wriggled out of his clutching fingers, moving far enough away to avoid capture.

Christy knew Roy was replying to Frank's mind-speak, but everybody else seemed to think he was agreeing with Dawn. Except...

Mason Tohme laughed. "Whoever described the old lady as an evil harpy was spot on. She's no better than her daughter."

"Dad," said Austin, sounding despairing.

Across the table, Elsa Tohme said, "Mason! What a dreadful thing to say. We hardly knew the woman. You should apologize."

"Ha," said Mason. "It wasn't me who made the comment. I just repeated it."

"You're a loony tune," Lincoln said, sounding and looking indignant. "No one at this table said anything about anyone being evil. Your wife's right. Apologize."

"I will not," shouted Mason, getting red in the face as he glared at Lincoln, who glared right back.

By this time, Stormy and Roy had connected and Roy was stroking the cat in a soothing way. "Time for everybody to stop talking and take a deep breath. Shouting at each other is only going to make it more difficult for your two families to learn to live with each other for the sake of young Carson."

His statement, uttered in tones of severe disapproval, had everyone staring at him. Christy was quite sure it was mainly meant for Frank, but if it quieted the rest of the group, all the better.

Surprisingly, Nolan Walker chuckled. "I fear that's an impossible task, Mr. Armstrong." He pointed a finger at Lincoln Muir, completely ignoring Dawn. "Mr. Muir, if you persist in your quixotic quest to prove your grandson is a Jamieson, you will have to wait for Ms. Ellen Jamieson to return from her travels abroad."

"Quixotic? What does that mean?" Dawn asked.

"It means Ellen is a full Jamieson and she was Frank's aunt," Christy said. "When she's tested and her DNA compared to Carson's the results will be exactly the same as those of Noelle's to Carson's."

"Nonsense," said Dawn. "Carson is a Jamieson. Of course, Ellen Jamieson must be tested. Why haven't you contacted her and demanded she return immediately?"

Nolan looked at Dawn for a long moment, his face expressionless, then he said, "Because she's climbing Mount Everest and is out of cell phone range."

His bland comment had Mallory's brows rising and Isabelle, at the other end of the table, looking astounded. Christy was amazed too. She had no idea Nolan was capable of uttering such a whopper.

Dawn, however, appeared to take the statement as absolute truth. "Mount Everest? People die climbing Mount Everest." She brightened. "That's good. Maybe she won't come back."

That was too much for Christy. "Mrs. Muir, that's unacceptable—"

Mason Tohme jumped to his feet. "And I suppose if she didn't return, you'd continue your money-grubbing plot to insert my grandson into the Jamieson nest forever! You're worse than your slut of a daughter! She laughed at me and told me I'd never be Carson's grandfather. She said she had the Jamiesons' lawyer in the bag and she didn't have to worry about producing real proof that Carson was Frank Jamieson's son. She wouldn't listen to me. All she cared about was money."

Austin Tohme had risen too. He put his hand on his father's shoulder and said, "Dad. Stop. Don't say anything more."

Why not? Are you afraid he's Pam's killer?

CHAPTER 29

Christy sucked in her breath. Could Frank be right? There was no time to consider his theory, though, because Mason's words had sparked a conflagration.

"I wasn't in her pocket," Mallory said, sounding angry—no, miserable—at the accusation. "Pam came to me with obviously forged marriage and birth certificates. I told her the Trust wouldn't accept them, and that we'd need to have DNA testing done. She laughed at me and said it was in my best interests to be accommodating. Then she reminded me that when I was part of Austin's defense team I discovered Pam was more than a simple accounting clerk at FPS, the company both she and Austin worked for. In fact, she was the brilliant mind behind the database system that masked the real results of their drug trial, not Austin."

"That's a lie!" Lincoln roared.

Mallory shook her head. "It's true."

"The police never did more than question Pam about Austin's activities. They never even considered she was involved," Dawn said.

Her eyes were narrowed, her lip curled with scorn. She wasn't about to let her daughter be slandered by anyone in the Jamieson camp.

"They never investigated her because I didn't pass my information on to the prosecuting attorney as I should have," Mallory said. She looked down the table, avoiding eye contact with the angry Muirs, regret evident in her expression. "I didn't even tell the senior lawyer on our team."

"Why not?" Walker snapped. He was frowning and his usually impassive features were tight with disapproval.

Mallory sighed.

Austin said, "Because I told her she was wrong. I said I was the one who developed the database, that Pam's only role was to input the data I gave her. I said she wasn't part of the fraud, not in a conscious way."

Elsa Tohme stared at her son, her lips trembling. "Was it true? Was she involved?"

Austin nodded.

"Why would you do that, Austin? Condemn yourself to years in jail for... for that woman?" Elsa's voice shook as if she was holding back tears.

"Because Pam was carrying my child, Mom. I knew there was no way I could avoid incarceration, but I couldn't let Pam go to jail too." Austin's expression pleaded for understanding. Elsa raised her hands and put her fingertips to her eyes, wiping away tears. Then, after a sound that was more of a hiccup than a sob, she nodded and said, "I see."

"None of this is true," Lincoln said. His eyes blazed and his face was a mask of outrage.

"I'm sorry, Mr. Muir, but it is," Mallory said. Her gaze briefly met Lincoln's, then settled on Christy. "I was infatuated with Austin, even though he was the client and I was part of his defense team. I didn't know he was the father of Pam's child. I thought he was being noble and protecting a pregnant employee. I found that incredibly romantic." She shrugged. "I was an articling student then, young and stupid. I let him convince me to stay silent. I shouldn't have done that. All these years I wondered—if I'd disclosed Pam's involvement, would Austin's fate have been different? Would he have served less time? Could we have we have won his case? I don't know."

She shook her head, then drew a deep breath. "Christy, when Pam came to me with her obviously altered documentation, she told me that if I didn't tell you her claim was valid, she'd contact the Bar Association and lodge a complaint against me. If they wouldn't do anything, she'd go to the press. Whichever way it went, I could kiss my career good-bye."

There was pleading in her eyes, shame in her expression. Mallory, the hotshot shark of a defense lawyer, had learned what it was to be on the wrong side of the rules. Christy thought her feelings for Austin had bonded with the guilt she carried for her youthful poor judgment and fueled her aggressive style ever since. But seeing her actions through Pam Muir's lens had shaken her confidence and put her into a position she loathed.

It could be motive for murder, but if Frank was correct, it wasn't Mallory who killed Pam Muir, but Austin Tohme's father, Mason.

Mallory might have directed her confession toward Christy, but she had Nolan Walker's full attention. His usually supercilious expression had hardened and he was tapping his forefinger on the table in a regular, annoying, rhythm as he stared at Mallory. "We will discuss this later, Ms. Tait. I don't believe we should pursue this further in the present circumstances."

Mallory nodded. She stared down at the table, biting her lip.

Lincoln pointed his finger at Nolan. "She should be fired!"

"The matter is no longer under discussion," Nolan snapped. He raised his brows in a condescending way.

Lincoln reddened.

Dawn Muir had apparently decided that with Mallory

vanquished, it was time to refocus on the Tohme threat. She pointed at Mason. "How dare you call my daughter that awful name! Pam was a hardworking, decent woman. She loved Carson. She'd never lie about who his father was, and certainly not for gain."

But she did. Sitting neatly in front of Roy, the cat lifted one front paw to give it a good clean with his tongue, an act as disdainful as Nolan's raised eyebrows and contemptuous expression.

"She did not. How dare you!" The outburst was uttered by Lincoln Muir.

Christy's gaze swiveled his way. His jaw was working and his upper body was stiff with outrage. It appeared Frank had reached yet another participant in this morning's drama. She looked down the table at Roy, who shrugged. No help there.

Christy said, "Mr. Muir, Mr. Tohme—"

Lincoln rounded on her. "That man..." his arm shot out, finger pointing to Mason Tohme. "That man has slandered a fine woman who happened to be my daughter. A daughter who is dead and cannot defend herself!"

At this statement Mallory looked his way. Some of her old fire flashed in her eyes. "Of all the things Pam was, Mr. Muir, fine and decent weren't among them. She manipulated men, then blackmailed them for her own profit. And if she found a weakness in another person, she took advantage of it for her own benefit. I'm an example of that. Mr. Tohme is right. She planned to palm off her son as a Jamieson—"

"Lies!" shouted Dawn Muir. Her voice was strident, but her expression showed desperation. Christy wondered if she'd begun to rethink her impression of her daughter.

"Were you aware she claimed to have been married to Frank Jamieson prior to his marriage to Christy, here?" Mallory asked. Her voice was cold now, her legal instincts kicking back to life.

Dawn was silent.

"She asserted the wedding took place long before she started at Future Pharmaceutical and met Austin Tohme. The marriage certificate she produced was so obviously a fake I told her I couldn't accept it. Do you know what she said then?"

Dawn stared at her mutely. Lincoln said, "I don't believe you."

Mallory's voice, ice cold and filled with anger, cut like a knife, slicing through Pam's character without a shred of remorse. "She said proof like a legal document didn't matter. She'd rouse public opinion and get all the idiots on the Internet believing she was a maligned heroine, shunned by the rich, elitist Jamieson family because she wasn't good enough for them. By the time she was finished with Jamiesons, she said, they'd be begging her to become one of them." Mallory stopped, drew a breath. Shaking her head, she said, "Your daughter was an opportunist, Mr. and Mrs. Muir. I'm sorry, but that's the truth."

"Pam had her good points," Austin said. He spoke calmly, in a dispassionate way, despite the fraught emotions swirling around the table. Whatever she had once been to him—lover, mother of his child, betrayer—he'd come to terms with it, accepting her for what she was, then moving on. "She was smart and capable. Yeah, she looked out for number one, but when Carson came along, I think she also looked out for him."

"She loved him," Dawn said. Her shoulders hunched and her voice lowered. "We love him."

"I'm not trying to take him away from you," Austin said. "I want to know my son, I want to help raise him, that's all."

"I wouldn't let my grandson near a convicted felon and a family like yours," Lincoln said. It was a statement and an ending. While Dawn had crumbled after Mallory's scornful deconstruction of Pam's character, Lincoln remained firm. He wasn't about to budge.

Austin pursed his lips, holding back annoyance.

While Austin might be able to contain his emotions, Christy

wasn't having the same success. Irritation made her snap, "Why are you being so unreasonable? The DNA proof is conclusive. Carson isn't Frank Jamieson's son."

Lincoln jutted out his chin. "He is and I'll fight to prove it if it takes the rest of my life."

Christy stared at him for a moment, then she sighed. "That's all very noble, Mr. Muir, but it's a losing proposition."

Still standing, Mason Tohme pounded his fist on the table. "And every day that fight continues, you'll keep the boy away from his father and his grandparents."

Lincoln's gaze, cold and mean, glittered. A nasty smile curled his mouth. "That's right. No Tohme will ever soil my grandson's life."

Both Austin and Mason stared at him. Austin's features were expressionless, except for the narrowing of his eyes, but Mason's face had reddened, and he flexed his jaw with a violence that spoke of anger barely contained.

Across the table, Elsa Tohme's gaze swiveled from her husband to Lincoln Muir and back. She put her hand to her throat and said in a soft bleating voice, "Oh no!"

The anger on Mason's face turned to outright fury. He pointed toward Lincoln, his finger jabbing dangerously. "You better watch yourself, Muir, or one day you'll find yourself in a back alley with your head bashed in."

Mallory's eyes widened and her gaze flicked from Austin to his father. "Mr. Tohme, it's not wise to threaten someone in that way in a charged situation such as this one. Particularly, when you don't mean what you're saying."

Nolan said, "It's not our place to offer free advice—"

Mason rounded on Mallory. "What makes you think I don't mean it? I got rid of the daughter, didn't I? I'll get rid of the father too." He turned his attention back to Lincoln. Pointing at Elsa, he said, "You heard my wife. She's torn up thinking she'll never meet this grandson

245

of hers. Her first. Her only! Your daughter did that to her. She deserved to die."

He stopped to draw a deep breath. A babble of voices broke out. Lincoln was on his feet, shoving back his chair, clearly on the move.

Dawn stared at Mason, tears in her eyes. Her voice wobbled as she said, "What are you saying? Are you saying you killed my Pammy?"

Austin said, "Shut up, Dad," and turned to Mallory. "He needs a lawyer, Mallory. Will you represent him?"

"I remind you, you're on suspension, Ms. Tait," Nolan said. He sounded prissy compared to the rampaging emotions emanating from the other speakers at the table.

Mallory cast him a cool glance. "I think the accusation that I killed Pamela Muir has now been put to rest. I'm free to take clients again."

"McCullagh, McCullagh, and Walker hasn't yet lifted your suspension," Nolan said.

"Oh, for heaven's sake. Mallory, will you take the commission or not?" Austin demanded impatiently.

After one long look at Nolan, Mallory turned back to Austin. "Yes. Austin, change places with me. I want to sit beside your father." She stood and they made the switch.

Across the table, Lincoln had ignored the exchange between Mallory and Nolan. Focused only on Mason Tohme's admission, he pushed past his wife's chair, intent on getting to the other man.

Roy stood, his arms crossed over his chest, his stance braced, blocking Lincoln's route. "Better not go any further, Muir. I've texted Detective Patterson. She's on her way. She'll sort everything out."

Lincoln's hands were balled into fists and his gaze flicked across the table longingly, but he stopped and didn't attempt to fight his way past Roy.

"I'd better go and unlock the door," Bonnie said. Her voice was high and nervous, and she looked relieved as she jumped to her feet to hurry from the room. From Isabelle's expression, Christy guessed that she wished she could go with her.

Christy drew a deep breath. "Mr. Lincoln, Mr. Tohme, perhaps you could both sit down. Whatever you've done, I do not want fisticuffs—"

"Whatever I've done?" Mason shook his head. "Woman, have you not been listening?"

Mallory's voice, sharp and commanding, cut through the noise. "Mr. Tohme, do not say another word!"

He turned on her. "I'm proud of what I did! Pamela Muir used everyone she met. She manipulated them, she lied to them and about them, and she would have destroyed the soul of that little boy she was blessed with."

Dawn Muir emitted a low moaning groan. Pain shivered through the sound. Lincoln lunged at Roy, making a sudden effort to get round him. Elsa Tohme screamed as Roy stumbled backward toward her chair, but he reached out and shoved Lincoln who lurched to one side, bouncing off the wall and almost losing his footing.

Stormy padded across the table. He sat in front of Mason and stared up at him. *Look at the trouble you're causing.*

"So what?" Mason said.

"Who are you talking to?" Mallory asked, looking around.

Me. Open your mind and you could hear too. How hard can it be? Even that dolt, Lincoln Muir, can hear me.

"Hey!" said Lincoln, looking around, a frown furrowing his brow.

Nolan's eyebrows rose toward his hairline. "Are you trying to build evidence for an insanity plea?" he asked, leaning around Austin to catch Mason's eye.

"I'm not insane!" Mason said.

"Of course you're not," Nolan said. "That wasn't my question."

How did you kill her? Pam, I mean.

Mason, finally heeding Mallory's advice, didn't reply.

Across the table, Lincoln jeered at him. "Yeah, you say you killed my little girl. So, prove it. Tell us how you did it, 'cause I don't believe a runty little guy like you is capable of anything as monumental as this!"

That infuriated Mason in a way Frank's question hadn't. His eyes blazed and his mouth opened.

Mallory said, "Don't!"

Totally focused on Lincoln, he ignored her. "When I read the report in the newspaper that Carson was Frank Jamieson's son, I knew that if someone didn't convince Pam to acknowledge Austin as Carson's father soon, it would never happen." He pointed at Lincoln. "She wouldn't talk to Austin and his lawyer kept saying he should leave it to the courts. Someone had to do something." He reversed directions, jabbing his chest with his finger instead. His face had contorted into a rictus of rage. "*I* had to do something!" His voice lowered, but his eyes still burned. "So, I went to her. Asked her not to do this, to acknowledge Austin instead." He shook his head. His jaw jutted forward, and his lips curled into a snarl. "She laughed at me, so I pushed her and she fell—"

"You hurt her?" Lincoln's voice was a wail of outrage. If Roy hadn't grabbed him by the shoulders, he would have surged around the end of the table and attacked Mason.

Mason laughed and nodded. "The next day—"

Mallory said, "Mr. Tohme, your admission proves assault, nothing more. You've said enough. Please sit down."

There was a silent sigh. *Where are the cops when you need them? It's time to finish this. Everyone here but me got to eat those luscious pastries and I'm hungry.*

Lincoln frowned and looked around the room. "What are you talking about? Everyone took a pastry when we first sat down."

"Except the cat," Mason said. He laughed in a rather menacing way and pointed at Stormy.

"What has the cat to do with anything?" Mallory asked.

If you listened, you'd know.

She paled and her eyes opened wide. She shut her mouth firmly.

"Definitely an insanity plea," Nolan said.

Christy texted Bonnie. Is Detective Patterson here yet?

Just coming through the door, she wrote back.

Thank heavens, Christy thought. She stood. "Mr. Muir, would you please sit down? You too, Mr. Tohme. Ah, Detective Patterson," she said, as Bonnie ushered Patterson, Detective Jones—the cop who had first scored the case—plus a couple of uniforms, through the door.

"An interesting group of people," Patterson said, gazing around the room.

"We came together today to discuss Carson Muir's parentage, Detective. Instead, I believe we have solved Pam Muir's murder," Christy said.

"I'm sure you think you have," Jones said in a patronizing tone, "but civilians rarely do. Leave it to the professionals."

Stormy turned away from Mason to stare at Jones. *Who is this idiot?* Jones frowned.

Mason noticed his expression. He grinned in a demonic way. "It's the cat," he said, pointing.

Patterson looked at Stormy, then brows raised, at Christy, who shrugged. Patterson turned to Roy. "You asked us here, Mr. Armstrong. Tell us why."

Roy had been soaking up the rampant emotions that had fueled the morning's meeting and his cheerful expression said he was having a lovely time. He nodded and happily provided Patterson with a quick précis of the action. "DNA testing proved Austin Tohme is Carson Muir's father." He pointed to Lincoln who had backed away from Roy when Patterson entered but hadn't retired to his seat as Christy had asked. "Lincoln Muir, Carson's grandfather, didn't believe it. In the discussions that followed, Mason Tohme, across the table there, admitted he'd killed Pam because it was the only way to stop her from successfully planting her little cuckoo in the Jamieson...er...nest."

Patterson's brows rose higher. "I see." She turned to Mason Tohme. "Well, Mr. Tohme, what do you have to say to that?"

Mason shrugged.

"I'm representing Mr. Tohme," Mallory said. "I've advised him to say nothing more."

"What's this about a cat?" Jones burst out.

"The cat is Stormy, the Jamieson family cat," Christy said quickly. "He thinks he's a person and likes to be involved in everything we do."

Stormy walked over to Roy, who was the closest friendly human, and butted his hand. Roy tickled him behind his ears. Stormy began to purr.

"Thinks he's a human," Jones said, sounding uneasy. "Sure."

"Enough about the cat." Patterson, who usually let people burble on and incriminate themselves, sounded impatient, even irritated. "Mr. Tohme, we'll continue this down at the station. You'll come with us."

Mallory stood. "I'll bring him, Detective."

Patterson shook her head. "In this case, no, Ms. Tait, I'll be taking Mr. Tohme with me."

With Mallory a former suspect, probably still a suspect, Christy figured Patterson wasn't about to trust her.

Mallory colored. Nolan cleared his throat. "I will escort Ms. Tait and Mr. Tohme, Detective. Is that acceptable?" He raised his brows and achieved a quite astoundingly supercilious expression.

Patterson studied him. "And you are?"

"Nolan Walker of McCullagh, McCullagh, and Walker."

"Ms. Tait's firm."

"My firm," Nolan said, annoyed.

A smile hovered at the edge of Patterson's mouth. "Of course. Well, then, Mr. Walker, we'll follow you to the station. I'd like to get this accusation cleared up."

Nolan nodded stiffly and rose. Along with Mallory and Mason

Tohme, he left the conference room. Patterson followed, with Jones and the uniforms tagging along behind. Jones cast Stormy one last look as he left.

Bye jerk!

Jones' eyes opened wide, and he hurried after the others.

Lincoln Muir began to laugh.

CHAPTER 30

Annoyed, Dawn said, "What are you laughing at?"

Grinning fiendishly, Lincoln pointed at Austin. He was still standing beside the table, his gaze fixed on the door, even though his father was now gone. "He claims to be our boy's biological father. Well, too bad! Even if he is, no court will ever give custody to an ex-con with a murderer for a father."

"He murdered my Pam," Dawn said, her voice wobbling as she wiped away a tear. "Carson will never understand."

Christy thought that was true, but it wasn't her problem. She was glad, however, the Muirs seemed to be accepting the reality of the DNA results, even if it was only subconsciously.

Austin dragged his gaze from the doorway. When he spoke, it was clear he wasn't giving up hope. "You'd be surprised what can happen in the judicial system when you have with a good lawyer. Pam brought about her own death through her greedy, selfish actions. A judge will be sympathetic to my case."

Apparently remembering that he still wanted Carson to be a Jamieson, Lincoln said, "It doesn't matter. When Ellen Jamieson comes back from Mount Everest and gets her DNA tested, you'll be out of the running."

Still seated, Elsa Tohme had been quietly crying as she watched her husband being led away. Now she said, "Does it matter which family Carson belongs to? That child has ruined my husband's life."

"Mom, that's not fair," Austin said. He looked like she'd just slapped him across the face for no reason he could fathom.

Enough, thought Christy. These two warring families needed to find a compromise they could live with, but it wouldn't be easy. They would battle it out, but not in her conference room with her and her staff as witnesses. "Mr. and Mrs. Muir, Mr. Tohme and Mrs. Tohme, I think we've argued the issue of Carter's parentage as far as we can today. Without lawyers present, we should terminate this meeting. Mr. and Mrs. Muir, should you wish to continue your suit asserting Carter is a Jamieson, please contact Mr. Walker at McCullagh, McCullagh, and Walker. With that, I'm concluding this meeting. Thank you all for coming." She gestured toward the door, a hardly subtle invitation for them to leave.

Austin was to first to react. He nodded to Christy, then rounded the end of the table to Elsa's seat. "Come on, Mom. We'll head down to the police station and see what we can find out."

She nodded and he helped her feet. They left, with Austin holding her arm protectively when she wobbled a little as she walked.

Dawn Muir sent Christy a venomous look. "This isn't over, no matter what you think."

Talk to the lawyers and leave Chris alone.

Lincoln frowned. Dawn didn't appear to have tuned into Frank's mind-speak so she didn't notice.

"As I said, Mrs. Muir, all further communications should be with Mr. Walker." Christy kept her voice steady and her expression bland. She wasn't going to be baited by Dawn into another argument.

They locked gazes and it was the other woman who looked away first. That didn't stop Dawn from rising with a slow deliberation that suggested she wasn't going to allow Christy to chase her away.

Stormy sat down and contorted his body so he could clean his inner thigh. *Will these people never leave?*

Roy laughed.

Lincoln reddened. "Come on, Dawn. We're not wanted here."

Stormy looked up from his cleaning. *You finally figured it out. Took you forever. A bit slow, are you?*

Anger deepened the red in Lincoln's cheeks, but he didn't reply. Dawn brushed past Roy without speaking. After a venomous look at Christy, Lincoln followed her out. Moments later they were gone.

"I'm glad that's over," Isabelle said, shaking her head as she gathered up file folders, her laptop, and the recording device. She looked from Christy to Roy. "Do you think the Muirs will continue trying to prove Carson is Frank's son?"

Christy nodded. "When Ellen returns from her holidays, I'll ask her to do a DNA test. I'll also have her DNA tested against Noelle's. With both Ellen's DNA and Noelle's not matching Carson's, and Ellen's matching Noelle's, the Muirs will have to give up."

"And even if they don't, they'll lose the case," Isabelle said. "I'll get Bonnie to type up the notes from today."

Christy nodded. "Thanks, Isabelle."

She left the room, lugging her armload of documents and technology with her.

Christy looked at the cat. "You're a troublemaker."

Just trying to help! The voice sounded indignant.

Christy sighed. That was the problem.

∼

A week later, she was at the arrivals gate at Vancouver International Airport, waiting for Quinn's flight from Toronto to deplane. This was her second trip to the airport in the last few days. She'd also picked up Ellen and Trevor, back from their South Seas getaway.

When the situation with the Muirs was explained to her, Ellen had immediately agreed to have her DNA tested. The results were already back. Ellen bore no relation to Carson Muir but had a strong relationship to Noelle.

Christy caught sight of Quinn's tall figure and thick dark hair. She waved. He saw her and waved back, then headed in her direction. She made her way along the low wall that marked out the baggage claim area to a gap and crossed into the open space, meeting Quinn halfway.

The next few minutes were spent greeting each other with a long and satisfying kiss. "I missed you," Christy said when they finally broke apart.

He smiled down at her and brushed a stray lock of hair from her face. "Goes double for me."

He slipped an arm around her waist and together they strolled over to his flight's designated luggage carousel. "I saw a news bulletin that Mason Tohme was arrested for Pam Muir's murder."

Christy leaned against him and nodded. "According to a piece in *The Sun*, he confessed. For years, he'd been trying to convince Pam to agree to acknowledge Austin as Carson's father, but Pam not only refused, but she taunted him that it would never happen."

"That's why she was searching for a blond man in a position of power. If she was married to him, she'd have a reasonable chance to convince the world that he was the father, not Austin," Quinn said.

Christy nodded. "Austin didn't claim paternity before his trial in case the prosecution discovered that he and Pam had a relationship and that she was deeply involved in the scam. He was afraid they'd charge her too. That made Mason even more upset. His son was sacrificing himself for this woman because she was the mother of his son, yet she was denying that very fact."

"Then his son is convicted and sent to prison." Quinn shook his head. "It must have been tough for him."

Nodding, Christy said, "He became obsessed with forcing Pam to acknowledge Austin was Carson's dad."

"When did obsession turn into violence?" Quinn asked as the carousel began to move.

"Not for a while," Christy said. "Austin was convinced that once he'd served his sentence, Pam would relent, and Mason bought into that." She shrugged. "I guess it was a form of hope—when the worse is over, things will get better. But that didn't happen. Pam still refused to acknowledge that Austin was the father. His lawyer told him to get a job and rebuild his life, then when his sentence was over, and he could show that he had a steady job, he could sue Pam for custody."

"I'm guessing that wasn't enough for Mason," Quinn said.

Christy shook her head. "Mason became more and more frustrated. He stepped up his campaign, even though Austin wanted him to wait."

"So, with Austin out of prison and his father putting on the pressure, Pam decided it was time to provide Carson with a father, in the form of Frank Jamieson."

Christy sighed. "Not quite. Yes, she'd been trying to find someone who could pass for Carson's father for years, but it hadn't worked. I think she was getting desperate." Christy glanced at Quinn. "I have no proof, but I think she'd decided to take Carson and disappear. That's why she began her blackmail scheme. She needed the money. Then Austin decided to sue her for custody, and she had to act quickly."

Quinn nodded as if this all made sense. "She remembered Frank and thought she'd give using him as the father a try."

Christy nodded. "He was dead, after all, not able to deny her claim. If she could convince the Trust that Carson was Frank's son, she'd have a powerful ally against Austin."

"I suppose seeing her claim in black and white in the newspaper convinced Mason she would succeed in locking out the Tohme family?"

"Even worse—Mason believed her statement that she'd been married to Frank. If that were true, Carson's parentage wouldn't matter. Legally, he'd be a Jamieson."

Suitcases started to slide out onto the carousel. Quinn leaned forward and grabbed his. He pulled out the handle and took Christy's hand. They began to walk, Quinn towing the case behind him. "Mason figured he had to stop her before the decision was made."

She nodded. "He went to her on Tuesday, the day before Pam was supposed to meet us at the Trust offices with her documentation. He says he asked her to rethink the Jamieson claim, but she laughed at him, and told him that after tomorrow he could kiss ever seeing his grandson good-bye. He was furious, but he was also terribly, terribly frightened she would make it happen. He apparently spent the night brooding and decided he'd do anything necessary to stop her. The next day, he went to the Trust's building and waited in the parking garage for her to arrive. When she did, he accosted her. He pleaded, but she sneered at him and turned her back on him as if he was nothing. His temper snapped and he stabbed her."

"Premeditated murder," Quinn said. "Mason Tohme will spend the rest of his life in prison."

Christy sighed. "Well, maybe. Maybe not."

Quinn looked at her, brows raised in question.

"Frank," she said, by way of an answer. "Mason kept talking about voices in his head, and because witnesses—notably his lawyers, Nolan Walker and Mallory Tait—stated that he was acting erratically during the meeting at the Trust offices, the police subpoenaed the tape-recording Isabelle made of the meeting. On the tape, Mason seemed to be responding to questions that hadn't been made. In addition, there were several times when he was asked what he was talking about, and he indicated he was replying to the cat. As a result, the

Crown accepted an insanity plea. He'll be going to an institution, not a prison, and he'll probably be out before you know it."

Quinn shook his head, then he laughed. "We've managed to make sure Frank's interference didn't muck up a few other cases. I guess you can't win them all."

IF THE CAT'S AWAY

THE 9 LIVES COZY MYSTERY, BOOK EIGHT

Patterson didn't move. "I understand Jodie Webster is staying with you."

Roy nodded.

"Is she here? I'd like to speak to her."

Frowning, Roy said, "She's in the kitchen, having breakfast. What's going on?"

Probably something to do with the murder. The cat's voice was loud in his head.

"Would you ask her to come down here, please?"

Murder? What murder? No one had told him about a murder. And how would Jodie be involved in a murder? Roy contemplated the detective. "I could if I knew what this was about."

Annoyance flashed in Patterson's eyes. "It's a private matter, Mr. Armstrong."

Roy blinked and smiled in a fatuous way that he hoped would get under the detective's skin. He liked Patterson, but Jodie was family, even if she was irritating family. "Come back in a couple of hours.

That way, Jodie will have finished her breakfast, and Trevor will have arrived."

Patterson's jaw flexed, and her mouth tightened into a hard line. "This is not a joking matter, Mr. Armstrong."

Roy raised his brows. "I wasn't joking, Detective Patterson."

"Stupid cat," said Jodie's voice. From the direction of the sound, she was in the living room and coming closer. "Uncle Roy? Why did you let this awful beast in?" Any moment now, she'd be at the top of the stairs.

"Mrs. Webster, I'm Detective Patterson from the Vancouver Police department. I'd like to have a word with you." She was looking over Roy's shoulder as she spoke. Jodie must have arrived at the top of the stairs.

Roy slowly turned, and yes, indeed, there was Jodie holding the cat, who looked remarkably smug. Roy wasn't sure why Frank had fetched her from the safety of the kitchen, but he could guess. Jodie could hear the voice, but she refused to acknowledge it. The cat was annoyed with her. He figured Patterson would make her uncomfortable, and he'd be there to enjoy her unease.

"About what?" Jodie put the cat down. Stormy crouched beside her, paws tucked under his body, sphinx-like.

Patterson looked at Roy. "If you wouldn't mind leaving us, Mr. Armstrong?"

Roy opened his mouth to say, "no way."

Might as well. We won't find out what Patterson wants until you're gone. Don't worry. I've got this.

Roy thought about the way the cat had influenced the results of other investigations. He closed his mouth, shrugged, and went up the stairs. As he passed Jodie he poked her in the arm. "When she asks you a question, say 'no comment' and tell her you want to see your lawyer."

"Mr. Armstrong!"

Jodie's eyes widened. "I don't have a lawyer."

"Yes, you do. I'm phoning him now." Roy went into the kitchen to call. Trevor promised to come as soon as he could. Roy quietly returned to the living room to listen to the voices that drifted up from the front foyer.

"All right, it's true! I had an affair with Clay. That's why I'm here, camping out at my uncle's instead of home with my husband." That was Jodie, sounding agitated, her tone strident.

Hey! Give the old man a break. He's offered you sanctuary. Don't diss him because you're upset.

"I'd like you to come down to the station with me to answer some questions, Mrs. Webster," Patterson said, apparently unaffected by Jodie's rising emotions.

"What? No! Why?"

It's obvious. She thinks you killed Clayton Green.

"If you'd come with me, please."

"No!"

Roy couldn't tell if Jodie was refusing Patterson's request or denying the cat's observation. Either way, he should probably intervene.

Good answer. Now say you want your lawyer and tell her to go away.

"I won't say anything until my lawyer is with me!" Jodie sounded panicked now, as if she was teetering on the edge of a precipice, and she was afraid of heights.

Roy ambled to the top of the stairs. "Trevor's on his way. It would probably be best if you waited in your car until he arrives, detective."

Patterson shot him a frustrated look. "Tell Mr. McCullagh to have Mrs. Webster at the station by one this afternoon."

Roy nodded amicably. "Will do."

Patterson shot Jodie one last searching look before she opened the door, closing it behind her with a quiet click as she departed.

Jodie looked up at Roy, her eyes wide, her lips slightly parted as if she wanted to say something but couldn't quite manage it. Roy and the cat stared back.

You are in so much trouble.

∼

Available in Paperback and eBook from Your Favorite Bookstore or Online Retailer

ABOUT THE AUTHOR

The author of the 9 Lives Cozy Mystery Series, Louise Clark has been the adopted mom of a number of cats with big personalities. The feline who inspired Stormy, the cat in the 9 Lives books, dominated her household for twenty loving years. During that time he created a family pecking order that left Louise on top and her youngest child on the bottom (just below the guinea pig), regularly tried to eat all his sister's food (he was a very large cat), and learned the joys of travel through a cross continent road trip.

The 9 Lives Cozy Mystery Series—*The Cat Came Back, The Cat's Paw, Cat Got Your Tongue, Let Sleeping Cats Lie,* and *Cat Among the Fishes*—as well as the single title mystery, *A Recipe For Trouble*, are all set in her home town of Vancouver, British Columbia. For more information please sign up for her newsletter at http://eepurl.com/bomHNb. Or visit her at:

www.louiseclarkauthor.com

facebook.com/louiseclarkauthor